Swimming in Sky

Swimming in Sky

A NOVEL BY INMAN MAJORS

SOUTHERN METHODIST
UNIVERSITY PRESS
Dallas

This novel is a work of fiction. Names, characters, places, and incidents are either the product of the author's imagination or are used fictitiously.

Requests for permission to reproduce material from this work should be sent to:
Rights and Permissions
Southern Methodist University Press
PO Box 750415
Dallas, Texas 75275-0415

JACKET ART: Magritte, Rene (1898–1967). *The Connivance*, 1965. Oil on canvas, 33 x 41 cm. © 2000 C. Herscovici, Brussels / Artists Rights Society (ARS), New York. Private Collection, Antwerp, Belgium.

JACKET AND TEXT DESIGN: Tom Dawson

LIBRARY OF CONGRESS CATALOGING-IN-PUBLICATION DATA

Majors, Inman.
    Swimming in sky : a novel / by Inman Majors.—1st ed.
        p. cm.
    ISBN 0-87074-455-0 (acid-free paper)
    1. College graduates—Fiction. 2. Knoxville (Tenn.)—Fiction. 3. Mothers and sons—Fiction. 4. Unemployed—Fiction. 5. Young men—Fiction. I. Title.

PS3563.A3927 S95 2000
813'.6—dc21   00-057398

Printed in the United States of America on acid-free paper
10   9   8   7   6   5   4   3   2   1

for my brother

I would like to thank those who have meant the most: my wife Christy, my mother, and my father. Thanks to my grandparents, Nina and Bob Winton, and Elizabeth and Shirley Majors, whose influence is with me always. Thanks also to Chris Vescovo, the Vanderbilt Dogs, Stan Braun, Mary Jo Potts, Dick Paddon, Walter Sullivan, Allen Wier, Tom Rabbitt, and all my friends and relatives who had the right word at the right time. A special thanks to Ray Murray, whose early editing proved so crucial. Finally, I would like to thank the University of Alabama, Motlow State Community College, Southern Methodist University Press, and my friend and editor, Kathryn Lang, without whom this book would not exist. Bless you all.

Swimming in Sky

May

You can turn on the light. I'm awake.

My mother turns on the light and stands whispering on the stairs, thinking she must be quiet, unaware she whispers still. I'm sleeping downstairs on her couch.

Did I wake you?

No. I was up.

Can't sleep?

Not that great.

Did you drink a Coke before you went to bed, she asks, and I'm reminded I have a sense of humor.

No ma'am. Must be all the hard work I been doing. Better take today off.

Oh hell, she says, halfway between a laugh and a curse. You take any more time off you're going to disappear. And seriously now Jason, I expect you to pull your weight around here. I've left a list of things I want you to do today.

Not a list.

Yes a list. I'm not running a free soup kitchen here.

You're not? Well how much is soup then? How much for a nice steaming bowl of chicken and rice?

Laugh now. This gravy train has about run its course. You're a grown man. It's high time you started acting like it.

But Moooommmy, I cry, I want free soup. I must have soup. My kingdom for some soup. But Ma Kettle's out the door, slamming it hard.

The darkness is not bad now since it's light outside. I stay on the couch, snoozing intermittently between phone calls and the Mexican jumping bean changing of channels on the television upstairs. Maximum volume and a rapid-fire remote drown out the phone. Nothing but bill collectors and bankers. Tom's been out of work for some time now. I never knew exactly what kind of job he had, some kind of sales, but now the money is tight. This house, that they went in on together, is up for sale and they don't talk about where they're moving. Four years of living together has just postponed the obvious. My mother is working fifty hours a week as a sales rep for a trucking company. All day she calls on good old boys in the trucking industry and she holds her own with them. She's started working out at a gym and chewing ass like the old days. A sturdy ship she is. In other lives, however, Tom and I sank the Titanic.

The phone rings for the zillionth time and I scream hello like I've just dislodged my hearing aid in an enfeebled scramble for the phone.

Hello, may I speak to Tom Laymon please?

Anyone who doesn't ask for Sweet is no one Tom wants to talk to. Tom has lots of friends, good old boys in a good way, and a ton of relatives. They all call him Sweet. I'm friends with Tom. He's never even insinuated I call him Sweet. For this I am grateful.

He's not in at the moment, I say, earnestly now, a kindly grandmother, an orphaned, invalid nephew.

When he gets in will you tell him that Dillard Tunney from First National Bank called. I've called for several weeks now and it's very important I talk to Mr. Laymon today.

Yessir. I'll tell him as soon as he gets back in town.

Will he be away long?

I really couldn't say. I don't live here, I'm just visiting.

Haven't I talked to you before?

Not that I recall, I say, looking at a granddaddy longlegs walking on the ceiling, but I'll be sure to give him the message as soon as I see him.

Yes, it's very important.

I go upstairs, unable to sleep any longer. Out the kitchen window the dogwoods hold their color, the sky is blue and blue, and this behemoth of a yard needs mowing. The steep hill on the other side of the swimming pool intimidates. Both the lawn and the pool are on the dreaded list my mother's left for Tom and me. The realtor will start showing the house soon, and Tom hates the work like a man digging his own grave.

The pool itself is a nasty gangrene shade of green, a pond of primordial scuz, the chlorine we used either the wrong kind, or not enough. Like the house, it's older and needs much care. Yesterday, much to Tom's delight, I gagged when he scooped out a floating dead rat with the long-handled skimmer.

I grab a Coke out of the refrigerator, one of those little six and a half ouncers my mother buys because I like them, and fire a Winston from the pack Tom's left on the table. Then I walk out to greet what's left of the day. Right away, Pookie jumps on me. She's Tom's oldest son's dog, left here when Tom's son moved to Birmingham. She licks my hand with her black chow's tongue. She knows all about me. I come in late at night and lie in the grass and don't really have to tell her I'm crazy. She's smart and sympathetic, not at all churlish as chows are thought to be. For my benefit, I start running madly around the yard with her chasing me, round and round the pool, Pookie barking and faking as if she'll bite me, until my knee starts to hurt. Then I let her out the back gate, though I'm not supposed to, so she can tear around the neighborhood taunting dogs dumb enough or tame enough to allow their humans to keep them under lock and key. It's not as if she needs me to let her out. All around the yard boarded up holes under the fence show the futility of trying to keep her in. As of late, Tom's stopped trying. Pookie will have her fun.

I turn on my old stereo which I've moved out to the gazebo. Painting the gazebo, which is one strong storm from falling down, also is on my list to do, but for now I sit by the pool to catch some sun. My knee really is hurt. Not that anyone necessarily thinks I'm faking. My health insurance lapsed while I was stumbling around Australia with my friend Pel last fall. When I heard it pop playing basketball back in March, I knew I was in for a long stint of limping. I was hot as hell too when I got hurt. I keep thinking one of my parents, or maybe a grandparent, will step up and offer to pay for the operation I need, but since the divorce wars, whose first official volley was launched many moons ago, are still raging, it will take several summit meetings and a possible exchange of prisoners before I'm able to run full speed or play ball again. My right thigh has already started to shrink, and for the time being I pass the days trying to remember if it was Chester or Festus who had the limp, and reminding myself I can always ask for an operation for Christmas. I'm working on the Tiny Tim motif.

The shadow is still with me during the day, but not as bad. Something behind me, unshakable. I can forget about it for long stretches, especially when my mind is on something else. No one knows exactly. It's not really fodder for casual conversation and I fake a normal existence pretty well.

Tom comes outside shirtless. He's a big man with some rough scars on his chest, operations, machinery accidents, I'm sure a fight or two. Perhaps the fight stuff is the romantic in me. Regardless, Tom's been kicking against this life for a long time now, and he's starting to look tired of the battle. Damn that phone rings, he says.

Ain't that the truth, I say, aware I can good old boy as situation dictates. That asshole from the bank.

Figured.

He unravels the garden hose and puts the nozzle in the chewy green water of the pool. The other end he drags through the chain link fence and down the steep hill of the driveway. He's draining the pool for the second time this spring. Pookie get out? he asks me.

I let her out.

He nods. Might as well. Seen any rats this morning? And saying this he smiles, looking like a grown man who would be called Sweet, like a man who would treat your mother the best he knew how, which he, and your mother, probably knew all along would not be quite good enough. The drinking got you Sweet, I want to say. I say, no, I hadn't seen any rats today, but I keep hoping.

Yeah, I bet you do. You and your mother. I never seen two people so scared of a little rat.

I grab a cigarette off of him, and go down to the garage for the hydrochloric acid we'll bleach the pavement around the pool with. The garage is filled with paints and tools and ladders, all the things a man would need to take care of his own business. And old furniture is scattered about, piled in corners, stacked crazily on boxes with legs and cushions all akimbo, my little brother's old bedroom suite, outdated love seats and bean bags, various desks that belong to Tom or one of his kids. It's always strange when your parents are split up, how you'll see a glass from the old house at your mother's new house, and then see another from the same set at your dad's. Old chipped glasses that you used to drink Kool-Aid out of during the summer. The furniture and glasses just follow you around, reminders, ghosts, from another life. Pictures taken by Tom's wife mixed in with pictures of me and my brother in anachronistic baseball uniforms. Strange such things, but not bad, little ghosts.

I come back to the pool with the acid, and we spread it around with long scrubbers. It smells bad, like rotten eggs that have been electrocuted.

Shit that smells, I say, watching the acid sizzle and fry on the concrete.

Yeah but you're not gonna believe how white this concrete's gonna be. Make it look brand new.

Tom's smoking a cigarette and I wonder vaguely about combustion. I stop wondering long enough to bum one from him and light up. Mortal fire seems mundane and overrated.

Your mother said that girl called for you last night, Tom says, leaning against his brush, yellow acid smoking and hissing all around his feet.

What girl, I say, lying, him knowing I'm lying. He's talking about Penny Jackson.

That redhead that was out at the pool the other day. With the big ones.

Oh. Her.

Oh her. Listen at him.

The redhead dumped me.

What for?

Pool turned green.

Oh hell, Tom says, laughing, yellow smoke billowing around his knees. Always somebody waiting with a blue pool. You need you one like I had. Redhead. Six foot two. I was living in this little log cabin outside of Vonore. Cold as hell. The bedroom had one little old floor vent for heat. This redhead, she had to be at work before I did, so she'd get up early and take her shower while I was still in bed. She'd get out of the shower and I mean it was cold. What she'd do is, see, is stand spread eagle over that little heat vent and dry her hair. Stark naked. I tell you I'll never forget it. You ain't seen nothing until you've seen a six-foot redhead standing naked over a heat vent drying her hair.

Tom goes in to cook dinner and I start the lawnmower. The grass is tall, reaching over the tops of my tennis shoes. The yard is three tiered, the bottom of which is flat and easy to mow. The second tier is the pool, and above it a steep hill, and then a larger flat spell. I dread the hill, and what it will do to my knee. What I need is a nice herd of marauding mountain goats.

The sky is perfect blue and the sun feels good on my back. This mower has an automatic propeller, but I never use it, the yard having many trees and tight turns around the pool area. I like the workout too, getting a sweat for the first time in weeks. I knock out the bottom part first, cranking it, powering the mower. The vibration saps some of the tension from my arms and back, and the steady drone takes my mind. I have a good rhythm. Around the pool I'm careful to always have the mower facing out so the grass won't blow in the pool. When Tom mows he just slams, grass flying everywhere, the heavy crunch of sticks being chewed. It drives me nuts, grass in the pool.

I save the hill for last, and start on the large third tier. The mowing is slow for the picking up of sticks, and the circular maneuvering around trees. In places the grass is thin and I don't enjoy mowing. Somehow there's less a feeling of accomplishment when the grass is thin, like what you're doing isn't fundamental to the existence of things. I'm the same way about vacuuming. Give me a really dirty carpet with lots of lint balls any day, so I can see where I've been.

My mind is good for awhile with the vibration, the drone. A squirrel in a tree hangs impossibly far out on a tiny limb. He will fall, he will surely fall. My thinking this, knowing well that squirrels test fate on a regular basis, invites a shadow. The squirrel will fall because I think he will fall. And then, inevitably, it's last month and I'm back with Pel and Jimbo at Jimbo's cabin. It's Good Friday and Pel is placing a clear drop in the palm of my hand and I'm licking it off. Pel says, nice to know you. Then, later, we're in the car and I've begun to feel woozy, slippery and gelled, and we're passing a trailer where a little retarded kid is kicking a kickball against the back of a broken couch that sits in the front yard. As we pass, he picks up the ball and fakes as if he'll throw it at the car. He has a huge head and thick glasses and I think about waving, but too late. I'm glad I don't live there, I say. And quickly Pel has turned, he's driving, he hasn't tripped, it's Jimbo and Pel and me, quickly he's turned and said, maybe they're glad you don't live there too. And his glance has lingered.

I lack humility.

I go faster now, afraid to look at the tree, not wanting to kill the squirrel. I go and go, bullying the mower, this shadow and these thoughts all just craziness, residual. Lions and tigers and bears oh my. Lions and tigers and bears.

I start on the top part of the hill where it's less steep. I sneak a look at the tree for the squirrel. He's safe. The shadow lingers.

Going down the steeper part of the hill the grass is a little slick. I will definitely slip and cut off my foot. I have a slight panic going when Tom comes through the gate with the weedeater. He's the youngest of ten children. When his mother was old and cranky and dying, no one could talk to her. Her mind was slipping, little light left from a hard life. Tom stood behind her chair and brushed her hair. He brushed and brushed, joking, pacifying. Sometimes mothers love their youngest sons too much.

You saved my ass Tom, I say.

I bout busted mine on that hill last time. We need us a rider. This damn yard's gonna kill somebody.

I cut off the mower and go inside for a Coke. The house is nice and cool. I smoke a cigarette. Outside, Tom raises hell on the hill, swinging the weedeater like a sword.

The phone rings and I consider not answering. Hello.

What you up to boy? Jackie says. He's Tom's best friend.

Bout six feet, I say.

Shit. You getting any?

Nary a bit.

Well why not?

No gas in my car, no money, very little personality.

Well hell, me and Sweet need to fix you up. Get you one of them wild little Vonore girls. I'm serious, we could do it.

Sounds good, I'll get Tom, I say, a little Jackie going a long way.

I trade places with Tom to finish up with the weedeater. I sweep back and forth. I go in circles. Until the yard is done. I carry the weedeater back to the garage, and fill it with gas and oil. A growing affinity for my couchbed, infinitely preferable to sleeping under the bridge like a troll, constantly reminds me that indentured servants must properly care for and maintain another man's tools.

When I come back to the yard, Tom is sitting under the gazebo with Pookie and a bourbon and water. He's smoking his two thousandth cigarette. Pookie stares at me, looking wild and untamed. She's taunted many dogs today. Her fur is unruly and covered with burrs. Her paws are muddy and her black tongue hangs out loosely, saliva slobbering out by the bucket. She is perhaps rabid. My girl.

We're done, Tom says with finality.

Now you're talking.

He pushes his cigarettes over and I sit down at what was the kitchen table in our old house to smoke. This is the slow time of day, the giving in, the sun somewhere else to visit. I smoke my cigarette and it tastes good, the dusk, the birds quiet, no wind, the gentle leaving of the light, death near, perhaps not bad.

Concrete's white, I say.

Like brand new.

We gonna have to paint this gazebo?

It's on the list.

God I hate a list.

She aims to keep us busy I reckon.

I reckon.

We sit in the early evening, the yard mowed, the concrete bleached. The pool is nearly drained. Dark green residue of yick covers the bottom. Tomorrow we'll scrub the pool for the second time. The gazebo will wait.

Tom clears his throat and I have a premonition what he'll say.

Your mother said anything to you about what her plans are?

No sir.

I didn't figure she did. I don't even think she knows.

No, I say, I don't think she knows.

Tom rattles his ice a little, looking off somewhere I can't see. Far away.

I always tried to do the best by your mother.

I know you did. I appreciate it. I think you helped her out a lot. I think she feels good about herself now.

He doesn't say anything. We sit in the fleeting grey, the smell of cut grass in the air. The pool drains.

Got some red beans and rice on the stove if you're hungry. Cornbread too.

Sounds good.

I sit for a while more. Pookie sleeps. It's nearly dark when I go inside. I grab a beer out of the refrigerator and microwave the red beans.

I'm downstairs eating when my brother Pete calls from Nashville. He's three years younger and a senior econ major at Vanderbilt, where I earned my completely useless liberal arts degree, earned my passport to this life of leisure. How's it going, he asks, trying his level best to sound casual.

Okay.

Okay better or okay the same.

The same I guess. Maybe a little better. Had a good day today. Worked on the pool with Tom.

Well that sounds good, he says. Then he pauses, trying to decide if sleeping dogs should lie. He thinks I'm at the end of my rope. You talked to Pel?

No.

You planning on it?

I don't know.

Well listen. I've thought about what you told me. That shadow stuff. It's like you've had a shot to the head. It's going to take awhile to get all the way back.

I don't say anything.

Your friends saying that religious stuff just made it worse. I mean who says that kind of stuff?

I don't know. It was Good Friday. It was on everyone's mind I guess.

They didn't know how messed up you were?

Maybe they were just trying to give me a humility lesson or something.

Yeah. That's it. You need a humility lesson. You're brimming with con-fidence. It's just a bunch of drug talk. Pothead shit. They were fucking with you.

I don't say anything.

Good God. Isn't there anyone else in town to hang out with? Why don't you give old Barry Paige a call?

He moved to Atlanta.

What about Coffey, Allen McDuffie, Vescovo?

Gone, gone, gone.

Well come see me. See Dad.

How is Dad?

Good. You ought to come visit.

I will, I say, I will.

Just call me man. Anytime. I'm up late.

I know it, I say. I appreciate it.

And then we hang up and I finish my dinner, wishing I'd never said anything to my little brother about what it is that ails me.

When Mom comes in I'm lying on the couch in the dark watching television.

You been on the couch all day? she asks. She's kidding.

Go check the yard. We kicked ass.

Well good. It was a nice day to work outside wasn't it?

Real nice.

Are you going out tonight kiddo? I owe you some money for your work. I've got a twenty.

Thanks, but I'm going to hang in. I'm not really getting along with the guys right now. I'm kind of slightly crazy.

Maybe you're just growing up. Ready to get going.

Maybe. I doubt it.

Well I'm going upstairs. Come up in a little bit and talk. Did you get any supper?

Yes ma'am. Tom cooked. It was real good.

Okay, good. Come on up in a little while.

I will.

She walks up the stairs, her hand sliding along the wall, feeling her way in the dark. I assume Tom is still outside. They will probably not eat at the same time. Mom will watch a movie in the upstairs den. Tom might watch the movie with her. Maybe they'll talk about my mother's day. I will lie on the couch and watch TV until I try to go to sleep. I'll probably read some more of the Bible and smoke some more cigarettes if I can find them. Train whistles will blow throughout the night, interrupting my dreams. The toilet will run. I'll hear the clink of ice on glass hollow from the kitchen. It will be so dark I won't be able to see my hand in front of my face.

I'm sitting in someplace familiar, maybe this very den, surrounded by Pel and Trick and Bobsmith and Jimbo. We're talking about something inconsequential, but not funny, and my friends, who are all facing me, smile sardonically. There's some joke I'm not getting. What, I ask. Why are you laughing? Pel smiles, nothing, nothing, he says. I feel the flames before I see them. There's a small fire behind me. I stomp it out quickly, and my friends continue to laugh. I'm more confused, they saw the fire after all, Pel saw the fire, and they're looking at me smiling and behind more fires and I am stomping them out stomping them out stomping them out until there's too many and my friends at my back do nothing until all is fire and my friends are gone and I'm left alone in roaring fire.

I turn on the light and search along the coffee table and among the scattered pillows on the floor for cigarettes. Finding none, I walk to the garage to look in Tom's Lincoln. I start to panic when I fail to spot a pack, not wanting to hike upstairs and risk Tom in full brood at the kitchen table, though I doubt he's up now. I find a nearly new pack in the glove compartment, thank you Tom, and vow to buy my own the next day.

I come back into the den and turn on the television. I flip through the channels but nothing's on. I turn to the preview channel, mute it, and go to the bookcase for the Bible I've been reading lately. I'm obviously whacked. My brother says I suffer from post-traumatic shock. My friends laugh and say I suffer only from a bad trip. They smile. I think they can read my mind.

I smoke Tom's cigarette and watch the minutes change on the preview channel and read in the New Testament. Sometimes it helps me sleep. I haven't slept well in awhile, since before Australia really. Australia is when I first started getting a little wiggy, thinking too much, partying too much. I'd be in some rundown hostel, Pel snoozing away in the next bunk, and my mind would just race. Pel was on this self realization kick. I guess I was on some kind of kick myself and didn't know it. Pel thought you could will things to happen, that there was energy in the world you could tap into and that if you concentrated hard enough and wanted things badly enough, they would happen, you could get what you wanted, whatever you wanted.

I'd say, what about God?

Never met him, Pel would say.

Some nights, on some of the long nights when I couldn't sleep, I'd find myself thinking about Reverend Madden, the chaplain at my high school. He was a cool guy, funny. I'd hated Chapman at first, thought it was too preppy, and I guess it was pretty obvious. But Reverend Madden would go out of his way to say hello in the halls, would make me, all five feet of me, be Goliath to his David in religious studies class. It was a good class too. His favorite story was the one about Jacob changing his name to Israel. It seems Jacob was mad at the world, mad at God, and dreamed one night he was wrestling one of God's angels. Israel, Reverend Madden told us, means one who wrestles with God. When he was telling the story, he'd get in a sugar foot wrestling stance and hop around the room saying, okay Big Man, I'm ready for you. I'm mad at you and I don't agree with you, so let's see what you got. Let's see how you like it. It was funny. This skinny, scattered, chalk-covered egghead from Harvard hopping around the room giving the business to God. Think about the Jewish faith, he'd say, lunging at his desk, jabbing at a filing cabinet, a whole religion based on wrestling.

I go upstairs to get a beer, moving along the darkened stairs by feel and I like the way the wallpaper feels, smooth and cool. In the kitchen there's a light on over the sink and in the sink, Tom's glass. On the table an ashtray filled with tense and mangled butts. It's so quiet in the kitchen, the silence seems to move. Like the silence has a tangible weight, heavy and slow around the lighted sink, quick and harried and flitting in the darkened hall, the shrouded dining room.

Back downstairs again, the silence is the same. Electric and crackling. Then thick and slow. Then stopping. I drink beer and smoke cigarettes in the muted spectral blue of the television. And again it's Good Friday. It's dusk on Good Friday and I'm out of my mind. We're in the yard at Jimbo's cabin and I reach down to pick a dandelion.

Don't pick the dandelions, says Pel, they're alive.

And the air has gone thick and electric. I think, small murder is mass mayhem. Small murder is mass mayhem and Pel can read my mind.

And I'm outside of myself watching myself watching myself. I watch myself walk through the den to the bathroom. The carpet is thick, seventies shag. In our old house, I rubbed my knees raw playing knee football with my little brother. I never let him win. I watch myself walk through the den. A shadow is behind me. I never let my brother score. Younger brothers learn early that life is not fair. I'm the oldest son. Sometimes mothers love their oldest sons too much.

In the bathroom there's a cricket in the corner, quiet, aware that I'm watching. I consider crushing him into the carpet. I consider catching him and letting him go in the garage. He's very still, numb to destiny. I do nothing. I jiggle the toilet handle to no avail, turn out the bathroom light and walk back to the couch that is my bed. I put out the cigarette and turn off the television and the light. Lying down and pulling Tom's old army sleeping bag around me, I listen for the cricket's chirp. But the night is still, save for the whir of the running toilet.

One hour, two hours, three hours pass, until I hear my mother at the top of the stairs. She opens the door and starts down the stairs, her hand brushing softly against the wall. I wake softly, surprised I was asleep. Outside it's raining, not daylight yet. I lie still, like I'm not even breathing, like I have enough air to last awhile. The rain outside is nice, and I'm warm and cool under my blanket.

Turn on the light, I'm awake, I say, and she does, continuing gingerly down the narrow stairs.

Can't sleep, kiddo?

No, I slept all right.

Well good, she says. I'm going to be up in Morristown today on business, but I should be back around noon if you want to get some lunch.

Okay, where?

Meet me at Starnes?

Yeah, that'll be good.

It's nasty outside.

I'll wear a hat.

I've got an umbrella you can have. Let me get it, it's in the closet.

Mom don't worry about it, I'll wear a hat. I hate umbrellas.

You're a strange boy.

Yes mother, I'm strange. Dad says I get it from you.

He's one to talk, she says, taking the bait, willing to argue in the dark at seven in the morning with her unemployed twenty-five-year-old son, who won't leave the couch until twenty till noon, and then only to receive his free meal for the day, about whose gene pool was the major contributor to this abomination of normalcy swaddled in old army blankets before her.

He's one to talk, she repeats, hoping I'll elaborate on the psychological profile Dad submits of her to the world at large, but I back off a little, it being early in the day for a full goad session.

I'm just kidding.

I know.

No you don't.

Just hush, Jason. Go back to sleep. On second thought, why don't you get up and vacuum the den.

I feign snoring, loud, Three Stooges style.

I'm serious, there's plenty of work to be done in the house.

I snore louder.

I should have spanked you as a child.

You did, I say between snores.

Obviously not hard enough.

I know. We never told you, but that spatula didn't hurt.

Your brother did one time, she says, remember?

She's laughing now, remembering five-year-old Petey saying, that didn't hurt, one time when she'd halfheartedly spanked him.

I wore his butt out good after that, remember? He wasn't quite as smart there for awhile after that.

Oh, those were the days, I say, smart as ever.

Those were the days. And I've still got my spatula upstairs.

I know you do. Why don't you go fry me some eggs.

I'll fry your butt, she says, shaking a skinny fist. Then she turns, says with John Wayne finality, Noon, and is out the door, leaving the stairwell light on on purpose.

I get out of bed around eleven, having smoked two cigarettes while watching an invigorating sequence of game show repeats. I go upstairs and Tom is reading yesterday's paper. We mumble hello and I grab a Coke out of the refrigerator. No work today, I say. Need me to pick up anything while I'm out?

Nah. I'll run by Kmart later on and get that paint for the gazebo.

All right, I say, walking down the stairs, a lot less cute than I felt earlier, the gloom of the day through the kitchen window, Tom at the kitchen table smoking, popping the pages of the paper hard, a slow brood working, the sun and the softness of the day before washed away dirty, the just-drained pool filling again with small leaves and grass clippings and water run scummy through the soil.

After I shower and dress, I step into the outside world. The rain is cold, hitting my back and bare neck hard. I run to my car aware that Mom's umbrella would have kept me dry, but not too worried about it. The windows are fogged, and the engine is cold, stuttering. I haven't left the house for three days and with a solid dread of confronting the rainy grey of Knoxville, I put the car in reverse, ease with trepidation down the driveway, past the For Sale sign in the yard, and into the real world.

The dogwoods are shivering in the rain, and greyer somehow, Easter past. I pull out of Bearden Heights and onto Kingston Pike. The Pike runs parallel east and west with Interstate 40 from Dixie Lee Junction, west of Knoxville, for fifteen miles up to the University. I used to live out west in Concord with the rest of the nouveau presumptuous before my parents split up. Now my mother's house is closer to town, and actually just a couple of miles from the split-level we lived in when we first moved to Knoxville, the house we could actually afford. My life has been a series of split-level houses, excluding our brief attempt at the upper middle class, and I've come to conclude I was never meant to live anywhere else. Life is a circle. Life is a split-level house.

Knoxville should be a pretty city, set in the foothills of the Smoky Mountains, which sit old and brooding and constant in the east, and with the Tennessee River running through, and the TVA lakes, and the Dogwood Trails, but malls and carlots and vacated ghost shopping centers and other concrete generica have overrun the city. Paved hell.

The rain continues and the wipers have a hard time keeping the windshield clear. I drive a little Hyundai that my grandfather bought me. The thinking in the family was that if someone bought me a car, I might be more inclined to get a job. This, as it turns out, was not the case. I've not so much as sniffed at one since I got back from Australia in December. It's a decent car, more than I deserve. It runs well, and won't go fast enough to get me a speeding ticket or killed in an accident. The door handle is broken on the passenger side, so if I ever have another date she'll have to get in my door and straddle the stickshift to get to her seat. Not that women don't like contorting their bodies into awkward positions in the first ten seconds of a first date.

Turning on Middlebrook Pike, a bird flies in front of my car and I have to hit the brakes hard to miss it, nearly going into a hydroplane in the process. This happens a lot lately, birds flying in front of my car out of nowhere like some video game. But I always miss them.

I turn into Starnes and circle the parking lot looking for my mother's car, but I'm a little early. The line is already into the far dining room and it'll take us fifteen minutes to get to the front. Good country cooking at Starnes. The walls are filled with pictures of this year's Tennessee Volunteers football team, and pictures and collages of former UT All-Americans.

My Uncle Clay is on the wall. He's probably the most famous football player to ever play at UT. At least in the state he is. Wherever I go in Knoxville I see his picture. Or drawings of The Catch. A play where Clay dove and just barely kept one foot in bounds to beat Alabama in 1962. I'm sure there have been dissertations written on the Southern affection for football, how it is an intuitive communal reflex to the loss of an old and bitter war, and perhaps there's something to that. Perhaps we just like the game. I do know that Uncle Clay was about as famous as you could be at the age of twenty. And that for as long as I can remember, whenever I intro-duced myself, people asked if we were kin. Cleancut, Clay Sayer was, said ma'am and sir. Life magazine wrote a feature on him in 1963. His statue stands in front of the athletic dorm.

Mom pulls up and gets wetter trying to get her umbrella up than she would have if she just walked the twenty feet to the cafeteria. I get out and meet her at the door. We walk in together and go to the back of what is about a thirty-person line. My mother is fifty, but men at tables check her out. Some make the quick neck jerk to their friends. She knows, la de da, what else is new, yes hello boys, a general smile to the cafeteria at large, and her entrance is complete. My father is good-looking too. I, on the other hand, am Mendel's favorite recessive gene case study.

We talk about the rain as we move slowly toward the front of the line, passing a watercolor of The Catch and a black and white photo of Clay after a game with his hair wet, wearing a skinny tie and a wide grin.

I love that picture of Clay, my mother says.

How come?

He just looks so happy, so world by the tail. I don't know. I just like it.

Who was the best-looking?

Oh your father. At least to me. A lot of people would say Clay. But your father, when he was younger, he was really a handsome man.

What happened to me and Petey, I ask, and she laughs.

We get to the front of the line and there's a handwritten sign reading

Tennessee 35

Ole Miss 3

The season opener is only three months away. One year Tennessee started out 0 and 6, and the whole town had given up on the team and was ready to kill the coach, but every week Mr. Starnes was putting up those signs, saying Tennessee 13 Alabama 6. Even though the whole town knew the Vols had a mule's chance in the Kentucky Derby of winning. My dad doesn't have much use for Tennessee fans. He played at Memphis State and remembers the fans booing Clay when he was a sophomore and being carried off the field with broken ribs. Of course Tennessee was losing at the time.

While Mom is paying the cashier, I see a couple of guys I went to high school with. Jody McDowell is one of them, the other's name I can't recall. Jody's a nice guy, one of those Fellowship of Christian Athletes who wasn't an athlete type. He drove a BMW, a lot of kids at Chapman did. But it galled me, I guess, that Jody had a Prince of Peace bumper sticker on his. Rich guys and camels through eyes of needles and all that. I guess I wasn't into the whole FCA thing. I thought half the guys were in it just to meet girls. And I heard one too many chapel talks, with slides and obligatory James Taylor soundtrack, about the hugging, tug of roping, sing alonging, picture posing weekend retreat to Vanilla Mountain. I'm sure there were a lot of sincere kids in it, and Jody's all right, everyone in high school a rawer form of themselves, but I slide on by his table without speaking, using my mother as a shield.

We sit down in the back room and before Mom is all the way down I'm shoveling in those beautiful artery-clogging deep-fried chicken livers that are Mr. Starnes's specialty. Mom, graceful Southern girl watching her figure, has been hypnotized by the Starnes zone and has loaded down her plate with chicken and dumplings, fried okra, creamed potatoes, and turnip greens. A piece of pecan pie for good measure. She sees my admiring stare. Hungry, she says.

Maintaining a vigilant pose as I eat, I sweep the floor with my eyes to ward off sneak attacks from other old schoolmates, ex-girlfriends, fathers of ex-girlfriends, former employers, and a host of other must-miss Knoxvillians. During one such sweep, I spot an older man sitting down to lunch. He looks familiar, friendly, someone I've seen at a Little League ballpark years back. Some rural area. Karns maybe. Or Powell. Places where folks come out to the games even when they don't have kin playing, sitting quietly in the stands, then saying afterward to some kid they'll never see again, good game son, that's the way to throw that bean. He looks a little country, like he used to come in here before the cat was out of the bag about the good food and cheap prices and still finds the expansion hard to believe, the crowds of men in suits mixed in with old regulars like himself. After he pulls the plate and silverware off his tray, he bows his head and closes his eyes. Then he puts his napkin in his lap and digs in.

We eat in silence until Mom says, I met a girl you might like at O'Charley's the other day.

This is an instance where Mom cannot let well enough alone. Let her brooding son, who up to now was enjoying her company, eat in peace. Oh swift run the gamut of emotions when mothers and sons lunch, mercurial the shifts in tone.

Uh hm, I mumble.

Really nice girl, advertising major at UT. Just your type, nice legs. And she doesn't have that Dolly Parton hair you're always talking about.

I don't respond, my mute boy routine indication enough I don't want to continue this conversation, that Mom is in danger of losing all grumpy son bonus points for buying me a good lunch. But my mother, half masochist, half kamikaze, has an unfathomable streak in her that is fueled entirely by silence, specifically silence by the males of the species, and the quieter I get, the more likely she is to keep talking and dig herself deeper into a hole. What I should do is feign interest in this waitress from O'Charley's, promise to go by and meet her and that Mom will have grandchildren before the year is out. What I do instead is remain silent and wait for her to piss me off like I know she's about to.

I told her about your trip to Australia, she continues blindly. She seemed interested. I got her name if you want it.

No you didn't.

Yes I did.

No you didn't tell her about my trip to Australia. That's horrible. You didn't really tell her about my pathetic trip.

She doesn't say anything. I swallow half a glass of iced tea and shovel into my coconut cream pie.

Mom, I'm telling you, all I did in Australia was get drunk. I might as well have been in Ohio.

She's looking at me kind of wild eyed, a deer blinded by headlights in the middle of the road.

But it was something. Not everyone gets to go overseas. I never did.

Good God she can't be serious. Surely she is baiting me. Hunched over my tray, leaning close to her, a snarl through tight teeth, I say, please get it into your deluded mind that my trip to Australia was a total fucking waste of time. If you must have something to chat to waitresses about, you're going to have to be a little more creative than that.

She doesn't cry, but gets up and goes to the ladies' room, leaving me staring wildly about the room before my squinting snake eyes settle on an older couple that I'm sure were eavesdropping. I stare at them, bullying their eyes back down to their plates, and then sit, soaking in unreasonable anger, until I have the overwhelming urge to fork myself in the face.

She comes back from the restroom, eyes slightly red, and the older couple look up from their sweet potatoes, pity in their eyes, Mom's presence giving them strength now to reproach me, she's walking so straight and unbowed. The old woman turns full around to watch her take her seat, giving me a you ought to be ashamed look, a look that says yes, I am a doddering old nosey woman out of touch with this crazy modern world, but I still know that any boy, a man for crying out loud, should have more sense, more rearing, than to put that awful look on his mother's face. The old man, stoked by his wife's bold indignation, wants to say, I could eat a pound of baloney and shit a better man.

Uncle Clay, on the far wall, smiles from 1963. Cleancut he is, well reared. The old couple sit wondering what ever happened to young men like Clay Sayer.

Mom, I say, and then stop, nothing new to say, we've been here before.

I just want what's best for you, she says, composed, a professional mother nearly. She's seen movies about angry young sons.

I know.

I'm just so worried about you.

I know, I'm worried about myself too.

Uncle Clay smiles, bring on Bama.

You could do anything, you can do anything, I don't care. You could collect garbage and I'd still be proud of you.

Which is true. She'd brag to her friends about my daring and innovative way of throwing trash into the back of a truck.

But you have to do something, anything.

Yes, I say, for she is right, I must do something. I'm sorry Mom, I'll get better.

My mother smiles at this mystery of her own flesh before her eyes, convinced more than ever by my skittishness that I'm destined for some great endeavor, that I've just not found the right outlet for my particular genius, that any baby who could say his ABC's before he was two years old is bound for some sweeping success in this grand old world of ours.

I'll do something, I say, beaten down as always by unbridled and ridiculous optimism.

Thatta way, Uncle Clay smiles from the wall, that's my nephew.

I know you will. I'll help as much as I can, okay?

Okay, I say, blindly, dumb and dizzy in a world where childhood precocity counts for so little. We get up to leave, me a skulking wet dog in the rain, Mom bright and cheerful in her dutiful mother role. She is beyond happy, her catharsis complete, her son will do her proud yet, and she will have had no small role in his comeback from she knows not where, but somewhere awful and unfair.

We walk past the older couple. They remain unconvinced.

Outside the rain continues, seems always. Mom kisses me, puts twenty dollars in my hand for the yard work I did. Just to get you by for awhile, she says. Then she walks to the car in the rain without bothering to put up her umbrella. The rain must feel good, for she doesn't walk fast. The rain makes my knee hurt, and I limp back to the car, not sure, not even concerned, whether the limp is affected or not.

Coming out of the parking lot, I don't know whether to turn left or right. A miserable country song comes on the radio. Not wanting silence, or the possible pandemonium on the rock station, I leave it. I have money for cigarettes, but hate to break the twenty, a twenty broken soon gone on gas and beer and smokes. I search the ashtray for a good long butt, find one, wipe off the ashes, fire it, and then that sweet nicotine that soothes for a moment before putting the shaky edge back on my shaky world.

I turn left and feel a shadow behind me. I check the rearview for visual proof, find none. I turn off the radio. A light flashes in my eyes, something that happens with great frequency now. There is nothing there, no light, just a flash, like something in the imagination. The flashes are a residue from the acid trip, Pel says. But that was over a month ago, and they're more frequent than ever.

I pull in a Weigel's convenience store and fill up with gas. I go in the store, buy a quart of beer, some smokes, pay for the gas, get back in the car and head the other way down Middlebrook Pike toward home. I fire a cigarette and take a long pull at my beer. They both taste fresh and good. The rain has slackened, coming down now a little beaten, in short spare whimpers. I take a right on the Pike, then veer off quickly to Deanne Hill. Mom's house is about a mile up the road, but the thought of Tom at the kitchen table, not wanting to see my sorry ass, wanting only to brood, and the For Sale sign in the yard like a reverse gargoyle inviting bad spirits in, makes me take a quick left into the Deanne Hill Community Center in the hope that Beth's working today. But she isn't. Her car's not there. The parking lot's empty and I'm back ripping down Deanne Hill Drive, water off my tires hissing clean like snakes.

I come to the end of Deanne Hill and take a left on Morrell, go over the railroad track fast without looking, and then make a right on Westland. I go two miles down the road, take a right up an embankment and back over the train tracks, and park my car on a side road of Westwood subdivision, next to the train track, a hundred yards from the nearest house.

Uncle Clay was in the backseat of a car that got hit by a train at this spot. He and two other UT coaches were on their way to practice. All three were killed. I was five months old at the time and Dad was twenty-four, two years younger than Clay.

I get out of the car and walk up the steep embankment. This is still a dangerous crossing. The weeds are high, as they were that day, and with the steepness of the hill, and a heavy fog that morning. If only Clay had been driving, everyone says.

I walk a ways down the tracks. The rain has stopped, but the trees lining the track are heavy with water. I keep walking, then running, high step chopping on every tie like a tire drill. The running hurts my knee, but I keep going, breathing out hard, humping it, getting that rhythm, going through the tires in my mind, late August, Chapman High two-a-days, thin legs trying to take big feet through tires fast. I've got no speed. Technique, concentration. Coach, let's go now go now go now go now. Carryokie drill now, turning sideways, left foot over right, right out, left behind, front-ward over then backward behind. Backpedaling now over the rain-slick ties, ball drill, get back get back get back, react to the ball, planting, ready for the oskie, then my foot slipping, bad knee buckling, hands down just fast enough to keep my face from smashing the railroad tie.

Not far off, near the intersection close to my mother's house, the shrill of a train. I pick myself up slowly, hands cut from the rocks between the ties, wrists jammed, probably sprained, the throb in my knee constant, the pain good, real. I stand on the tracks and face the direction of the whistle and wait to see what synapses take charge. The train comes into sight a half mile away, a black monstrosity out of the rain-hazed grey. I stand still on the track, wanting to hear the whistle. It will mean something if I hear the whistle. With the train a quarter mile away, I walk off the track and sit on the bank under some trees. Cold drops of rain hit my head intermittently. I sit with the seat of my pants wet from the ground. The train comes even, the engineer looks at me, a haggard bum, a ghost on the bank, and I look back, and then he's past, my ears gone deaf, swoosh of wind like a blow to the head. The train rolls by and I turn to watch the caboose rattle out of sight. Then I walk to the car, limping slightly, the smell of anticlimax in the air.

Coming up to my car, I see I've left the lights on, and know right away it won't start. I've needed a new battery for months. I try to start it, but nothing. I check the trunk for jumper cables in case someone drives by, but no go, just my golf clubs and some old tapes.

I sit in the car and wonder where the hazard button is, but don't bother to look for it. The rain on the windshield is soft and steady. I recline the seat. I'd like to have seen Beth. We're pretty good friends. Since she works so close to my mom's house I go by and see her on occasion. I've known her for awhile. She used to date Pel. I knew her before she dated Pel, but that's mostly how I know her.

The rain keeps coming down, easily, running in slow blurry waves down the windshield, down the hood, and I feel myself going to sleep, and I don't fight it.

I'm awakened by tapping on the window and young male voices asking if I'm okay. I keep my eyes closed even though I'm pretty sure I'm awake. When I open my eyes there's two high school kids in the window. What do you say boys?

You all right?

Still reclined, I say, sure I am. What's going on?

We saw your car and thought you might need some help.

I can hardly keep my eyes open. Beside me, wedged between the seat and the emergency brake, is the quart of beer. I appreciate that, I say, bringing my seat upright.

You out of gas? one of the young Samaritans asks.

Battery's dead. I must have dozed off waiting for someone to come by. I take a gulp of warm beer and it doesn't taste good and light a cigarette, which also doesn't taste good. I look at myself in the rearview, and wipe some dried spittle off the side on my mouth, and then get out of the car. It's stopped raining.

The boys stand back a ways, eyes curious, Lazarus back from the dead and looking dangerous. They're looking at my hands, so I look at them too, muddy and blood-streaked. I wipe my hands on my dirty shorts. Fell, I say.

One of the kids has a smile wanting to form on his lips. They're rich kids, their Maxima parked thirty yards behind. Ragged cutoff Duckheads, white T-shirts. One wears a Ski Breckenridge baseball cap, the other a faded UT cap that he waterskis in. Irony plays a symphony on their lips. Ski Breckenridge asks, you Pete Sayer's brother?

Chapman boys, I say, showing them the proper prep school way to look ironical. I used to live in Breckenridge for awhile, I say, pointing at his hat. Right after college.

You did? That place is awesome. Did you ski a lot?

Not much.

What did you do?

Not much, bartended, drank for about a year, I say, slipping way too easily into my casual, too cool for school, this life is so easy it's a joke demeanor. They laugh.

We thought you were dead, Waterski Cap says, a bit overeagerly. It took us awhile to wake you up. What're you doing over here?

Uhm, I say, trying to think up a lie. Just watching a train. I smile. They laugh nervously.

Were you on that state team, Ski Breckenridge asks.

Yessir. Damn right. State champs.

What position?

Corner. A very speedy corner. A blurred number ten streaking like a phantom across the field.

Man I think I saw you get kicked out of a football game when I was in fifth grade, Waterski Cap says.

I laugh. That was the next year.

You threw the ball at a guy.

He late-hit me.

Did he? I don't remember that. It was homecoming though. My dad was an alum and he thought it was so funny that someone got kicked out when everybody was in town.

Yeah, well, I say. Nothing to be proud of Rusty. I want you to know that that penalty cost us a touchdown. And good ole Chapman could have lost the game because of it. There's a valuable lesson to be learned here youngsters about losing your temper.

They laugh, roll their eyes. Hey, Ski Breckenridge says, didn't you used to date Leslie Ellis?

Yeah.

Man she was hot.

Indeed she was.

Where is she now?

Couldn't tell you bud. Couldn't tell you. But if you fellers will help me push this here car up that there hill yonder, I think I can jump her off.

They get behind the car. I jump in, turn the starter on, put it in neutral, get myself ready to one-leg, and we're off, up the hill, then cresting the hill I put my hand up for the boys to stop pushing, put the clutch in, shift to second, pop the clutch, the motor kicks in, thumbs-up out the window, the Fonz lives, and I'm gone.

Oh glory days at old Chapman High, Knoxville's finest. Where, like most young men of a certain inclination, my imitation of teenage rebellion was fairly predictable and, in hindsight, a bit stale. I'd been sent freshman year kicking and screaming and tearing at the tie looped round my neck. My parents felt I'd garnered more jockish provincialism than any young man would ever need and that public Concord High would offer little else. So after eight perfectly relaxed and enjoyable years of public schooling, there I was in a coat and tie, in docksiders for crying out loud, butchering the French language, je ne sais pas madame, hacking my way through essay exams on Beowulf, and otherwise distinguishing myself with unstifled mediocrity in Algebra I, Religious Studies I, and Western Man. And oh the dreaded chapel talks. A Chinese water torture whereby every able-bodied student addressed the whole of the assembled student body at least once a year. Mumbled accounts of summer vacations in Hilton Head. Sniffling biographies of sisters gone off to college. The Jody McDowell rhapsodic slideshow. Pel and my other friends at Concord High found me too pitiful to ridicule that first year at Chapman.

Here now, I'm winding my way through Westwood, the subdivision adjacent to my old one, West Trails, developers in the seventies emphasizing that yes, this is West Knoxville, home of the momentary middle class. I'm tracing my old bus route from Cedar Bluff Middle School, pre-Chapman days, when I was the young go-getting student council president. I drive past the small trailer park near the train tracks that the whiff of upward mobility never quite found, where kids with nicknames like Junior and Democrat lived, kids with pants an inch short who shut up as soon as we boarded the bus, who carried their gym clothes in grease-spotted paper bags, and how nice it must have been after the suburb boys were dropped off, when they had the bus to themselves again, and Albert the bus driver would say, tell me about the world, Democrat. Tell me about the world.

I take a right off Gallaher onto Apache Trail, and here I am in West Trails, in split-level heaven. They're kit houses really, the colors varying somewhat, yellows, browns, and whites, but no mistaking the fact that there's little variation in this litter of West Knoxvillia. Not a bad thing. Everybody's house seemed equal.

I drive past Drew Deaderick's house, which was the start of the sledding hill. Drew Deaderick, who in 1983, on his nineteenth birthday, drove up to the Great Smokies National Park and shot himself in the head. Crazy Drew with the long, flaming red hair, who always wore a Boone's Farm Strawberry Wine T-shirt and went around the neighborhood screeching KISS songs in a loud falsetto. Even the older kids were scared of him.

One time a possum got in our garbage can, hissing and spitting like a camel. Drew hopped over the fence with a stick in hand, Mom screaming from the kitchen window, and all the kids in the neighborhood gathered around, but at a distance, that possum like a huge primordial rat, its tail pink and skinny, Drew poking with a stick, calmly saying, go on, git on out of there, and finally the possum scooting off past us. Mom gave him five dollars afterwards.

A collie I don't recognize walks in front of my car, and I come to a stop in front of Barry Paige's house. His dad, Big Barry, used to coach us in Little League. He called us the West Trails Allstars. Good old Barry Paige. We used to brainwash his little sister Janet into thinking her name was Joshua Pudge. What's your name Janet?

Janet.

No, it's Joshua Pudge.

What's your name?

Janet.

No, it's Joshua Pudge. What's your name Janet?

Joshua Pudge.

That's right, good girl. Now go tell Mom what your name is.

I take a right onto Brushy Trail, and stop to watch a couple of kids I don't know splashing around in the drainage ditch. It's strange how few of the same people live here, though this was not a starter neighborhood for everyone. This small subdivision of apparent suburban normality was an accomplishment in itself for some, a yard to mow once a week, a bedroom for each of the two children, a paved driveway for a basketball hoop, and good Americans like yourself minding their own business, saying hello at the mailbox. Halloween parties for the kids, and Fourth of July picnics, but of course that is not the way, not anywhere, the American dream like any dream, cloudy with dark splotches and suicides and divorce, and when do you open your eyes and say, this is all a sham. Or do you keep the blinders on and mow the grass, and let those who need to move on move on. You mow the grass, and greet your new neighbors at the mailbox, and isn't this house starting to feel small? Or do you put your foot down and say, I like this house and this apparent suburban normality. No it's not perfect, but life is not perfect and I'm not perfect and this house is okay and this neighborhood is okay and I don't want to divorce my wife and my kids may be confused at times but I'm pretty damn sure they'll never kill themselves, and I'm doing the best I can, and right now I'm sitting on the porch of the house I could afford to buy and the grass is mowed for the week, and if I look hard to the east I can see the Great Smokies and in the fall I'll drive up to watch the leaves changing to orange, yellow, and a hundred shades of red, and I will not listen to you who tell me this is not enough.

I start up again and there it is at the corner of Brushy and Sante Fe Trail, the split-level that started it all. The house, which still seems my house, remains the same bright canary yellow. The evergreens Dad planted to cover the wasteland gully behind our house are huge now. About seven of the neighborhood men helped him plant the trees, and afterwards he bought beer and grilled hamburgers for everyone. There were no other evergreens in the neighborhood and most people doubted they'd grow, they looked so thin and scraggly wrapped in ropes on the truck. But most were skeptical because we always had the worst yard in the subdivision, crab grass, and what good grass there was worn bare by West Trails Allstars scorching lawn with hot grounders and hotbox games, and any time my mother could get Dad and me to work in the yard somebody would come by the house to make a crack about calling Better Homes and Gardens.

Those evergreens are close to sixty feet high now, like huge Christmas trees, and I bet Mom and Dad haven't seen them since they were ten feet tall.

Driving out, on the corner, I see two little kids trying to spray their sister with a water hose. She's older, maybe fifth grade, and rides her bike in the driveway, just out of range of the spray, inches from it, taunting her brothers, them straining the hose, thumbs over nozzle for distance, soaking themselves, the sister not even looking, dry as a bone, the yard wet and mud-streaked from the rain and it still too cold out with no sun to be playing with the hose, and I turn my head before I start to think.

I turn right on Gallaher, then left on Gleason. The car is driving itself to the other house that is no longer my house in farther west West Knoxville. I come to the end of Gleason and take a left on Ebenezer, serpentine through this new West Knoxville, past subdivisions with names like Windrush and Hampton Chase and Richmeade Place. It's the old Richmeade Place, rustic and subdued in the quaint British countryside just north of Essex. Notice the bleating lambs, the charming pubs. Then farther out, gunning the engine on the winding roads, past rolling farms and small old houses, trees here, and cows, getting my car up to eighty where it shakes, like the old days, Duke Boy driving, yee-hi, the General Lee purring today.

When I was in Australia with Pel, we bought an old Ford Falcon for about six hundred American from some Kiwi guys in a hostel. It was a road warrior, had been passed around from traveler to traveler, no papers, expired tags, broken gas gauge, an accident and a deportation waiting to happen. It would go though. The Falcon was the best part of the trip. The rest, I don't know. We traveled up the east coast from Sydney to Cairnes, but in the second month of what was to have been six, I began to perceive that all was not as it should be, at least as my life was concerned. An anxiety came upon me unawares. I was four thousand miles away yet Knoxville bound. And Knoxville meant, what next? Before, I could answer that question from presupposing relatives and unduly concerned parental friends with, Australia, I'm going to Australia. Something about traveling to another hemisphere tended to keep the inquisitive wolves at bay. I'd saved three thousand dollars in two years after college. I bartended with Pel in Colorado right after school for about a year, a very good time, spent a summer with Trick in Atlanta when he was trying to flunk out of med school, then finished up with nine months in Indianapolis with a college friend who was trying to get into law school. Putting my good as gold BA to work as an itinerant mixologist, a fill-in roommate, sleeping on couches, bare box springs, the floor, who would not, no hell no would not, join that nine to five sleepwalk to death.

After our stint in Colorado, Pel had gone back to Knoxville to work. We were still planning our trip to Australia over the phone and when I was back in town for the holidays or an odd weekend. I was planning a trip I was sure would somehow define me, put into context this vague vain notion that I was different. Jethro Bodine, international playboy.

I spent about three weeks in Knoxville before we left, hanging out with Pel and Trick. Trick had just quit medical school. And perhaps it was then I noticed things were not the same. I couldn't tell before, just hitting K town for a weekend every five months or so. But now, it wasn't just a little beer, a little hooch anymore. The pace had quickened while I was shooting one-handed set shots in the old Hoosier state. Acid and other stuff. I was used to the smarty-pants college graduates in the bar crowd scene, those like myself too smart for the sap's play, the old suit and tie. The red-eyed philosophers, the goateed gurus, Knoxville's earth mothers and starry-eyed boys who couldn't quite make it to New York or San Francisco, who couldn't quite make it in Atlanta, the scarred and wounded, the jive asses and profound, all looking for they knew not what in Knoxville, this island of Misfit Toys. I knew and liked that crowd. But this was different. It was a new breed, young and edgy, and a Pel I no longer knew was all grown up and leading the parade.

We were in Townsville, Australia, not long after we bought the car. We were sitting beside a large salt water pool fed by the ocean. Though it was cheap, buying the Falcon had hit our wallets. The money was running out and we didn't have work visas. Knoxville loomed. Pel was reading the newspaper, folding it neatly in squares against the wind, something I never could do, read a paper in the wind, and I was watching a little Aborigine boy who was running around the pool and going up to everyone and saying allo. He came up to me smiling and said allo, and I said hello back, and then he said good, which seemed right, and was off again alloing as he went.

I was thinking about Beth, who was Pel's girlfriend back home, who was a lifeguard in the summer, and how I never did like swimming lessons when I was a kid. And I was watching this little boy, wondering where his folks were, wondering if he could swim, watching him walk down the stairs of the pool, gripping the rail. Pel was reading the paper. I was thinking that I had changed and he had changed and that this trip wasn't like our trip to Colorado. I was starting to see that Australia was not the answer I thought it was going to be. So Australia was a failure. A private failure. I would have to tell my family, my friends, what a great time I'd had, how it was a once in a lifetime experience, etcetera. But I would know. I had thought there would be answers. That if I kept moving they would come to me. That if I just avoided becoming what I was not, I would become what I was. I was mistaken. Twas the end of the road. And the fiddler who'd accompanied me was asking for his pay. I had begun to pray by then. Furtively, constantly. I'd be at the hostel, drinking and laughing with friends, and in my head I'd be saying, just stay with me God, just stay with me.

The little boy was playing on the stairs, just splashing around with his hands, and I was thinking about Beth and this new Pel and how tired I felt, how tired I'd felt ever since I got to Australia, and then the little boy falls off the stairs. He's flailing about in the water. I'm running, but see everything slowly, I'm in my tennis shoes, my only pair of shoes, then I'm in the pool, his arms windmilling every which way. I grab his waist, it's unbelievable how light he is, and just scoop him out with one hand and place him on the concrete right on his feet, him motionless, things still slow motion, a blonde guy in a thong saying, good job mate, I was just after him myself, and I'm out of the pool, with everyone looking at us, me and the kid, and then smack smack smack, some Aborigine woman is slapping the shit out of him. She's holding a fishing pole in one hand and wearing him out with the other, and he's begun to cry into her skirt. I walk in slow motion back to Pel, his face still buried in the paper. Should have taken your shoes off first, he says, and this life is odd I think, sitting down again to watch the pool, and what you think, is.

On Northshore Drive, Fort Loudon Lake appears quickly to the left. A TVA project overcome by the sewage treatment plant. I cross the bridge we used to jump off and remember teenagers in OP shorts waiting for a boat below to pass, sharing the bridge with older, drunken men, whose pale skin is frying red in the sun, a general unease between the two groups, Pel's nice car parked shiny a few yards off the road, their car nowhere to be seen, as if perhaps they lived under the bridge. These were Concord men before Concord became West Knoxville, farm boys before the concrete invaded, this bridge, this land, slipping away from them, their small houses, shacks, smaller with the tide of suburban gargantua.

I like them flowery shorts, one of them says to Pel, who is half a foot shorter than anyone else on the bridge, who has cut school to join Trick and me who have yet to start back for the fall. Their parents are already divorced. And mine can see the writing on the wall.

You're not going to try to kiss his ass are you, I say, smirkiest of the smirking suburbanites. Perhaps I am the only one smirking. Trick is the shy future Chapman valedictorian, Pel is still in the early rounds of his bout with the puberty monster.

What'd you say?

You heard me you fucking red, I say. Then I'm off the bridge, Pel and Trick laughing nervously above me. I hit the water and go down deep, staying down as long as I can, drunken redneck trouble coming. When I come up, flailing sickly white legs of irate hickdom flying at my head. I push hard in the water, then hard-swim to the shore as a barrage of bodies hurls toward the lake.

I scramble out, hands muddy from the shore, and run up the embankment over rocks and broken beer bottles, the reds screaming from the water, come on you little pussy!

They are poor swimmers. Their long, greasy matted hair flops in the water like drowning squirrels. They swim in that awkward, head out of the water semi-dogpaddle, choking as they scream.

I'm nearly to the top when the one who admired Pel's shorts is just getting out of the water. I'm laughing now. Pel has the car waiting. He's sixteen years old and looks about twelve, but you could count on Pel in a deal like this. Trick too. And below us the lead red slips down on the muddy embankment, too drunk and old for this business. Then I'm out of the car before telling Pel to stop, the car still rolling, because there's a big pile of beaten up, misshapen shoes, Kmart tennis shoes, workboots that must belong to the big fellow swimming in his long jeans, and then I'm flinging them off the bridge, the shoes splashing ugly and poor and grotesque in the water against a backdrop of wailing, luckless poverty. Learn to read you fucking necks! And then back in the car as the instigator is just to the top of the bridge to see his pitiful shoes drowning in the thick, muddy, shit-filled water.

I turn on Concord Road, and pull into the old Russell's Bait Shop. And walking in, past crickets chirping in wire cages, and shad swimming in rusted, topless coolers, I wonder how I could be so mean. But I know how I can.

Inside the bait shop it's cool and dark. No one minds the register. An overhead fan swirls dust off candy bars and moon pies and peanut butter crackers still in boxes. Last year's baseball cards. Mounted largemouth bass and pictures of smiling kids bracing a hip to hold their catch.

I walk to a stand-up cooler and start to pull a Coke out of a six-pack. Got some cold ones up here, an old lady says from the front.

I walk up front and she's sliding open an old floor cooler. Got some real cold ones here.

I didn't see you.

Watching that durn TV in the back, she says, going around to the register.

I nod, pull out an icy bottle of Coke. You weren't lying.

Hurts my teeth. Folks seem to like em though.

I pull out a dollar and hand it to her. On the register, small packets of fishing hooks, a hand-scrawled sign saying Sharp Hooks Catch More Fish.

You fish?

Some, she says, handing back the change. Not like I used to. Don't like them durn ski boats slapdashing all over. Scares the fish.

I nod. How long you been here?

Opened up in nineteen and forty as a pool hall. After my husband got back from the war he didn't want to mess with the drunks no more so we went to bait.

Area's changed some since then I reckon.

Area's changed. Folks is the same.

I laugh. So sharp hooks catch more fish?

That's a fact. And good bait. You needing any?

No ma'am. Just the Coke.

She nods. I done took out for the deposit. If you want to drink your Cocola here, I'll give it back.

That's all right. I better get going.

I figured. Come back.

I get back on Concord Road and drive past new subdivisions that were built last night, huge houses crammed on top of one another, with tall fences and expensive grass, the occasional tree looking embarrassed and old. Past abandoned plank houses too close to the widened road, with sagging wraparound upstairs porches, and windows with boards like eyepatches, and No Trespassing signs swallowed by weeds. Past Concord Cemetery, where some former ghost of myself should pop over the graveyard wall and pelt the car with a water balloon. I'd chase him down too. No fun throwing water balloons if some idiot doesn't engage in a futile chase. Especially at night when your eyes have adjusted to the darkness, and the marble tombstones and crosses whisper just beneath the breeze, just a hint of moon, a spring storm coming in soon, quick clouds across the sky, feet fast carried by specters, and down fast, hiding on a knoll in the darkest part of the cemetery, a whistle whist to your little brother to let him know where you are. Face down in the wet grass, cool, heart flying, not breathing, the ground damp, moist with death, and the tickle and rush of the wind through the grass alive, you alive, the thump of that balloon and the screech of tires ringing thick in the air. Lying perfectly still, buried in the night, hearing everything, the slam of car doors and hollow profanities, hearing the clouds pass overhead, the quietness of the quiet, and no way this chump is going to catch you in your own graveyard.

I turn right into the neighborhood just opposite the cemetery and here I am, home again, in Concord Village. I turn left on Pleasant Ridge Road, and my how pleasant is this life. No split-levels here. The yards run in constant perfection one into the other into the other. I park in front of one of these perfect yards, in front of an old white mailbox painted with faded robins, dowdy bluejays.

The house is large and brown and ugly. A three-story monstrosity, the bottom floor almost completely underground and almost completely unused. The current occupants have torn down the basketball goal and planted a flower bed along the front walk. And a new-looking fence in the back obscures the Dunstons' house. A notable improvement.

One winter when I was in seventh grade, school was canceled because of snow. Even most of the parents stayed home from work. I think Dad was out of town, he was out of town a lot, but almost every other father was out with his kids sledding or watching. All the kids were sledding and throwing snowballs. It was a hell of a snow. Jimmy Dunston, a pain in the ass kid who would no doubt grow up to be a pain in the ass macho man like his father, was throwing snowballs at sledders and catches this kid named Smooth right in the face, not hard, but still, in the face. Smooth wasn't all there. He was a couple of years older, one of those guys who hangs out with little kids, and even the little kids know he's a loser, if for no other reason than he's hanging out with them. The kind of kid who's still trick-or-treating in ninth grade.

So Smooth, dragging his sled back up the hill, stops, makes a snowball, and fires it at little second grade Jimmy Dunston, who was at that time busting a six-year-old girl in the back. Smooth catches Jimmy on the side of the head, just above the left ear. I saw the whole thing. It was a pretty good shot, but Smooth couldn't throw that hard, and it was from a distance, so there was some lob to it. It might have been hard enough to make Jimmy cry, but I think he was more embarrassed about the tables being turned, and Smooth down the hill laughing like a hyena. Mr. Dunston is at the top of the hill and hears Jimmy crying. He tears down the hill, dragging his sled blades-up, saying, what the hell happened? What in the hell happened?

Smooth knows he's in trouble, and is in half slink toward home when Mr. Dunston comes flying over, screaming about hitting little kids with snowballs, and I think he's just going to dress old Smooth down. I'm maybe twenty feet away, ready for a couple of more runs and then home. But Mr. Dunston grabs Smooth by the back of the head and trips him over his ankle. Then he gets on top of him, his knee smashing into Smooth's back, and grinds his face in the snow, saying, how do you like it? How do you like it when someone bigger than you rubs your face in the snow?

I'm in shock. None of the adults are even saying anything. Smooth is bawling, his face being ground in the snow, his arms and legs flailing, making perverse, dying snow angels. And it was such a helpless feeling, wishing Dad was there to take care of it, to say something or beat Mr. Dunston's ass or whatever it took to stop Smooth's legs and arms flying every which way, to get that look off Mr. Dunston's face.

Let him up asshole, I say.

What? Mr. Dunston says.

Let him up.

Did you say what I think you said?

Just let him up.

He hit my eight-year-old in the face, he says, getting off Smooth and heading my way. You think a big guy ought to do that?

Your kid hit him first, I say, backing up a step or two. He's right on top of me. Crazy-eyed.

I don't give a damn. He's too big to be picking on little kids.

I don't say anything but my throat's getting tight like it does when I'm mad and about to cry. Another man comes over and stands between us, putting what he means to be a calm hand on Mr. Dunston's shoulder. You best run on home son, he says to me.

No, I say, legs shaking.

Kid's got a smart mouth, Mr. Dunston says. Meanwhile Smooth, red faced and hunched up, is walking toward home.

Mr. Dunston smiles. My brother Pete has come up behind me, mad or scared at seeing my eyes watering. His eyes are watering too. Mr. Dunston does anything and Pete will be all over his ass, chewing on his leg or whatever he can.

Kid's really got a smart mouth, Mr. Dunston says, walking away. He's going to get his ass kicked one of these days.

Not by you, I say.

Mr. Dunston's smile broadens, like I'm cute or something, but he's mad as hell, smiling like a boxer who's been tagged. The man with the calm hand starts telling him something about Uncle Clay. I hear him say, Clay Sayer's nephew.

I don't give a shit, Mr. Dunston says. That kid gets old enough and I'm going to kick his ass.

A car pulls up behind me and a man in a uniform gets out. He walks toward me, moustache bristling. I place my hands on the steering wheel.

Can I help you, he asks.

I don't think so.

Neighborhood security, he says, pointing to an emblazoned patch on his chest.

I nod.

You looking for anyone?

No sir.

May I ask what you're doing here then?

I consider the question. I don't know, I say. Just sitting.

May I see your license?

I'm leaving.

Not yet you're not.

I hand over the license and he goes back to the rentacopmobile to call it in. I'm sitting there waiting when a car pulls in the driveway. A lady gets out and stands there in a jogging suit with a worried look on her face, looking first to the security car and then to me. She's got a bag of groceries in her arms. A little girl, maybe nine years old, gets out of the car and starts running down the driveway. Get back here Monica, her mother says, but the kid just stops and stands there, looking at me, then to the cop, then back at me. She turns to look at her mother who's started down the driveway. Then again at me. I give her a little half wave. In slow motion, like she's going to get in trouble if she does it, like she knows she ought not do it, talking to strangers and all, she raises a hand and waves. Then the mother is grabbing her by the arm and marching her to the house.

The cop does his own little march back to my car. Mr. Sayer, he says, other than just sitting, what are you doing here?

Nothing, really. I had an old girlfriend used to live here. I was just reminiscing.

He looks at me awhile, looks around my car until his eyes come to rest on the half-drunk quart of beer. You been drinking?

No sir, I say, holding up the empty Coke bottle and kind of shaking it.

He points at the beer. That ain't Coke there.

Just dropped a friend off. I meant to throw it out.

I could take you in for having an open container.

I'd appreciate it if you didn't.

He's got my license in his hands, almost resting it on the windowsill. He looks up the hill and back down. He scratches his security badge. He looks at my old house, my mother's old corny, cheerful mailbox. You need to find somewhere else to do your reminiscing, he says. This is a good neighborhood. Don't you reckon you scared that lady?

I reckon. I didn't mean to.

He nods, looking the car over one more time. Then hands over the license. I don't want to see you back in this neighborhood, Mr. Sayer.

You won't.

On the interstate, on my way to see my brother in Nashville, on my way out of this shithole of a city, I pass under the Watt Road Exit where someone has spray painted an upside down cross and 666 and THIS IS WAR and I feel sick to my stomach and can't shut my eyes fast enough or drive fast enough away.

In Kingston, I'm still paranoid about the crazy graffiti and start to sense a shadow, a shadow perhaps of my own volition, the amputee's sensation of having a leg, real and unreal at the same time, and I'm checking the rearview, checking that there's nothing behind me, when from nowhere a bird flies in front of my car and I have to slam on the brakes, just missing it, its black eye and fast fluttering wings a blur in the headlights, phantom bird, ex-suicide, then gone into the night.

Pete and I are in the back parking lot behind his apartment building. We've been out for a few beers. He's paid for mine and loaned me clean clothes. He's listened to me ramble about my insane weekend. He doesn't like it that his big brother has lost his nerve, that whatever swagger I once had has gone to slump.

You've got post-traumatic shock, he says, like I told you. It's like a blow to the head. Going two days without sleep, you're going to keep hallucinating. And it sounds like your friends were doing parlor tricks with your brain.

I don't know what they were doing. Maybe they were just kidding around. I was out of my mind.

They knew you were fucked up. They know how your mind works. They knew whatever they threw out there you were going to chase.

I don't say anything.

At any rate, taking your first hit of acid on Good Friday wasn't the smartest thing you've ever done.

No.

So it makes some sense that you're going to have some religious thoughts if you take acid on Good Friday. Like you said, it was probably on your mind to begin with. Whether you knew it or not. You probably said something and they jumped on it and the next thing you know we've got a theme party going.

Maybe.

But man those guys used to kiss your ass. Do you not remember that? You were the balls of that bunch.

I lost my nerve.

Well get it back.

I've been reading the Bible.

Okay. Fine. Whatever helps. Whatever it takes.

I keep hearing trains everywhere.

Listen, Mom lives half a mile from a train track, you're going to hear trains. It doesn't mean anything.

He stops talking. He looks tired. I want to tell him I'll be okay, that I'm just out of it right now, when far away, so far away you'd think it wasn't even coming from Nashville, a train whistle blows. Thin, hollow, so distant Pete cocks his head to make sure he's hearing right.

He keeps his head cocked for a second more, straining to hear what he knows he can't be hearing. The whistle blows again, far away.

I guess there's not a lot I could say right now, he says.

And I start to talk, but there aren't any words.

The next day, after lunch, Pete tries to talk me into staying with him for awhile, or at least for another night, and he means it, he wants me to stay. And I really ought to see my dad. He only lives a couple of miles from here. But I can't. It's a strange kind of loneliness, one where you want to see people and don't want to see people all at the same time. And Pete looks so run-down, fifteen hours with me enough to do the job, mine a contagious strain of malaise. We're standing by my car. I'm wearing one of his old shirts. I've seen my face in the mirror and scary scary scary it is. Puffy and wide-eyed. You need any money? Pete asks.

No man.

Enough to get you home?

Give me a five.

He pulls out a twenty and waves off any protest on my part.

We shake hands and I get in the car. I'll be all right, I say, and saying it, I hear a shaky facsimile of my voice, sounding old.

I know.

Then I try to start my car and the battery's dead. Meat, I say, using the nickname Pel hung on him long ago, give me a little push here.

Your battery's dead?

Eah, I say, chagrined country boy too tuckered to enunciate.

Good God, he says. But Pete's had to rollstart a jalopy in his day. He pushes from the front, me one-legging it backward, until I'm out in the road, then the quick hop-in, coast downhill in reverse, pop the clutch, sputter sputter, come on baby, and it starts, and I'm driving back past Pete, and begin to give him a cocky smile, then settle for the half salute. Pete waves, a good wave, not too much head-shaking in it. Enough though. Plenty.

On the interstate I drive beneath an undefined sky. A shadow is behind me. I roll down the windows, but it's too cold still after yesterday's rain. I try the radio. Nothing. I grip the steering wheel hard without realizing it, until my hands start to sweat, until the sweat starts to burn the cuts from when I fell on the train tracks. I ease my grip. My mind will not ease. Pel's your best friend, I keep thinking, Pel's your best friend. Why would he try to screw with you? Why would any of them? I was just too messed up. It was the worst weekend to try that. And at Pel's house on the Saturday after Good Friday, after I've stalked the streets in search of my sanity, after no sleep, Pel says, whenever you need healing, just water these flowers beside the porch. If you need to be healed, water these flowers. And at the bar, later, with Trick and Pel and Jimbo, I found a quarter on the floor, then a nickel. When I told Trick, he said, Judas Iscariot sold out Christ for thirty pieces of silver. Am I Judas, I said, am I Judas. And Trick said, there's a lot of Christian imagery here tonight, don't ignore it.

But am I Judas I wanted to know. And if I'm Judas, then who is Christ? Who is Christ is what I needed to know.

And Trick said, well it's not me. I'm not Christ. But feel free to ask Pel.

And late that night, still on no sleep, after I've stood in the dark and watered Pel's flowers while my friends drank beer and listened to music inside, after Trick and Jimbo have left, after Pel and Bobsmith have gone to bed, I decide to walk home to my mother's. I'm too hyped up to sleep. I walk, alternately jog. There's not a car on the road. I get to the railroad track, about halfway between Mom's house and Pel's, and it's still and quiet, empty warehouses and weeds. I walk over the railroad track towards my mother's and then back again toward Pel's. There's not a sound in the world. Nothing at all to help me decide. Back and forth, back and forth. I get two hundred yards away toward Pel's and back again, half a mile towards Mom's and back again, and there is no sound and nothing to look at but warehouses and weeds, not a car on the road, nothing at all to hear or see, and all I can think is what Pel said before he went to bed, that you always end up right back where you started. And I'm back and forth, back and forth, pacing, unable to slow down, and what I'm trying to think, trying to get my mind to slow down to remember, is where did I start. Is the place I end up back where I started? But I can't end up and I can't start and I'm back and forth back and forth over the tracks over the tracks over the tracks.

After a long while I walked back to Pel's. I sat on the porch and watched the sun come up. And it was Easter Sunday and I had not begun and I had not ended.

Approaching Knoxville, I begin to anticipate the graffiti of the day before, and at the Watt Road Exit, I don't look, have no need to be reminded. I get off at the West Hills Exit and start for Mom's house, but keep going, to the Deanne Hill Community Center, where I spot the car I'm looking for. I drive around the lot and park on an incline, so I can rollstart the car when I leave. I start to look at myself in the mirror then don't. I grab my smokes. I get out of the car and make myself walk slowly to the pool, though I have the urge to run.

Beth has her back to me. She's trying to coax a six-year-old boy into swimming to her in the middle of the pool. The kid holds tightly to the pool wall, he's crying a bit, blubbering that he can't, that the water's too cold. Come on, Beth says, you're tough, it's not that cold. You knew how to swim last year.

The kid shakes his head, no way, tightens his death grip on the wall. I walk to the edge of the pool, still behind Beth. The kid's seen me. I put my hand in the water. Whoo that's cold, I say.

Beth turns around. Hey Say.

Man that water's freezing.

Shut up, she says, laughing.

I'm serious, you'd have to be really tough to even jump in that water. No way I'm getting in. No way. No sir. Not me.

That's because you're a sissy.

Yes I am. I'm most definitely a sissy.

Paul's not though. Paul's tough. You should have seen him last year. He had his face in the water.

No way. I don't believe it. I'll have to see it to believe it.

Sit over there and watch, she says.

Blubber Boy looks up at me, blubbering away, having none of it.

Beth has unhinged Paul from the wall and walks beside him as he dog-paddles, refuses to really swim. Every now and then his head goes under and he comes up choking and crying, clutching for Beth's waist. Finally Beth picks him up and holds him. She looks at me and shakes her head. There will be no swimming today. Okay Paul, she says, I'm letting you off the hook.

Paul pulls his head off Beth's shoulder to look her in the eyes, disbelieving his good fortune. His mother leaves her card game to bring a towel over. Paul scrambles out of the pool to his mother, and oh that big towel looks warm. You gave it a shot, his mother says to Beth.

It is a little cold, Beth says.

The mother rolls her eyes, turns to look at me. Would you swim today?

No ma'am. Not unless Beth made me.

Right, Beth says.

The lady smiles at me, at Beth, thinks we're a couple. She leaves a check for Beth on the table.

Burrowed beneath his towel, Paul's already started toward the car, hot-stepping it before someone's mind gets changed.

Beth gets out of the pool and goes to the outdoor shower. She stands underneath it, head back, running her hands through her hair, trying to get the chlorine out. She's already midsummer tan, though her hair is not yet as blonde as it'll get. Her hair looks nice wet. Girls always look good with wet hair. She turns and sees me looking and smiles, still thinking about the butchered swim lesson probably, and I feel a little odd looking at her and give an awkward wave, then just to do something I go to the back corner of the pool, next to the dressing rooms, and smoke a cigarette.

When I first met her, she was a fifteen-year-old lifeguard at Country Manor Apartments. I was nineteen and working at the Quality Inn over summer break. The Quality Inn was having its staff party one Sunday at Country Manor and Pel and Bobsmith and Jimbo and I had all shown up together. I'd worked at the Q the summer before as a barback and had gotten Pel a job doing the same thing. Jimbo, a big good natured guy from Lenoir City who had just started running around with us a little bit, worked in banquets. Bobsmith was the twenty-six-year-old bar manager and head bartender. The Old Man we called him. He didn't date much, was always too nice to the girls, already perfecting his Uncle Bobsmith routine, the proverbial shoulder to cry on. At this same juncture, however, the dual nature of my faux persona was rounding nicely into form. The coeds seemed to think of me as a rakish tomcat in their plaid and khaki world, whereas country girls and older cocktail waitresses found me fancy as a French poodle. In other words, as the four of us pulled up for the Quality Inn staff party, with bikini clad waitresses and their bar crowd friends drinking frozen margaritas in the hot sun after a long weekend of work, I liked my chances.

So just as we're getting out of the car, Bobsmith says, Say, if you talk to the lifeguard, I'll cut your balls off.

What?

I'm serious. You think you're hot shit right now. But she's only fifteen, she lives next door to my parents, and she's like my little sister.

I laugh.

Pel, you and Jimbo are my witnesses. We're talking Vienna Boy's Choir.

All right Bobsmith, I say, laughing, and Pel and Jimbo are laughing and Bobsmith is shaking his shaggy head, making scissor motions with his hand.

I did end up talking to her. Bobsmith introduced us. He was always introducing me to girls. And man she was good-looking. Not flashy-looking like some of our waitresses, just real nice, classy. You could tell she was fifteen though, shy and self-conscious, laughing at everything.

Three years, I told Bobsmith in the car when we were leaving. In three years, the moratorium is off.

She turns off the shower and goes to the women's room to put on dry clothes. It's quiet now and we're the only ones left at the community center. I walk around the pool looking for a ripple, some movement, this quietness unnerving. I get up on the diving board and think about diving in or at least jumping up and down on the board, anything, a rash gesture of some sort, then I remember my knee, that the water's cold, and when Beth comes out I'm standing on the diving board doing nothing.

Jump on in, she says.

It's too cold, my belly hurts, I'll get water in my nose.

She laughs, a big one, not too loud, not exactly a snort, but far from demure, a laugh without self-consciousness.

Did you snort?

No.

Are you sure? I thought I detected just the slightest snorting of nose.

I didn't snort. I laughed.

A semi-guffaw?

You're just so funny, she says.

And I am. Ooh boy am I funny.

Beth takes the skimmer and begins fishing leaves out of the pool. I sit on the diving board and watch. She scoops the leaves and places them in a pile. The skimmer is a long one and heavy and when she reaches for a leaf in the middle of the pool, she has to bend her knees and brace her back. Hunker down Beth, I say.

She laughs, straightens herself, looking self-conscious for a minute about the awkward position, then thinks to heck with it, and hunkers down again. The leaf she's after proves elusive, and after several failed attempts at gathering it in, she lays the skimmer down. Christ, she says.

I don't say anything, let the word hang in the air so she can hear it, see if she realizes she's picked that up from Pel, though they've been broken up since before Christmas.

She laughs, not a good one.

Want a break, I say.

Yes, please.

I come down off the board and start skimming. Beth folds chairs. Pel hovers around the pool.

When I'm finished, I help her with the last of the chairs. She locks up the storage room and the dressing rooms, then the main gate to the pool and we walk out to her car together. She sees mine parked on the hill and makes a face.

My battery's dead, I say.

Do you need a ride?

No I can roll it off.

She laughs. Are you doing anything tonight?

No plans. Taking offers.

We could go get a beer if you want.

Okay, I say. That sounds good.

Can you drive?

Is there a hill near your house?

Yes.

I can drive.

She laughs again and man I love it when women laugh.

About eight, she says.

All right.

She gets in her car, starts it, and follows me up to mine, waiting, I guess, to see if the Argo will start.

I put the clutch in and get a good run down the hill and pop it easy, no problem. I circle around past her and she gives me a big thumbs-up, I've just jumped the Snake River, then follows me out of the parking lot and I head toward my house, she toward hers.

I'm due a lecture from my mother, queen of perfunctoriness, for not telling her I was going to Nashville, so I'm a little disappointed when her car's not in the driveway. Tom's is and I'm glad. I hustle around back and there he is, sitting by the pool reading the paper.

Howdy, I say.

He made it back, Tom says, looking up from his paper to acknowledge me. Then he's reading again.

I go in the house and grab a Coke and come right back out. I take my shoes off and sit by the pool with my feet in the water. I work my knee a little and it doesn't hurt and it doesn't feel great.

Water cold? Tom asks.

A little. Be all right tomorrow if we get some sun. It looked like it wanted to come out today.

Can't shit, can't get off the pot.

Yep.

Picked you up a battery today, Tom says, not looking up from the paper.

Did you really? You shouldn't have done that.

He doesn't say anything.

I was getting good at the old roll start.

He smiles. Let's go see if she fits.

All right, I say, and Tom's already halfway to the driveway. I walk behind him, barefoot, cool grass on wet feet familiar and nice.

I park at Beth's house and consider leaving my lights and radio on just for the fun of it. I have a fresh twenty in my wallet, compliments of Mom, who skipped the lecture, who nearly broke into tears when I told her I had a date.

I walk toward Beth's house with a decent dread going about meeting the Reverend Blaylock. He's one of the university chaplains, a big shot, and I'm sure a nice guy. Nonetheless, entering the palace of inquisition is never good. My dread proves warranted when the Reverend opens the door. He isn't a small man, nor particularly affable to the guys who come to pick up his youngest daughter. His eyes fill me in on the night's dinner table conversation. So who are you going out with tonight Beth?

Jason Sayer.

Pel's friend?

Yes.

Awkward silence.

And what does Jason do?

Nothing.

Well what does he want to do when he grows up?

I don't know.

Long silence ensues. Mrs. Blaylock, out of sheer embarrassment, leaves the table to check on the brownies she put in the oven not thirty seconds before.

Hello Reverend Blaylock, I say.

Good evening, he says.

We stand there looking at one another for a nice long time. Rather he looks at me while my eyes do a little dance all around his chest. I decide to take off running for the woods. I decide to say, I enjoy your intimidating presence quite a lot.

I may be a little early, I say.

No, Beth's ready. Beth, he says, not in a yell, but loud enough. I'm about to point out that I don't wear an earring or a ponytail when Beth glides by him with a pat on his broad shoulder. I won't be late, she says, breezy as only a youngest child can be.

Good to see you, I say, knees twitching in anticipation of departure.

His head moves a millimeter, slowly, a pantomimed nod, perhaps just a twitch of the nose, and walking away I'm waiting to hear the door close. Not that the Reverend wouldn't enjoy the sight of his daughter scrambling over the gearshift to her seat. The door does close, not softly, not too firmly. Just right.

At the car, I say, my other door handle's broken. You'll have to get in on my side.

You know how to treat a lady.

I've been told that.

But she skedaddles in without a hitch. And when I start my car, the battery cranking strong as a bolt of lightning, she looks a little disappointed that she didn't get to watch me rollstart it, that she didn't get the full treatment.

Your battery works, she says.

Oh yeah, it's a new day for me. I got it going. Get your dad out here, I want to show him my battery.

She laughs.

No it was fun, I say. We had a nice talk. Shared a firm handshake. I think I made a good impression.

She laughs again, then we're down the road, heading toward the Old Pub.

The Old Pub is a decent bar. It's on the Strip but isn't too collegiate for its own good. You walk in the front door and the bar is on the left. A long row of booths runs down the right side and past the bar a few more booths on the left. It's dark, but a soft dark. Not a lot of junk on the walls. The crowd is a mix of yupwads, college kids, the occasional longhair. A few good-looking girls scattered about as visual stimuli. Stevie Ray Vaughn on the stereo.

We grab a booth toward the back and talk for awhile, drink a couple of beers. The bar gets more crowded, with people standing around waiting for booths.

Do you remember when we first met, I ask her, just for the hell of it, just to be reminded that I once had a game.

You mean when Bobsmith said he'd cut your balls off if you talked to me?

Yeah that day.

Yes I remember, she says, and smiles, and then laughs and I'm glad I asked.

You were about eleven years old then.

Fifteen. I was fifteen.

Man that was a fun summer. I thought I was so cool. I thought I owned the town.

You seemed to have a few girls floating around. All those little Quality Inn waitresses. It must have been the earring.

Good gosh. I didn't really wear an earring.

I liked it. I thought you were nice.

I wasn't nice.

You were to me.

Well I didn't mean to be.

Okay cool guy, I forgot. You were so cool trying to impress all your buddies that I didn't even know you were faking it. You must have felt sorry for me.

I laugh. She's got me. She gets up to go to the bathroom and gives me the double thumbs-up, the double Fonzie.

While she's gone, good old Jody McDowell comes in the bar. I don't have my mother to hide behind, so I'm a sitting duck when he walks over.

Hey Jason, he says.

Hey, what's up.

You know I saw you yesterday down at Starnes. I tried to get your attention but you didn't see me.

Yeah, I was with my mom, I say, as if being with one's mother affects the ability to see the Jody McDowells of the world.

Beth comes back to the table to save me before the interrogation can continue. Hey Jody, she says, sliding into the booth.

Hey Beth, he says, looking shy and sheepish.

Do you want to join us, she asks, and involuntarily my eyes roll to the back of my head.

No. Thanks. I'm meeting someone. I'm just going to wait for him up front.

My eyes roll forward again. My escape plan, which had just begun to jell, but was to be initiated with a bloodcurdling scream and a roundhouse kick to his head, dissolves into thin air. I smile easily. Good to see you Jody.

Likewise, he says. See you later Beth. Then he's walking back toward the front.

Beth's smiling at me, her back to Jody, knowing she can smile whereas I can't. How do you know him, I ask.

Campus Crusade.

And.

Well, he called to ask me out today.

Shew.

I know. I can't believe I saw him.

You already had plans though. You would have gone otherwise.

Yeah.

You would have?

Yeah. He's a nice guy. It's just awkward seeing him. I don't want him to feel bad.

I went to school with him.

I know. He told me. I said I had plans, then he asked what I was doing, which was really none of his business, but I said I was going out with you. Then he said he went to school with you. And that was it.

Good old Jody McDowell. You know we didn't really hang out that much in school.

That's surprising.

I laugh, and right when I do, Jody happens to turn around and see me, and I feel bad about laughing. It's bad enough being by yourself in a bar, even for a little while, without having to see a girl you asked out that very day laughing and cutting up with another guy, especially a guy you would consider an asshole if you considered anyone at all an asshole, and then you'd start wondering if they were laughing at you and you'd wish you hadn't dropped by the table and tried to be nice to a guy who, if you were paranoid, you could have sworn was trying to avoid you the day before.

I get up to go to the bathroom, though I don't really have to, just to give Jody a chance to melt into the crowd a little more, let him know I'm not laughing so hard at his expense that I can't break myself away from the table.

Walking back to the booth, I look toward the front and see that Jody's friend has arrived. They're sitting at the bar talking, enjoying their diet Cokes, their frozen virgin daiquiris, and all is well at the Old Pub.

Beth and I drink a couple more beers, get a little giggly. I begin to entertain the notion that perhaps we should get married. Perhaps tonight. Let's get married, I say.

Okay.

Tonight I mean. We'll wake your dad up and he can perform the ceremony in his pajamas.

She laughs. Maybe we should wait until tomorrow.

Tonight, I say. Right now. Let's go right now.

She laughs and looks at me and I give her a crazy look, all desperate and happy and insane. A dose of sincerity thrown in for good measure. A look that leaves no doubt that I am the valedictorian of my charm school class.

For some reason I look to the door, it's like I'm drawn, an intuition, a thing to happen I knew was going to happen. In walk Bobsmith and Jimbo and Trick and Pel, all in shorts and T-shirts and basketball shoes. Tuesday night. I'd forgotten. It's been a long time since I played. And besides, you can't go anywhere in this one horse town without running into every single person you know. The boys just walked in, I say.

Pel?

Yep. The whole crew. I forgot it was Tuesday.

They play basketball on Tuesday.

Yes.

And then they come to the bar.

Yes.

And what has not been said about me and Pel and my insanity, what has not been discussed about Beth and Pel and why I'm with her now dances around in my eyes, makes Beth's face look a little drawn. And Bobsmith has seen me, pointed me out to Trick, who gives his recently trademarked smile, the cat who ate the canary, and Bobsmith is walking towards us and Trick points at me and makes a motion asking if I want a drink, but I wave him off and he laughs as if I've done something funny. Pel is at the bar, laughing about something with the bartender, and hasn't looked back, but he's seen me. He's got fast eyes.

Bobsmith sits down next to Beth. His shaggy hair is still damp. His legs are so long he can't fit them both under the booth and has to stretch one down the aisle. Beth's glad to see him. She pats his slouching shoulder like a favorite uncle. He looks at me and smiles. What say Say.

Nothing much.

I scoot over to let Trick slide in. You got the boy out, Trick says to Beth. I thought he'd retired.

Semi-retirement, I say, a little break in the action. Beth laughs, nervously.

How was your game, I ask.

Good, Trick says. Had about twelve to run. The old man was hitting his dusty running hook-sling, I was dribbling the ball off my foot every five minutes, Pel only needed CPR a couple of times. It was good. We missed you.

Say's the dishman, right, Beth says.

He fills the plates, Bobsmith says.

None shall go hungry, says Trick.

What they're trying to say Beth is that I can't shoot. And it's not that funny, but Beth laughs, and Trick and Bobsmith are red-eyed giggles and I'm thinking, these guys can read my mind.

Beth and Bobsmith talk about Bobsmith's nonexistent lovelife, about what bands are playing down at Mentors where Bobsmith and Pel and Jimbo work. Trick and I talk about the NBA playoffs, my knee, our high school basketball days. Trick could really play. He was All Knoxville our senior year. He'd practice four or five hours a day by himself in the summer and wouldn't call it quits until he'd hit fifty free throws in a row. If he missed number forty eight, he'd start over. We talk about particularly irritating players on other teams, Old Floppy Neck from Chattanooga Baylor, Mr. Exasperated from Knox Catholic. We talk about our joke of a coach, the bullshitter of all bullshitters. We do not, however, get around to talking about my bad night, or why when I was crazy Trick would say Judas sold out Christ for thirty pieces of silver.

Trick gets up to go to the bathroom, and I sit in the booth, needing a beer, not wanting to talk to Pel, who is still at the bar, his back to us, talking to Jimbo.

Do you need a beer Say, Beth asks. It's my turn to buy.

Which it is. But she's blocked in by Bobsmith. She pulls a ten from her pocket and starts to scoot Bobsmith out, but I say, that's all right, I got it.

As I near the bar Pel has his back to me talking to Jimbo, but just as I walk up, he turns around and smiles. Say, long time.

Been awhile, I say. Then I extend my hand to Jimbo, the former country boy muscle of the group, the king of the flunkies, who is smiling up a storm at me.

Big Say, he says, the mystery man.

What you been up to Say, Pel says, dragging on his beer, facetious earnestness in his voice, trying to make light of the fact that the last time he saw me I was insane, that I haven't called him or any of them in well over a month.

Oh, little of this, little of that. Trying to find my sanity.

Where you been looking?

My mother's house, I say, and smile.

Pel nods his head. We've got nothing to talk about.

Did you ever find Judas, Jimbo asks, and as soon as he does Pel cuts him a look with his asphalt at night eyes like he shouldn't have said that.

What?

Jimbo blunders ahead. He's either oblivious to the fact that Pel wants him to shut up or is experiencing a dope-induced straightening of spine. That night, at Pel's, you were yelling, who is Judas, who is Judas.

No I wasn't. I was yelling who is Jesus.

Are you sure, Jimbo says, small doll's eyes glistening in his big face.

I'm sure.

We look at each other. You want a beer? Pel asks, and I turn to look at him, but he's already got his back to me, waving down the bartender, and going out the door, out of the corner of my eye, it's Jody McDowell, a head nod, and then gone.

Pel hands me a beer. Did you see Jody McDowell?

Yeah I saw him.

The old Prince of Peace himself.

He's all right.

Pel nods, squints his eyes, looks far off in the distance to the land of acquiescent head nods, the village of good guys and warm sentiment. Jimbo thoughtfully strokes a phantom goatee.

Good imitations, I must admit. The all encompassing distant look-away, the old benevolent Sigmund Freud. Two of my patented routines. Do you guys ever footnote, I ask.

Never, says Jimbo.

Pel looks at me like he doesn't know what I'm talking about. And I remember how it is now. I didn't teach these cool guys a thing. Then he signals back to Trick, a quick pursing of lips, that he's going out to the car to smoke one. Say? Pel asks, motioning toward the door.

No thanks. You fellers go ahead.

I go back to the booth, ready to leave, but Beth and Bobsmith are still talking. Trick is at another booth talking to some girls. I would like to leave. I'm not having a bad time, but I can't stop thinking about the acid trip and the strange dreams. I keep telling myself this feels almost normal, almost like old times. But it doesn't. No matter how much I drink. So I ease back out of the booth, walk slow motion and shadowed to the bar to smoke a cigarette.

I'm standing at the bar when Pel comes in alone from outside. You forget how thin he is sometimes. Guys with a lot of hair, and Pel's is past his shoulder blades, look bigger than they are. He is tall though. One of those guys who grows about a foot senior year. His nose and chin are sharp, even his eyes. No wasted space on that face. Looking now like the front man for a rock band, like the cover of Rolling Stone. Hard to believe he was so little when we were kids. That every Saturday night I spent the night with him we got dragged to church by his mom the next morning. Pel in a three-piece. Pel in loafers. The two of us laughing so hard at a teenage girl's voice cracking during a solo that his mother yanked us out by the ear.

He approaches me, sees the cigarette in my mouth and my fumbling for a light and yells to the bartender for some matches. The bartender looks vaguely familiar, one of those guys on the periphery of this my new Knoxville, tiedyed, ponytailed, opaque eyes as if flipped inside out.

The bartender hands over the matches and Pel introduces us. Oh yeah, he says, I've met you before. Down at Mentors. You wouldn't remember man. You looked like you were kind of out there.

Could be, I say. You look familiar. I light my cigarette and hope he goes away.

Oh yeah man now I remember. You were telling me that Peter meant rock. That's my name. You're Jason, he says, pointing at me for my own edification. You've got a brother named Peter right?

Yes.

That's how we got talking. You were saying that Peter meant rock. That Peter was the rock of the church. You kept saying that over and over.

I don't say anything.

You were on some of that liquid Pel had. That's right. Now I get it. You were out there on that slippery liquid road.

Pel points down the bar to show Mr. Eager, Mr. Team Acid, that he has a customer waiting. And all smiles now, he gives me a sincere, I'll be back in a minute gesture.

He's a cool guy, Pel says.

Yeah, I say. And I want to say, now that my bad night has been brought up, I want to shake him and say, how can watering those flowers heal me? Am I dead now? You can tell me. Am I already dead? Is that why I have a shadow behind me?

How are your dreams?

What? I say. He's read my mind.

Whenever I trip I have weird dreams.

I've had weird dreams. I can't sleep.

He nods his head, looks in my eyes, and I know how they look, wide and scared. His eyes give nothing back. Say's got a restless mind, he says.

And yes indeed Say does.

Trick comes over and Pel goes to the bathroom. I watch to see if Beth looks when he walks by, but she doesn't. Jimbo's at another booth throwing some lame rap at two girls who both like Trick. Your protégé learning anything? I ask.

Trick smiles, a frat boy stoner smile. The full scholarship Dartmouth biology and religion double major, the Chapman wonderkid. Who looks now like a cross between a former med school student and a hippie. Jimbo's a hard worker, he says.

I'm sure he is.

Why don't you go give him some pointers? Some of the old mean boy tricks from the book of Say.

I forgot about the mean boy tricks, I say.

Never acknowledge a girl you like within the first thirty minutes of entering a room, Trick says. The second time you meet a girl, ask what her name is even if you know. If she's real good-looking, ask her again the third time.

I smile.

Go ugly early.

I shake my head, trying for the disclaimer.

Dog em up early and often.

Good gosh.

A finger in her butt doubles your nut.

Shut up, I say, that's enough, but I'm laughing, Trick's laughing, he's got a funny laugh because he'll straight-face it forever then he just can't hold it anymore and this high gasp giggle pops out of his mouth and he's done and you are too.

I turn to see what Beth's doing and am surprised to see Pel sitting at the booth with her and Bobsmith. Trick asks if I want a beer. I do. Pel's listening intently to something Beth is saying, a sincere look on his face, fake as hell, nodding his head up and down, index finger and thumb conscientiously stroking bottom lip, intermittently stroking his hair. And I turn back around to grab the beer that my good friend Peter, the rock of the church, is handing over to me.

You know Peter, don't you, Trick says.

Yes.

Peter smiles as if we share some secret.

You know, Trick says, that Peter denied Christ three times before the cock crowed twice.

I look at him. Then at Peter. Peter smiles. Trick nods his head as if he's just related a bit of trivia.

Yes, I say, I know that.

You've got a customer, Trick says, and Peter walks off, smiling to beat the band.

Why do you say shit like that to me?

Like what?

I look at him. Trick's smiling. His eyes meeting mine and not looking away. Then Jimbo walks up, following the two girls who are on their way out. Trick turns to talk to them. I stand away from them, away from the bar, in the aisle, and I don't want to look in any direction, so I turn and face the door and watch the occasional car drive by.

After awhile Trick and Jimbo walk by behind the girls. See you Say, Jimbo says.

See you.

Trick smiles. Give me a call, he says.

I don't say anything. Then they're gone and I'm standing in the aisle by myself and have no choice but to walk over to the booth.

I get there and Pel is saying, Christ Bobsmith, and Bobsmith is in full slouch, shaking his shaggy head and Beth's laughing at the funniest thing she's ever heard. Pel scoots over to let me sit down but I remain standing. Beth looks at me and the smile leaves her face. Have a seat Say, Bobsmith says.

I'm all right.

Are you ready to go? Beth asks. We'd better. I've got to be at work early.

You leaving us Say? Pel asks.

Yeah I'm heading home.

He nods understandingly, as if I look tired, as if he's not surprised at all that I'm ready to go.

Beth taps Bobsmith on the arm to scoot him out and says quick quiet goodbyes. I'm head nods, half waves. Bobsmith tells me to drive safely, and I say in a voice too deep, swallowed up in false backbone, that I will. Pel is smiling. I follow Beth to the door and am conscious of walking, and it's hard to put one foot smoothly in front of the other, so stiff are my legs, cumbersome my feet.

I open the car door for Beth and it's not as cute this time, her having to get in on my side, her awkward straddle over the gearshift, a forced laugh. I could do this better before five beers, she says.

I get in and nod as I do, to let her know I heard what she said. Then I start the car and head down the Pike toward her house. We drive in silence, wind through my open window the only sound. And I consider rolling it up because Beth is probably cold, but I don't. After awhile Beth holds her hand out in front of my face and says, how are you doing, I'm Beth.

I nod, having lost the ability to speak.

We didn't get to talk as much as I'd hoped.

Again I nod.

Are you all right?

Yes.

Christ Say, are you going to be like this all the way home?

That sounds great when you say that, I say, and I still haven't looked at her. Christ Say, Christ. That sounds great. You sound really good saying that. Christ Beth.

What's the matter with you? Something's happened. Bobsmith wouldn't tell me. But something's happened. I can tell. I know it.

I drive on, fast heart, dead eyes on the road. Beth doesn't say anything else, and sits without moving, without breathing. I try to hear her breathe. Cool wind through the window, sound of tires on road, headlights flashing lonely in the dark, and worse when swallowed by strip mall lights, cold light on faces, dusty dashboard, then dark again suddenly.

I pull into her neighborhood and with every turn my headlights flash a house window, intrude on someone sleeping. I pull even with her house and get out, leaving the engine running. I turn my head so Beth can make her ungraceful exit, but she's out almost as quickly as I am. She closes the door behind her, not all the way, but enough so she can stand next to me.

You're right about that word, she says. It doesn't sound good. I didn't realize I was saying it that much.

I don't say anything.

I'm not apologizing. I'm just saying I agree with you that it doesn't sound very nice.

Mute and hollow.

Are you mad at me?

No.

Because you're acting like you are and I haven't done anything. Will you at least look at me?

I look. I'm looking at Pel's girlfriend. I look away.

Goodnight Jason, she says, and she's walking down the hill toward her house, quick but unhurried steps. I wait, perversely, as if I were a gentleman, to hear the front door open and close. Then I get in my car and drive home, and all the way home, along the empty streets, with my window down and the wind through it firm and cool, my headlights flash and dart obscene among the trees and through the windows of the dead houses.

June

I come inside after swimming, and Tom and Jackie are at the kitchen table, drinking beer and smoking. They're laughing like hell. What say boy, Jackie says between snorts.

Not much. I didn't see you come in.

I'm sneaky like that.

I nod.

You getting any?

Not a bit, I say, trying to move fast.

Sweet, can't you get this boy laid? Shit, hell, this boy needs to get him some.

Tom grins a little, harumphs.

Well, I'll see you, I say, moving on through.

Downstairs I hear laughter, I assume at my expense. Boy wouldn't know where to put it.

Couldn't find it with a flashlight.

Have to tie a board to his ass.

Laugh.

Snicker.

Shit, we used to tear it up Sweet.

And Sweet, the front man for all those bachelor, six-foot naked red-head drying her hair over a heat vent days, nods his head and smiles. Money coming in hand over fist, the Butcher Boys not yet in the pen for bank fraud and embezzlement, the World's Fair coming to town. Everybody getting rich off the Fair, Knoxville in the boom years.

Jackie laughs again. A small, soft-faced man. Perhaps he reminds Tom of the time they sent me to the toolbox that first summer in the house, when they were running a phone line out to the gazebo.

Jason, how bout getting me a Phillips head screwdriver out of the toolbox.

Which one's that?

You'll know it when you see it, Tom says, not hiding a smirk for the college boy.

The college boy's been telling his friends that his mother's living with a truck driver, that his New Dad and mother are buying a waterbed for the back of his rig to honeymoon in the parking lot of Dollywood. His mother has started chewing tobacco, his mother who used to be his mother, used to be his father's wife, has her own handle, Tom's Cat, and Pel and Trick laughing and the college boy pouring it on, swear to God, we've got New Family Thanksgiving reservations for Stuckey's, my mother's running moonshine, my mother's taking clogging lessons. And pass that doob over, says the college boy, not even wondering what kind of narrow-eyed meanness his mother has brought into this world.

At the toolbox now, he's looking for a screwdriver so these blue collar farm boys can hook a phone to the gazebo, the redneck gauchery of it all too much, this run-down house, Tom's legion of country sisters and aunts and nieces calling day and night, Sweet there? Tell him Bobbie called, Jackie called, night and day, and the college boy, one generation off the farm, Chapman snob, Vanderbilt redneck, new money, no money, reaches into the toolbox with anger, pushes nameless and unknown tools about, Aaaaaahhhhhh! Holy shit!

Tom and Jackie laughing their asses off. What is it there Jason?

It's a damn snake.

Naw.

This little ole thing, Jackie says, coming over and holding it up, thin and squirming against the sky. This little old worm? Throwing it in the grass, where it slides in ssssses to the fence.

Pretty funny, says the college boy.

Wonder how that worm got in there, Sweet? says Jackie.

And Sweet, in a house with a pool and a good-looking woman, good luck time, looks to the blue sky, to the college boy. Ain't no telling Jackie. Ain't no telling.

I get in the shower with a decent dread going about my grandfather's imminent arrival. He's a former mule trader and auctioneer. Oats, Goats, and Shoats, Ray Crandall, Auctioneer, We Sell Everything! Dad used to say he could talk a dog down off a meat wagon. He's coming to Knoxville to take me to the doctor about my knee. He's got money and can afford to pay for an operation. When a man graduates from college he should know enough to check on things like health insurance, some would say. My grandfather would say I'm like my father, irresponsible and lazy. Dad used to call me Little Ray, meaning I was nosy and prone to ask questions. They didn't much like each other. About midway through college I'd had about enough of both of them. I told them so. A long poker game ensued. I wasn't bluffing. Now my father pretty much just calls me Jason, and unless my grandfather's been drinking, he doesn't bad-mouth Dad or me, and I don't mention the gun he pulled one fine Christmas morn.

I get out of the shower and it's girlish laughter from underneath the bathroom sink. Jason, my Playboys call to me.

What?

We're down here. We're waiting. We've taken off all our clothes.

Not today, I say, but they hear the wavering in my voice.

You won't even have to talk to us, and we're just the same today as we were yesterday, just as naked, just as awkwardly posed. We left our high heels on. We love washing the car naked in our high heels. You won't have to buy us dinner, or try to impress us. We know you're funny.

I'm getting tired of you. You're all just so easy.

Jason, it's me, remember, the one who looks like Leslie Ellis.

I'm over both of you, I say, with absolute lack of conviction, reaching under the sink, just, I tell myself, for one quick peek.

Jason, my mother calls, just outside the door, are you in there?

Yes ma'am.

Telephone.

I'll be right out.

I grab a towel and come out of the bathroom, trying to hide the old pup tent with my hand. Who is it? I say, irritable to be talking to my mother in such a condition.

Your cousin, I think. I thought you were going to cut the yard today.

You did think I was going to cut the yard today. But we weren't in total concordance on that plan.

Your grandfather'll be here any minute. I wanted the yard cut before he got here.

Hold on, let me get the phone, I say. I throw on some shorts underneath my towel, then say to my mother, if you mow the grass too much in this heat it'll kill it. Hello!

Cousin Spud.

Cousin Butch.

What are you doing?

Just haggling with Mom about the yard. She thinks it ought to be mowed every other day just to keep the mower in shape.

I look over at my mother who's trying to ignore me while she straightens out the pillows on the couchbed. I give her a raised brow Belushi look. She doesn't laugh.

You want to go to a movie tonight? he asks. His real name is Jim, though it ought to be Butch. Butch is a name for a guy who's never failed to throw cold water on a friend when he's in the shower, who never swims without trying to dunk everyone in the pool. Cousin Butch thinks I have the personality of an Idaho potato.

Mom, can your twenty-five-year-old son have five dollars for a movie?

She laughs in my face.

Butch, she's laughing, so either you're buying, or you're going without me.

I'll buy. I'll drive. Anything else you need?

No, that should do it.

All right, about six-thirty.

Yes boss.

When I come upstairs, Jackie's gone and Tom is well buzzed. He's sitting at the kitchen table with his shirt off, smoking cigarettes and drinking bourbon. There is about him some unspeakable doom. He's here with Mom, her son, and any time now his not quite father-in-law. This is more than he bargained for. Only in rare moments does Tom make me feel uncomfortable, but this is one of them. He looks at me and sees my mother, or perhaps he just sees someone my mother loves who doesn't even have to try for it. I grab a Coke, throw him a how's it going, and I'm out the door to look for Pookie.

At six o' clock my grandfather drives up. He comes around back, peeking around the gate like a little boy looking for Easter eggs.

Over here, Ray, I say, rising from a lawn chair to shake his hand. How was your trip?

Pretty good. Caught a little rain around Chattanooga. It rain here?

No sir. And I been right by the pool all day.

I want a job like yours. Your mother hiring any more like you? Or you got to have a fancy degree from Vanderbilt?

I laugh. Fancy indeed. And you see where it's gotten me. If I'm not lounging by the pool, I'm waxing the yacht.

I see, he says, I see. You're part of the country club set. Well don't forget us country folk when the circus comes to town. He smiles, looking me in the eyes, mirrors of his own, wide blue hoping eyes, hoping, it seems to me, with just a little too much fervor.

I'll get your bags. Mom and Tom are inside.

Walking to his Cadillac, I'm struck by how old he is, how short, remembering the first time I discovered he wore lifts in his shoes. Even with the lifts, he's nearly half a foot shorter than I am. Ray is old now, and sick. Two heart attacks, prostate cancer, old men diseases have caught up with him. He doesn't walk fast like he used to. When he was twenty-five he had three daughters and a business of his own. I don't have five bucks to see a movie. We've never really understood each other.

I carry his bags into the house, wondering which holds his bourbon. Pete, who always got along with everybody, says I wouldn't believe how little booze it takes to get Ray drunk. Pete goes to Florida with Ray and lets him drink without hounding him. My brother is practical. He has an MBA in his sights, a job in his future. He knows Ray will drink whether the doctors tell him he can or not.

I take Ray's bags to the guest bedroom upstairs. Ray and Tom and my mother talk in the kitchen, and I wish Butch was already here. Any of the three of us would probably be all right, but the four of us, none of whom is zippity-do-dahing through life at the moment, is too much to take. I'm already claustrophobic. Tom, no doubt, is climbing walls. An edginess permeates the house like a gas leak. We're all waiting for something unpleasant to happen before Ray's visit is through. It could be any of the four of us that blows, though I doubt Mom will. I'm impervious as well, at least I think so. I try to think of something someone could say that I haven't already said to myself.

In the kitchen, decorum rules. Small talk, chitchat, smiles smiles smiles. I assume Tom is wasted. His grin is perpetual, determined. I've seen the same look on mad dogs, on rednecks in pool halls who are smiling smiling while you notice their hands getting tight on the cue. At times like these I wonder if I could take Tom if I had to, but a look at his arms and that grin reminds me I best run if things ever get serious.

What you say there Jason boy, Tom says, smiling. His face will break.

Not a lot. Did you make some spaghetti? I say, my voice soothing as a mother's lullaby. Is that what smells good?

Be ready in an hour. You hungry?

Yessir, but I'm fixing to go to a movie with Butch. I'll just heat some up when I get back.

Janey, you got you a good cook here, Ray says, and his tone is hard to determine. Poker.

I wish I could cook half as good, Mom covers quickly, and by the speed of her reply I can tell she's trying to turn a backhanded compliment front-wards again. Jason won't hardly eat what I cook. It's all those years you were a bachelor, right Tom?

I'm going to learn how to cook, I say, throwing myself in front of the oncoming Ray truck with Mom. Tom, you're going to have to give me lessons. Lame. Butch, that bastard, has wrecked his car.

How bout a drink Ray, Tom counters, settling into the insane rhythm of things, and I casually consider diving out the window.

I guess a little one wouldn't hurt. That is if my daughter and grandson won't be offended.

I'm not going to tell you what to do, Mom says. It's your life.

Tom's already pouring. I never saw ice go into the glass.

Well thank you for reminding me, Ray says. He looks now, I can't tell, like he really is joking, that he can have maybe just one small drink, and sit around and discuss the weather. We're all smiling intently. Only Ray may mean it.

How's that leg Jason, he asks me. They going to have to amputate?

Maybe. I think I'd look good with a wooden leg.

And you don't have insurance, he says, a man sitting with a full house.

Not a lick, I say, my eyes meeting his. We look at each other for awhile. We're both smiling. I got nothing, he knows it. I'll gnaw my leg off before I ask. We both know he's come to Knoxville to take care of my knee. My PR team, Mom, Pete, and my grandmother, have been on him for months.

I've got an appointment for Jason to see the doctor tomorrow, Mom says quickly. But she needn't have bothered. Ray knows a mule trader when he sees one. His eggs at home may not be soft boiled just the way he likes them if he blows this one. My grandmother will not have her firstborn grandson limping, and she is tired of these fool men games.

I look at Tom and wink. My grandmother has four of a kind.

Tom, new to this game and wanting no part of it, lights a cigarette and sits down like a man real tired.

I guess you'll need a ride to the doctor, Ray says. Promise to tip the driver, and I might just take you.

I reckon I could scrape up some change, I say, and outside comes the heavenly blast from Cousin Butch's car. There's Jim. I'll be back about nine.

We may not be here when you get back, Mom says. Tom and I are taking two of my clients downtown to see a show. We shouldn't be late.

All right, I say, and then to Ray, the playoffs are on tonight. We'll watch them when I get back.

That's a deal, he says, and we look at each other and smile, John Boy to Grandpa Walton, and then I'm down the stairs and gone.

I come through the garage with arms raised. The fresh air, not so hot now, I want to breathe in all of it.

What say cousin Butch, I say, getting into the car.

Cousin Spud, he says, yanking the car into reverse before I get the door closed. You been kissing up to the old man? No guns this time?

Butch is a second cousin on Dad's side. He knows most of what's gone on between Ray and me, and Ray and my dad.

Fuck off Butch.

What, are you getting along now?

Yeah, we're getting along better. Now shut up about it.

Yessir, he says, just a bit sarcastically.

When I get back the house is dark, and Mom's car is not in the driveway. I assume Ray's already fallen asleep. It's nice outside, cool, an orange moon rising in the sky. A good night to sit out by the pool and drink beer and smoke cigarettes.

I walk in quietly, through the garage, and Ray is lying on the couch where I sleep. The TV is on, but no sound. Are you asleep, I say in a whisper.

No, he says, his voice catching in his throat. He's drunk.

The game's on. What are you watching?

Turn it if you want to, he says, not looking at me, not sitting up to talk.

I switch channels to the game.

The movie was pretty good, I say.

Who'd you go with?

I think he knows. I think this is a setup, a precursor to a steam-letting after a long night's brood. Jim, I say, hoping he's just tired, or drunk, and has forgotten.

Your cousin Jim?

Yessir.

He couldn't come in to say hello? I remember when he used to come down to the house with you.

We figured you were already asleep, or he probably would have.

Ah, none of you Sayers ever wanted to have anything to do with me.

I ignore him, standing in the glow of the television.

Of course, I remember a few times when your daddy needed me a little bit more than he let on. But you never did want to hear nothing about that.

I thought we agreed not to talk about my dad?

I never agreed.

Listen, I thought we put that shit behind us?

You might have, I never did. I remember you saying one Christmas you didn't need me, didn't need my money. You remember saying that?

I don't say anything, but I remember.

You tried to hit me. Your little brother had to hold you back in the kitchen.

Pete couldn't have held me back if he wanted to. I let him hold me. If I'd wanted to hit you, I would have. You're the one had the gun out.

It wasn't even loaded. Aw hell, you're just like your daddy. How long you gonna suck off your momma's titty anyway?

I don't have to listen to this shit. If you're drunk or not, I'm not going to listen to it.

And I'm out the door to the garage. The same old shit. But I can't find the keys to Tom's car, the keys to my car are on the coffee table in the den. I open the garage door enough for me to slide under, run around to the back of the house, through the door, grab Tom's keys off the kitchen table, run back around, get in Tom's car, the stale stench of cigarettes, nearly hit the garage door I'm going out so fast, get out, open the garage door all the way, try to get calm, don't want to wreck Tom's car, that's all I need.

Backing out of the driveway, I look up to the guest bedroom window and he's watching me. What is that crazy son of a bitch doing upstairs watching me? I back out of the driveway, get to the bottom and stop. Ray's small frame pressed against the window, against the dark house. He looks like a little boy.

I put the car in drive and ease back up the driveway and into the garage. I park the car and get out. I walk slowly around to the back and through the back door. I walk into the kitchen as Ray makes his way from the bedroom. He's wearing blue pajamas.

You can say whatever you want to me, I don't care, I say. I know you're drunk and don't mean all what you're saying.

I'm not that drunk.

Okay you're dead sober and you mean everything you said. I'm still not leaving. You can say whatever you want about me or my dad. I don't care. I know you don't believe it, but I love you. So that's all I'm going to say.

I walk downstairs, leaving him standing there with an odd look on his face. I never said that to him before. I don't know that I ever thought it before. I got enough to worry about. I don't need any extra. Ray's getting old. I'm not going to let him die on me without getting things straightened out a bit. What a look. Five years ago that shit wouldn't have flown.

I hear Ray and my mother talking upstairs before she goes to work. He won't mention our little episode, and I won't either unless I have to. Ray doesn't want my mother and grandmother on his ass, and they both know

I'm trying. I am the model of consistency. One can go far by holding one's tongue.

Mom comes downstairs and gives me twenty dollars to take Ray to breakfast before we go to the doctor. It's probably Ray's money she's handing me. Mom too is on the payroll.

She leaves and I go upstairs. Morning Ray.

Morning, he says. He's already dressed. The farm boy can never sleep past six. He's wearing tan pants, a tan blazer, and a tan hat. If he had on blue pants, the jacket and hat would be blue as well.

After I shower, we drive to the Waffle House for breakfast. We take his Cadillac but I drive. I wheel that baby out sweet, smooth, the largest automobile in the world, working the dials on the air conditioning and radio. It's near ninety degrees out and within a minute Ray will turn off the air and talk about being chilled. I've sweated through many nights at Ray's.

At the restaurant, Ray talks to the waitress. He calls her by the name on her name tag, Robin. He finds out where she's from and how long she's been working at the Waffle House. He finds out she's divorced, forty years old, and has two girls in high school. Her ex-husband ain't much good.

Robin, he says when it's time for the check, you got any dishes need washing? This boy promised me breakfast, but he's a little light on the hip.

We got a mess of dishes in the back, she says. You just leave him here and we'll put him to work. She looks at me and smiles a you've got the cutest grandfather smile. I smile an isn't he though back at her.

He's poor, but he's a good worker, Ray says.

Not that poor, I say, pulling the twenty from my wallet with a flourish.

He's robbed a bank, Ray says, eyes wide with mock disbelief.

In the parking lot Ray asks if I need some new shoes.

No sir.

Let's see.

I raise my leg over the hood for him to inspect my old hightops turning grey. I had a nice pair, the ones I hurt my knee in, but threw them away as jinxed.

I wouldn't slop hogs in those, Ray says. His shoes are brown, those Jarman brand, kind of a loafer with a small buckle in front.

Aw, they're all right, I say, picturing the new ones that will be on my feet in approximately thirty minutes.

That doctor won't even let you in his office in those. Let's get you a pair of shoes.

Well, I only decline once.

Sometimes not even once.

Ray takes small steps in the mall, shuffling nearly, looking around, malls still an interesting phenomenon to him. Winchester, where he's from, just got their first Wal-Mart. They got ice cream? he asks.

Baskin Robbins. You want ice cream right after breakfast?

Oh yeah. No I guess not. What's that kind I like?

Pralines and cream?

That's the one. Maybe a little cone here directly, he says, a small smile on his face. His mother died when he was two. Some boys never know their mothers.

I steer us toward Champs, and on the way a good-looking girl walks by, about nineteen, her high heels clicking loud and hollow in the near empty mall. She likes the way her shoes sound. I turn around to look at her nice thin legs and small bottom. She's wearing a tight businesswoman skirt, and probably works in one of the stores. What are you looking at, Ray asks.

You know. I like them little bottoms.

You can't always tell by that, he says, with an almost imperceptible shake of the eyebrows, a pre-Belushi move, perhaps Charlie Chaplin.

Tell what?

You know.

We get to Champs and when the salesman asks if he can help me, I say, those, pointing at some sparkling, shiny oh so white hightops. Size eleven.

I wear them out, carrying my old ones, my new grass-cutting shoes, home in the box. I'll be wearing hightops when I'm eighty. My grandchildren will wear brown Jarman loafers.

We get Ray his ice cream and sit on a bench. You need a pocketknife? he asks, pulling his from his pocket.

No sir.

You got one?

No sir. I don't have much need for a knife, I don't think.

I bet I use mine everyday.

What for?

Cut a thread off a shirt. Trim a hangnail. Peel an apple. Lots of things. You don't think you need one? I got a bunch of them. Boys don't use knives anymore?

Not much. Guys wear jeans mostly now. There's not a lot of room in the pockets.

I like deep pockets, he says, and gets up to throw his ice cream wrapper away.

We're on our way to Dr. Brimswick's office. Brimswick was a teammate of my Uncle Clay and is famous in Knoxville for throwing the block that sprang Clay on an 82 yard punt return against LSU that sealed Tennessee's 1963 SEC championship. He's operated on both my dad's knees without charging a fee, and I've been counting on those 82 yards, those white-boy hightop cleat long strides streaking past dull-footed purple and yellow Tigers that keep Brimswick's name alive in Tennessee football lore, to cover my doctor's fee, but so far, my third-generation nephew blood counts for squat. And there's no way Dad will ask him.

Clay played ball with this doctor, didn't he, Ray asks.

Yessir.

Wasn't his sister friends with your mother?

I think they were in the same sorority, I say, seeing the ducks lining up in a row in Ray's mind. I smile nervously to myself. I've seen Ray in action.

Let me do the talking when we get in there, he says, eyes gleaming at the prospective haggle.

Walking in the clinic, I tuck in my shirt. I hold the door for Ray and watch him shuffle his way up to the receptionist. He's a little hunched over too, trying to look small, look country perhaps. I sit down near the desk, a perma smile on my face, yes ma'ams and no ma'ams ready to fly out of my mouth at a second's notice. I slip easily into a farm boy grandson persona. Humble rurality seeps from my skin, the smell of rich soil on poor hardworking hands is in the air. I'm a threat at any moment to recite the Pledge of Allegiance.

I hear pieces of Ray's conversation with the receptionist. I hear, no insurance, mother working fifty hours a week, monthly payment plan. The receptionist smiles. She looks at me, empathy etched on her face. I'm thinking Ray's asked how many children she has. She's a mother. She knows what it is to work, to sacrifice for your children. She's thinking now of my mother, and how she wouldn't want her own son limping around just because she was too poor to afford his health insurance. Of course her son is probably a freshman in high school, not a twenty-five-year-old unemployed grimace of urban cynicism. I smile shyly back at her.

This is Mrs. Rembert, Ray says, and I walk over to meet her. Several people smile at me. They've been listening. I'm a brave young man. You can tell it in their eyes.

Jason's Uncle Clay played ball with your Dr. Brimswick, Ray says.

Clay Sayer? Mrs. Rembert says, and then points to an oil painting on the far wall. In it, little Jimmy Brimswick, homegrown Knoxville product, too small too slow, but fiery, little Jimmy Brimswick, is cutting number fourteen in purple at the knees, a prophecy of things to come, as speedy Clay Game Day Sayer eyes eighty yards of green and a runner-up finish in the Heisman voting.

Mrs. Rembert sends Ray back to talk to accounting, and I take my seat again. When my name is called I walk to the back, past Ray sitting down in the accounting office, his tan hat humbly in lap, the two ladies in accounting smiling as he nods to me walking by and then goes on about his retirement and social security not going as far as you'd like and his daughter trying to make ends meet.

I don't hear him mention my father or how I take after him, but I know he's dying to say it. Son of a bitch owes me twenty thousand dollars, he wants to say. Whenever I want to break up with a girl, I start giving her my good T-shirts and sweatshirts, postponing the inevitable, no longer able to drum up affection. When I'm older I'll buy her houses I can't afford. I'll borrow money from her father who I don't like and buy a house we don't need and one Christmas Day, after I'm divorced, my ex-father-in-law will serve papers on me at my mother's house, send a damn police car, even the cops looking embarrassed, my seventy-year-old mother having to come and get me in the den, a small sad look on her face. And I'll drive in a rage to my ex-father-in-law's house, where my kids are getting ready to leave, Christmas Eve with Mom, Christmas Day with Dad, the new arrange-ment. Christmas Day for God's sake and here I am without a pot to piss in, and twenty thousand dollars nothing to him, and him with my kids right now. When I get there, I'll tell my boys, you're taking every damn thing that son of a bitch gave you and giving it back. Leave your car here too Pete. And then my oldest son will lose it, go damn near crazy. I'll be in the driveway and can hear him screaming, crying, in the house, cursing his grandfather on Christmas Day in front of his mother and grandmother and aunts, and both my sons coming out of that house crying, getting in the backseat of my car, their mother, my ex-wife, shell-shocked in the den, everything slow motion, thick dread dreamlike death on this too warm for Christmas Day, my sons near grown, crying with their heads in their hands in the rearview mirror, driving toward my mother's house, and what in the hell kind of life is this? What in the hell have we done?

Ray comes in and asks if the doctor's seen me yet.

Not yet.

I talked to the accountant, he says. You can pay by the month. No interest.

That's a bargain.

We'll see what the Doc says. He might cut us a break. I think that lady up front might be talking to him, he says, giving me the slightest twitch of an eyebrow.

Little Jimmy Brimswick comes in the room, nimbly lugging his two hundred and forty pounds. He couldn't block Ray if he had to. I look at his hands. I don't want some chubby-fingered slob butchering my knee, but I needn't worry, the hands are long and fine and strong. Little Jimmy Brimswick will make the catch on third and eight.

What say there Jason, Dr. Brimswick says. How your folks?

Doing good. Hanging in there I guess.

Glad to hear it. Tell them I said hello.

I'll do it, I say, a bit put off by Brimswick's brusque manner and with a twinge of panic thinking what Ray might have said to the nurses.

Ray stands up and shakes Brimswick's hand. I'm Janey's daddy. I think I've met your sister.

Oh yes, Brimswick says, looking at Ray like he's got a purple 14 on his chest. Janey and Kate were in the same sorority.

Sweet girl, Ray says, as Brimswick starts yanking my knee around.

I'd say you've definitely got some torn cartilage, Brimswick says. It's not going to get much worse I don't think, but it's not going to get any better either. It's just a matter of how much it's bothering you.

Well I can't run on it.

That's no good.

Some of them young girls is pretty fast, Ray says, and Brimswick laughs.

We'd just go in there with an arthroscope and clean out that loose cartilage. You'd be in and out of the hospital in the same day. Well you know, the same thing your Dad had done. A couple of times.

What's a little operation like that run, Ray asks. This boy's got no insurance. His mother wants to help, but she's working fifty hours a week just to get by. And I'm going to do all I can, but I've been retired over two years now. Things is a little tight.

Well, Brimswick says with what looks like the beginnings of an ironic smile, your hospital and doctor fees are your primary costs. Mrs. Rembert tells me you'd like to come up with some kind of payment plan. That you'll have to work out with St. Mary's Hospital. And seeing as I'm an old friend of the family, I reckon we could just waive my fee.

That's mighty nice of you Doc. That sure would help out his mother an awful lot.

It's my pleasure, Brimswick says. Then he looks at me and smiles, and I swear I can't tell if he's smiling from warmth at the good deed he's going to do, or smiling because he enjoys the show, like at any moment Ray's going to offer to bring him some homegrown tomatoes or clean his gutters or something.

I appreciate it Dr. Brimswick, I say.

It's all right. We'll shoot for the latter part of June, if that's okay with you.

That would be fine, I say. I stand and shake his hand, then he shakes Ray's hand and is gone.

Ray looks at me and is about to say something. He has a small smile working. I put a finger to my mouth and shake my head toward the door in case Brimswick's still outside with my file. But Ray can't hold back. He grins. By God, I ought to have worn overalls.

Rachel's cutting my hair in the kitchen. She's Tom's oldest daughter, one of four kids. For awhile, after she divorced and moved back to Knoxville, she slept on the same couch I now call home. Now she's five weeks pregnant and will be married again next month. She and her fiancé were going to get married anyway, the baby just hurried things up a little. As money is tight, she's planning the wedding and reception herself. The reception will be here at the house. Tom's already paid for one wedding, and has tried in vain to talk her into an elopement. She's not biting. My mother and Tom will be the caterers, the florists, and all the other crap that goes with weddings. I will officiate.

My hair's getting a little thin on top and I don't like it a bit. My face is young, so if you've ever seen a sixteen-year-old with a receding hairline, then you have a pretty good idea how I look.

Rub my head a little Rachel. Make a wish for hair.

It's not that bad, she says.

Shit.

You oughta see Devon. When he gets out of the shower. Shew, skin city.

I think there's something in the drinking water that's making people go bald. I swear, half the young guys I see are losing their hair.

Devon thinks it's the ozone layer. He thinks the sun is burning holes in people's heads. She laughs at this. She's a good woman. She and Devon will be a good couple.

Tom's sitting at the kitchen table drinking a casual afternoon quadruple bourbon. Heredity, he says. If your mother's daddy is bald, you can just bet your ass you're gonna be bald too. Devon's been out in the sun too long, it's affecting his brain, not his hair.

Rachel and I laugh. We look at Tom sitting there, keeping his poker face, acting irritable just to act irritable, the long strand of hair pulled way from the back and then flipped over with defiance, a good cover job.

I hope I have a girl, Rachel says.

Tom laughs. That boy's gonna be bald as a bat.

Mom comes in as Rachel is finishing my haircut. She sits down next to Tom and counts to ten so that the word Rogaine does not find its way out of her mouth. It looks good Rachel, she says. I wish you'd keep it longer though. Your hair looks so good long.

I smile. Oh the thin ice she's on. Suggestion box is to the left, I say.

Hah hah hah, Mom says. Hah, hah, hah, hah.

After my haircut I'm outside by the pool with the portable phone trying to get myself to call Beth. I punch three digits, hang up. I look for

Pookie. She's out. I call Butch, get his machine. I call my old friend Barry Paige, but his parents aren't expecting him in from Atlanta this week. I call Beth and hang up before it rings. I go inside and get a beer and drink it in a nanosecond. I go back outside and remind myself that I'm twenty-five years old, that Beth and I are just friends, that she seems the kind of girl who would probably forgive a guy for acting like a jerk for no apparent reason. Then, for no reason at all, I call Pel. Bobsmith answers.

Old man.

Say.

What're you doing?

Nothing. Just pulled some tomatoes from the garden.

I was thinking about coming over.

Come on.

I might, I say, but as soon as I get off the phone I don't really want to. I dial Beth's number quickly before I have time to think about it and her mother answers.

May I speak to Beth please?

Beth's not in. She left today for Colorado.

Oh.

May I take a message.

Yes ma'am. This is Jason Sayer. I was just calling to say hello.

Oh hello Jason, she says, and it's hard to tell if I'm doghoused or not. Beth's gone camping with her youth group. She'll be back in two weeks.

Thank you, I say, I'll try back later, and when I hang up I wish I'd called her yesterday or the week before or the week before that.

I go back inside and everyone's gone. The house is quiet, palpably so, like all the couches and chairs and tables have sucked in their breath and are trying to hold it. I check the television, nothing. Pick up my address book. Set it down without opening. All my college friends are married. All my Knoxville friends are druggies. The only girl I know to call is Penny Jackson, who would probably sleep with me, but I'm feeling too sorry for myself even for that. I walk outside, look at my car. Walk around it, checking the tires. Pop the hood. Check oil and water. Close the hood. Call

Pookie. Walk down the driveway and check the mail. Walk up the driveway, get in the car, and head over to Bobsmith's.

Pel's in the front yard swinging a golf club. He concentrates hard on his swing. Few golfers have longer hair or smoke more dope on the course. He's good though.

What say Say. What've you been up to?

Been keeping a low profile.

Real low. Go check out our flowers.

I walk over to the side of the house where the bed of daisies and zinnias and sweet peas grow haphazardly, all mixed together. They look good, I say.

They need watering, Pel says, his back to me, swinging the club with smooth precision.

You got it, I say, fighting an urge to rip the club out of his calm hands and break it over his head.

Say, he says, with false hurt in his voice. You're just going to give up on your little flowers? It's been a hot summer, they're thirsty.

You know where the hose is, I say, hearing the overreaction in my voice.

He looks at me and smiles. Then he goes to the trunk of his car and pulls out a nine iron which he hands to me. When we going to play?

Not for awhile. After my knee operation.

No shit. You do need an operation.

Well I haven't been limping for the hell of it.

He shakes his head up and down. I guess not, he says.

Skeeter comes through the bushes that separate his mother's house from Pel's. He sees me and points at the sky. I look. Look at that airplane stuck in the mud, he says.

I see it.

Let me see that club. I hand it to him. Hit it a mile I could, he says, swinging the club in a jerky spasm. He points at his thin arm. Double jointed elbow, he says.

I nod, then light a cigarette for Skeeter and one for myself. He smokes it though he prefers menthol.

You still smoking those things? Pel asks.

Yep. Calms the nerves. I've been fidgety lately.

You? I have a hard time believing that.

After his golf clinic, Skeeter starts toward the gas station to bum a ride to the liquor store. Out on the road he stops and points at the thin shadow hunched in front of him. I'm outside in today, he says, taking one step forward, then shuffling two back. I'm walking frontwards in reverse, he says, his shadow growing larger the farther he back-steps. He points at the sky, but I don't look this time.

A helicopter?

You got to look to see, he says, and resumes walking toward the gas station.

I look at the sky. No airplane. No helicopter. A bird flies and lands on Pel's house.

I follow Pel into the house, where Bobsmith is dozing on the couch, his mouth open, catching flies, looking older than his thirty-one years.

Get up old man! Pel screams and Bobsmith jumps awake with a jerk of his head.

Goddam Pel, he says, then seeing me, what say Say. You've been hiding out again.

Trying to find my head.

Where'd you lose it?

Somewhere along the way.

Pel starts telling him about a dishwasher who hasn't yet shown up for work. I check out the maps on the wall, one of the U.S., the other of Australia. Pel's outlined our trips in black ink. Boy we had a fun time on our trip out west, Knoxhell in the rearview. Beneath the Australian map are old school pictures of Pel and Bobsmith in ridiculous seventies' wide collar shirts and various team pictures from Little League. A small picture, that once must have been in Pel's wallet, of Leslie Ellis and me at the Senior

Prom, my hair long and parted in the middle with the old feathered sides, an absurdly confident smile on my face.

I'm outside smoking a cigarette when Bobsmith comes out.

I'm going down to the bar for a minute to make sure the band's getting set up all right, he says.

What's Pel going to do?

He's coming down later.

I scrunch up my face like I can't decide what I want to do.

You want to ride down there?

Who's the band?

The Blueworms.

I nod.

Ever heard of them?

No.

Bobsmith smiles. Come on for a ride. What else you gonna do?

Lots, I say. Lots and lots.

In the car, we head down Lyon's View, past Cherokee Country Club, wee doggies, Knoxville high so-ci-e-ty, then the Pike, then Neyland Drive on our way to the Old City. On Neyland, the Tennessee River runs parallel, a slow-moving, muddy river, the south boundary of the World's Fair and the highlight, where visitors from across the globe came to spit in the water and watch the carp swarm over each other. Thousands of them coming from all over the river, millions of them, enough to walk on, fighting for lobbed loogies, the ends of hot dog buns, the dry edges of Danish strudels, falafel, Russian tea cakes, baklava, meat pies, Chinese egg rolls, Polish sausage, Australian lamb burger and Tennessee moon pies, the hordes of people swarming over each other to feed or spit at the hordes of scaly and scuzzed and hairy carp. More than one pale-legged Yankee in bermuda shorts and dark socks heard to say, Geez hon, would you look at the size of em, what I wouldn't give for the old rod and reel. And can't you see Cousin Butch, who has snuck darts from his job at the arcade, and is standing now at the dock, deciding into which horde to fling?

We pass the stadium, best in the nation, and Bobsmith asks if I've talked to Beth lately.

No, I say, and start to leave it at that. Not since that night we saw you guys.

He nods his head.

Why, have you?

Last week. I think she was going to Colorado today. Some kind of church camping trip.

I nod, play dumb.

Fucking Pel, he says, shaking his head from side to side, looking out the window at the hazed-over late afternoon sky.

We get to the Old City, with the newly cobbled road, the circa 1920s streetlights, and at any moment a toothsome ragamuffin in a floppy cap is going to pop out of the yogurt shop and start hawking the daily rag in a shrill but endearing voice. And all the while farmers are kicking dirt off their boots before entering the health food store and fatcats with watch fobs work toothpicks in well-rounded cheeks, deciding between the decaf espresso and that Knoxville standard, chocolate mocha cappuccino, after a hearty tropicana salad at the Sunset Grill.

Bobsmith dodges a couple of creaking streetcars, a gangster with a swell dame on his arm, and parks up on the curb behind a moving van. A couple of roadies and several guys from the kitchen are unloading equipment for the big Blueworm show. We walk down the steps and into the dank bustling bar. Waitresses are setting up tables, Jimbo sets up the bar, roadies on the small stage maneuver speakers. It's a pretty neat bar for Knoxville, in the basement of an old warehouse. There are no windows and if you think about it you can get pretty claustrophobic. They get a lot of rock bands, but also some guys like Jerry Lee Lewis and John Lee Hooker. Eclectic. Too fancy for Knoxville. It'll be out of business in a year. Not enough bands that play Rocky Top.

Bobsmith goes back to the kitchen and I head off for the men's room. Two doors, two restrooms, both with hand-painted emblems of obvious designation. Do I choose Day-Glo penis flying over cat doing handstand? Or is it witch with cat's face riding a broom over a dog with a penis growing out of his head. I choose flying Day-Glo penis, and I choose correctly.

When I come back, Pel's at the bar drinking a Coke. He offers me a beer but I pass. The tardy dishdog comes strolling in and gives Pel a combination sheepish, shiteating grin. Just a second, Pel says, getting up to follow the doo rag into the kitchen, I've got an ass to chew.

While I'm waiting, Jimbo points out some waitress he thinks he's got on the books. She's a chunky little country girl with a cute face, who for all her feigned indifference, her attempted haughtiness, for all her hippie bracelets and her stylishly unstyled hair, remains, eternally unmasked, a chunky little country girl with a cute face.

Jimbo tells me about the band, about other bands that are scheduled to play. He's excited to be working here, after running through the Quality Inn, O'Charley's, Fridays, and a couple of other chain bars. I listen to Jimbo, ask questions, try to seem interested in the bands, and all the while I'm thinking, Jimbo you don't have to be this cool, this is me you're talking to, you can say ain't, you can yee-hi. When I first knew him, back when he worked banquets at the Quality Inn, he'd enter every party yee-hiing and waving a beer funnel over his head. He'd make you funnel. Open up Say, open up.

I sit at the bar and feel a little bad about begrudging Jimbo his new personality. He's never really been out of Knoxville and he used to be a hell of a guy and probably still is, he's just having some growing pains, wants to try some of the A level women probably, wants to be hip, but I miss the shitkicking Jimbo and the way everybody was before, and I generally start to feel bad as I'm wont to do these days, when Angie strides in like she's walking on a conveyer belt.

Angie, UT junior, native Knoxvillian, Halls High School, rural but proud community, former waitress at O'Doyles, an Old City yup hang, who, having conquered the fern bar scene, is dipping her toes into alternative waters. She wears the healing crystal around her neck and is a recent vegetarian. She's thinking of changing her major from advertising to human development. She runs three miles a day, her long legs loping languidly across the hills and valleys of the campus, her mouth forming a perfect O while she runs and oh she sweats so nicely. These things I know from sleuthing missions around town and casual chitchat sessions after the bar has closed, waiting for Pel or Bobsmith to close out, and you bet I'm interested in hearing her proposals for saving the Nigerian titmouse. But now I am being snide. And she is such a nice young lady, earnest and hardworking, waiting tables to pay her way through school. And what I wouldn't give to hear more about her life at Halls, her thoughts of the modern world. And if push comes to shove, push to shove, I would not mind discussing her tawny brown calves.

She waves at Jimbo, at me. I wave, dizzy with the onslaught of blood rushing to my face. God, Jimbo says, with a look of pain.

I sob quietly into my hands. And now Jimbo and I have something to talk about.

Pel and Bobsmith start helping the roadies unload, so I go out and lend a hand. Longhairs and tattoos eye all four of my ninety degree angles, but don't say anything. I assist Bobsmith on two speakers and do a solo job on a mike stand. With so many helping, the whole of Team Mentors working as one, it doesn't take long to finish the job. After my ten minutes of exertion I accept the beer Pel offers. Take it with you, Pel says, I'll give you a ride to the house.

All right, I say, and follow Pel out to his car, my head spinning Linda Blair style for a second look at the imperial Angie.

Back at Pel's, I'm out in the yard smoking a cigarette in the last grey moments of dusk before nightfall. Pel and Bobsmith are inside preparing for work. Skeeter leans against my car, about as drunk as you can get and remain vertical. He's smoking one of my cigarettes.

People think I'm just a drunk.

They shouldn't think that, I say, looking to the house, hoping for reinforcements.

I drink. I get drunk. I am a drunk.

I kind of half nod.

But I'm not just a drunk. Do you understand?

Yes.

My eyes are blue just like yours are.

I know, I say, for they are. He is a black man with blue eyes.

My eyes are just as blue as yours.

Yes.

He points to the sky. Do you see an airplane stuck in the mud?

I look. I look for awhile. Do you?

Sometimes I do, sometimes I don't. I asked you.

I look to the sky again. I give it a good look. No, I say, I don't see an airplane stuck in the mud.

He nods his head. Then someone, a female, a mother or a sister or a daughter, calls his name. He starts off through the bush, wobbly man, bumping through the thin switches with his thin shoulders. On the other side he stops and faces me, outline of a man, scarecrow lifting his head to the sky. Can you see that moon behind you?

I turn around and there, just inching over the horizon, a pink moon ascending out of the grey and declining dusk. Then the sound of feet on a wooden porch, the squeak of a screen door.

Pel comes out and asks what I'm doing.

Talking to Skeeter.

He laughs. About?

Things in the sky. He wanted to know if I could see the moon.

That moon there, Pel says, pointing behind me.

Yeah that one.

Well can you?

Yes.

Well that's good, he says. Then he goes back inside and I follow.

Bobsmith is hitting the bong. Pel puts on the Grateful Dead. I'm heading, I say.

Stay awhile, Bobsmith says.

I'm gonna move on.

Come down to the club later. We'll put you on the list.

All right, put me down. I may or may not show. Then I'm out the door, heading home.

When I get home, there's a note from Mom saying that she and Tom are out entertaining clients. Under the note is a wedding announcement cut out from the paper. Thought you might be interested, the PS to the note says.

Before I see the picture, I know who it is. She looks good. Though the smile is slightly fixed, that born to be a bride look you always see. When I knew her, she glowed. I really liked her. She's going to marry a lawyer. Man she was pretty. And sweet. She played the piano and sang in the chorus at school.

I drink some of Tom's whiskey and go out to the back. I bring a left-over hamburger patty for Pookie. The half moon is blue in the sky. Few stars are out. I light a cigarette and watch the flame, the small orange a firefly in the darkness. Pookie eats her burger and comes over to lick my face. I could have been a lawyer. I'm lying on the concrete around the pool, near the freshly cut grass. I begin to be decently drunk. Pookie pookie pookie pookie pookie pookie. She yips at me, ready to play. Pookie is a shewolf, perhaps a banshee. She growls a little, deep in her throat, a Marlene Dietrich number. Pookie pookie pookie.

I walk toward the house, Pookie blocking every step, barking, no longer playing it cool. I bring her half a pecan pie from the refrigerator as a peace offering. Her black tongue laps it up and I cease to exist. When she's finished, I invite her in. She comes in the back door and walks immediately down the stairs, noses open the door to the garage, and is out the open garage and into the neighborhood for another night of havoc wreaking.

I walk downstairs in the dark and lie on the couch. I pick up the phone and dial. Hello, she says.

How you doing?

I'm fine.

You know who this is?

Yes.

You're getting married, I say, as if the idea just struck me, as if she didn't know.

Yes, she says, shyly, and I see a fifteen-year-old girl closing her eyes as I kiss her.

Congratulations.

She doesn't say anything. I consider asking her out. She's the best girl I've ever known. I love her madly. Your folks miss me?

She laughs. I love her a lot. I should have been a lawyer.

Do you still have my letters?

She pauses long enough for me to know the answer. I threw them out when I got engaged, she says. I couldn't keep them.

Why not? I've still got your letters.

What if my mom found them?

Fuck your mom, I want to say. I don't say anything.

I kept the pictures.

Well that's good, I say, and not in a smartass tone of voice either, though I want to. I'm pretty much not in love anymore.

I just felt I was starting a whole new life, and I kind of had to bury the past.

I don't say anything.

Are you mad?

No, I say, and I mean it.

You don't want an invitation to the wedding do you?

I don't think so.

I didn't think you would, but I thought I'd be sure. I'm in town for the rest of the summer.

We'll get together, I lie. Let her have her lawyer.

Really? I'd like to.

Sure.

I'd love to hear all about your trip to Australia. She laughs a little. Are you surprised I've kept up with you?

No, I say, just to be a cool guy.

She laughs again, a sweet chime of a bell in the night. But I tune out, become a small but solid slice of a vast and frozen tundra.

Well call me.

All right, I say, and then goodbye, and hang up the phone, and lie in the darkness of my mother's den.

I'm awakened in the night by the sound of water hitting pavement. At first I think it's raining, but then realize the sound is too singular, like a faucet running hard. I get up and walk toward the garage. The door's open. Tom's pissing in the garage, next to his Lincoln. Before I can say anything, he turns and sees me. Whatdoyousaytherejason.

Hey Tom, I say. I want to say, just watching you piss in the garage, but I don't.

He shakes off and I step back to let him pass. He walks upstairs and I follow him, ready in case he tumbles backwards. In the kitchen he sits down heavily at the kitchen table. There's a single light on over the sink. On the table a fifth of Dickel and a couple of packs of cigarettes. One cigarette burns in the ashtray. Ignoring it, he lights another. Have a drink, he says. I do, and sit down across from him.

Can't sleep?

These damn headaches, he says. I hadn't slept good in three months. He puts the palms of his hand over his eyes and massages his temples with his thumbs. I get up and come behind him and work his neck. That feels good, he says. I stand for a long time rubbing his neck and shoulders. He sits with slumped shoulders, closed eyes.

That's good, he says. I stop and sit down again. He pushes a pack of cigarettes over to me and I take one and light it.

We need us a riding lawnmower, he says. I'm tired of breaking my back.

That'd be good, I say. We sit in silence for awhile. Pookie's tail slapping against the screen door. Down the hall in the bathroom a faucet drips. I listen for a train. None sounds.

Your mother doesn't say anything about my drinking anymore.

I don't say anything.

Shit it's hot in here, he says, and stands to take off his shirt. What are you doing up?

I couldn't sleep either.

My head's going to split open, he says, and I see what looks nearly like fear in his eyes.

You want some aspirin?

I took three Tylenol.

Hold on, I say. I go downstairs to the bathroom and grab two Percodans from when I first hurt my knee. I come back upstairs. Take one of these, I say, laying the pills on the table next to his glass of whiskey. They're Percodans.

He takes one with a large swig of bourbon.

You don't want to drink too much with those things, I say.

Son, if I can get rid of this headache, I'd be ready to die tomorrow. I never felt nothing like this.

All right, I hope you feel better. I'm hitting it.

You're a good man.

You are too, I say, and turn and walk down the stairs. I stop in the bathroom to brush my teeth again. In the mirror I see a face that doesn't look that alien to me.

Mike Dorendo spreads eight crisp one hundred dollar bills on the coffee table. He's wearing a lime green Polo tucked into khaki shorts. Not really my look. I stand up from my couchbed to smoke my fourth cigarette of the morning. When we were in the ninth grade, Mike traded me a mint 1971 Roberto Clemente for the exact same card in just average condition. He knew I had a good number of cards, but that I wasn't much fooling with them anymore. I think he was probably hoping to give me a good turn on the trade, the swap being ludicrous from his standpoint, so I'd be a more active trader. He wanted to see my cards. Anyway, that was the last trade I made, the last new card I added to my collection. Mike is seeing my cards for the first time now, and I'm regretting taking advantage of his good nature on that first trade. He's a nice guy. Senior year he worked the PA for football games.

Eight hundred, he says, picking up the eight notes and sliding them through his fingers.

Eight Benjis. Right in a row. I can hear the neat granularity of the bills. They're in mint condition.

Shit, that '57 Mantle's worth four hundred by itself.

Yeah, Mike Dorendo says, if that person didn't write his initials on the back right corner.

I had seen the small RF before and not thought much about it. But now Robert Farmsworth or Ritchie Flowers or R. F. Dumshitty of Omaha Nebraska has initialed my card right out of the three-digit plateau. You know they're worth at least, at least, fifteen hundred, I say.

Yes. If you own a card shop. But take these down to any dealer in town and I guarantee you won't get four hundred for them.

The Stanford Law School has taught him well. I'm the only person I know who isn't a lawyer. And he's right of course. Two card shops I went to weren't buying at all, the other offered three fifty.

I want to keep the Clementes, I say, less businesslike, earnest even, a halfassed earnest, those Benjis already inching toward the black holes I call my pockets. Clemente's my favorite player, I say.

I'll give you six without the Clementes. Eight for all the cards.

Fucking hell Dorendo, you're robbing me.

He doesn't reply. The money sits on the table. I drag on my cigarette and try to look mean. I got nothing, he knows it. All right, I say, they're yours.

That's football too, he says, a point I hadn't considered.

Hell yeah, take em all, I think I've got some Charlie's Angels cards in there too.

He laughs a little, a little nervous. I'm unshowered and unshaven. I've not bothered to put on a shirt or shoes. I look like a man who would kill you for eight hundred dollars.

I put on shoes to help him load the cards in the trunk of his car. The good ones are arranged by year in plastic protective sheets of nine, then organized in colored notebooks by decade. The average cards are in old shoe boxes or old Topps boxes that the clerk at Weigel's would save for Barry Paige and me. Half the time Barry and I walked up to Weigel's without any money and searched the weeds along the road for returnable Coke bottles. Mantles, Mays, Clementes get loaded into Mike Dorendo's car. A Stan Musial my dad got me for Christmas.

When he hands me the money he has an odd look on his face, as if I'm blaming him for taking advantage of my desperate straits, as if I'm blaming him for profiteering, for buying my childhood. I am.

I appreciate it, he says, and sticks out a hand.

I wait a second before extending my own, just to wrench his gut a notch. Then I smile and shake. I needed the money, I say, you offered the best price. I didn't have to take it.

He turns to walk away. Hey, I say, I should have let you see them in high school. You did me a good turn on that '71 Clemente.

Mike Dorendo looks at his shoes, kind of mucks around. Aw, you were busy, he says. It's kind of kid stuff.

Well I appreciate it Mike. I needed the money. I really did.

He nods, waves, nothing to it, then gets in his car and drives away.

I'm back in the den before he's left the driveway. Call up the hookers, I scream to an empty house, and laugh loudly to myself. The laugh doesn't sound as hollow as it does coarse, a little cheap, a laugh for the boss's unfunny dirty joke.

I walk upstairs to get a Coke, there are none. Some old pineapple juice and a quart of buttermilk bought special for Ray last week are it. I pour a glass of tap water from the sink and look out at the back yard. I want to buy something.

Four huge crows are dive-bombing Pookie. They swoop down at her, pecking at her head, their caws piercing the window, harsh and unnatural and scary. Pookie thinks they're playing. Raising up on her hind legs she barks and bites playfully side to side at them. The birds dive simultaneously at her, landing on her back, flapping their wings all around her. Pookie's scared now, turning round and round in circles, dodging, not fast enough, her head jerking every which way. I run out with a broom, screaming at the top of my lungs. One swoops at my head and I swing hard with the broom, miss. Another one swoops from behind, caws, and I swirl and smack it with the broom. It falls to the ground flapping its greasy black wings, and I turn the broom over, ready for the kill, when another one flies at me. I swipe at the crow around my head and catch it with my arm, but not hard enough to send it down. The crow on the ground tries to turn back on its stomach and get up, but I pin it to the ground with the broom handle. It makes a thick soft sound, its wings flailing around the handle as I grind its spine in the ground. Another one swoops and catches me hard on the ear. I wave both hands around my head, drop the broom, pick it up and smash the crow out of the air. The other two keep coming. I run over to the crow that hit me and stomp on it with both feet, crushing its breastbone in the process, and take off to the house with the others flying at my head.

Pookie follows me in, and for once she doesn't head straight downstairs. I feel my ear and my hand comes away bloody. I run to the bathroom to wash it off with hot water and to apply alcohol. The alcohol stings, but my heart is still racing, and I don't feel it much. I grab an old towel out of the bathroom closet and hold it to my ear.

Back in the kitchen, Pookie cowers on the floor with a guilty look on her face, as if she's done something wrong. I pet her, it's all right baby. She licks my hand. Out the window, two large hulks of dead crow, a broom. In a tall oak in the far corner of the yard, the remaining two, dark, brooding, silent in the shadowed tree.

I shower and get dressed, and when I go upstairs the crows have gone. I go to the garage and grab a shovel and then to the back to move the dead birds to the far corner of the yard. Then I let Pookie out against her better judgment, leave her hovering around the house, near the door, slack shouldered and moping, not even following me to the gate to be let out in proper fashion.

I get in the car and head over to Pel's house. We're going to Atlanta, without hoods or ropes or missing teeth, to hear George Okeye speak, the former head of the underground newspaper in South Africa who was just pardoned from jail. Good liberals are we. Raised by the only two Democrats in this clodhopper Republican hotbed. And, of course, Roots the miniseries debuted during those sensitive formative years when I was still the upright Cedar Bluff Middle School student council president. We bought the tickets to the speech back in March.

I pull in Pel's driveway from the west as he pulls in from the east. It's noon sharp. Three cars are in the driveway. Trick, Jimbo, and Bobsmith. Good timing, I say, as we get out of our cars.

You're ready to go, Pel says, nodding his head in approval, a Little League coach encouraging a shy youngster with promise.

We walk in the house, I'm behind Pel, and there's some manner of hilarity, movement, a sort of flapping around that ceases when I'm seen. I have the feeling someone's just run out of the room, or they've hidden something under the couch. I am one paranoid freak.

Young Say, says Trick.

Say hey, says Bobsmith.

Jimbo smiles.

Boys.

I sit down while Pel goes to the kitchen to load the cooler with Cokes for the trip. What've you been up to? Bobsmith asks.

Oh, not much. Sold my baseball cards today and then got attacked by a bunch of crazy crows.

What? Trick asks, laughing.

Look at my fucking ear.

Good God, Trick says, horselaughing with the rest of them. I'm laughing too.

It was Hitchcock, these huge crows diving at me. It was like those flying monkeys in The Wizard of Oz. I thought they were going to carry Pookie off.

They laugh. Trick, the Chapman wonder boy, is in his suit, having what I reckon to be a four bong lunch before hitting the real estate salesman pavement again. It's about his fifth job in the last year. A lesson to the kids about the hazards of study burnout. Bobsmith and Jimbo are going to play golf.

I sit down in Pel's dad's old recliner, recently claimed from the storage box, the divorce box, his mother keeps for all the furniture that won't fit in her apartment. We're all divorce kids, suburban orphans of a sort. The stories are different and the same as we've fallen socially and economically down the food chain. But in a strange and sentimental homage to familial comfort, we've held on to that suburban love of the den, most casual of rooms, most comfortable. We've moved from rented den to rented den to rented den, with the same accoutrements, the same ragged couches, music posters, mismatched assortment of lamps and bookcases and end tables, the same beat up coffee tables strewn with bottles and magazines and dope paraphernalia and remote controls. The shut in, blinds down, stereo on, TV muted smell of dope. And the days I've spent in such a theatre, the years, watching the giggly houdini of passing time.

So you sold your baseball cards, Bobsmith says.

Yep.

Clementes too?

Eah.

From the kitchen Pel starts calling like a hot dog vendor, Childhoods, get your fresh sweet childhoods here.

And it's funny, I must admit.

Trick positions himself over the bong. Oh why can't I go play golf, he says. Oh why can't I go to Atlanta? Oh why must I list and show and try to sell all the livelong day?

That old SAT's not much good in the real world, eh Trick, says Bobsmith, the old man, the napping sphinx.

Trick flames, lights, swooshes and gulps. Oh what I wouldn't give some days for a grid sheet and a number two pencil, he says, wistfully, looking skyward.

We laugh.

Head to head with the population at large. Mental Darwinism at its finest. Don't know your logarithms? Then get on your tractor, hayseed, and get the fuck out of here.

Pel comes in and keeps the bong hot. Bobsmith dozes off, Geritol prune juice speedball overdose. Trick passes the bong over and I decline. They razz me a bit about not smoking. Just say no Say, just say no. Then Trick starts in on his Uberminch routine, standing at attention and saying, I am Nietzsche's Wonder Boy. There is no right or wrong, except what is in my own mind. I am my own god.

Jimbo laughs.

He reaches again for the bong, saying, my personal moral code says it is more important to take bong hits at this particular moment than it is to list or show or sell. On the other hand, if my moral code told me that Bobsmith had to be killed, then I would be obligated to slay him where he lies.

What, Bobsmith mumbles in ancient Sumerian, shaking his sleepy head.

I said that taking bong hits is more satisfying to my id at this moment than taking an axe to the back of your head. Though I reserve the right to exercise that option if at a future time my id requests it.

I thought you were Nietzsche's Wonder Boy, I say.

Freud loves me too.

Freud is a motherfucker.

But aren't we all, he says, making the bong gurgle, aren't we all.

On the road to Atlanta, Pel and I don't talk much. We used to not talk on long drives from Cairnes to Melbourne, from Chicago to Los Angeles to Colorado because we knew each other so well. Now we just have nothing to say. Around Lenoir City, Pel rolls a joint while steering with his knees, licks the joint to seal the roll, and fires up. He pulls on it hard, squinting, making a hyperbolic face of pain, the venerable shot through the head with the doobie gun. I laugh. Then it's Louis Armstrong hitting that note and holding, helium from a balloon. And it's like the old times, windows down, ripping along at eighty, moving down that paved road in a blue and green sunglass tinted world.

Let me hit that thing.

Now now Say.

Now now my ass, give me a little hit off that hoochie kooch.

He passes it over and I drag, that hot burn down throat and lungs, and exhale pretty quickly, not wanting my brain to explode on the first hit. Been awhile, I say.

I reckon it has, he says, taking the doob and dragging it halfway down.

We drive on, the interstate intersecting farmland, rolling is the land in this Cumberland Plateau, green still, though we're in the midst of a drought. Past cows and barns painted SEE ROCK CITY and abandoned cabins just visible through trees, cabins overrun with kudzu, cabins home now to field rats and rabbits and bluejays and copperheaded snakes, and what man lived in yon rickety pile of dilapidated planks, and were children conceived there, barefooted overalled blackberry picking youngsters? Can't they hear their parents in the bedroom, how that bed creaks, and the interstate not yet a dream in some engineer's mind, and maybe there's gold buried under the house, and all around unfound arrowheads, and this land is old that swallows arrowheads and Civil War musketballs and how long until the grey black tar and gravel is mixed and run over by dirt and rock, and the wood planks from the cabin soil for a new grove of trees?

We drive on, south past Sweetwater and Niota, Tom's old stomping grounds, then Athens and Cleveland. Past the sign for Highway 60 to Dayton, thirty miles northwest, site of the Scopes Monkey Trial. And they had to pick Tennessee, had to be Tennessee, where none of us could figger out what that Darwin man was saying bout great grandma being a monkey. And H. L. Mencken yukking it up for the slicks back east about life here in the buckle of the Bible Belt. And some of it's true, some is true. Today, on the interstate, we've passed more churches than I can count. White clapboard ones with gravel parking lots and faded revival tents in the back. Others with stained glass windows and signs out front saying everyone welcome. A couple are houses with makeshift steeples, pickup trucks in the driveway. But not all are of the snake handling variety. Not all are cross-eyed maniacs impatient for the vengeance of their angry God.

We pass through Chattanooga, site of the battles of Lookout Mountain and Chickamauga, and into Georgia. Near Dalton, we're passed by a Mercedes with a Confederate flag bumper sticker, the driver a college boy in shades and a Kappa Alpha baseball cap. And not too much farther down the road, we'll be passing the Redneck Rushmore on Stone Mountain, where Lee and Jackson and the other leaders of that ridiculous lost cause stare gravely and romantically through the smoke and haze of the nightly laser and fireworks show. I point at the bumper of the Mercedes. Can't say I much care for a redneck with money.

Hell no, says Pel.

No julep drinkers in the Sayer family.

Nor mine.

Can't say as I like Yankees much though.

No. And if the South's so fucking backward, why in the hell are they all moving down here.

Just took em two hundred years to figure out Buffalo's cold as shit.

Carpetbaggers.

Tearing up the land.

Screaming their lungs out.

Hairy assed women.

Farting at the table.

And so on.

An eighteen wheeler nudges into our lane from the right, and I jerk and grab the dashboard. I hadn't seen it. The truck rights itself back into its own lane. I sit there wondering if Pel saw me jerk. My heart is racing a little and my mind clips along at a decent pace as well. I'm very stoned. I'm very stoned, I say.

I bet you are, Pel says, looking at me with eyes not black exactly, but no other color either, eyes that absorb.

What do you mean by that, I want to ask, but don't.

South of Dalton, an hour out of Atlanta, we stop at a Cracker Barrel for lunch. I've forgotten what it's like to go into a respectable place with Pel. People stare. He walks to the hostess stand and old folks give him a wide berth, nearly knocking into each other to get out of his way. An old lady in a walker looks at me and I realize I'm no Rotary Club prize either, unshaved, untucked T-shirt, cutoff khaki shorts. I take off my sunglasses and smile, but she turns her head and I'm dismissed.

Sayer, two, Pel says to the hostess. There's a wait, so we wade through the legions of old folks and Canadians, station wagon and RV travelers all, milling about the down home blocks of cheddar cheese, the y'all come back pecan rolls, the crappy generically manufactured homecrafted crafts, and go outside to wait to be called over the loudspeaker. Pel grabs a newspaper and we sit on one of a row of wood benches that line the front of the store. If I had a quid of baccy and a good piece of cedar I could whittle me up a Jeff Davis doll. And any minute now Barney and Ange and Goober will be heading down from Floyd's.

There's a breeze blowing, but the air remains hot and humid, the water hanging near thick enough in the air to touch. Pel reads the sports, having handed me the comics, which I breeze through quickly. Nancy's funny today, I say.

Shut up.

I swear. Today is the first funny Nancy I've ever read. Not hilarious, but funny.

He reaches for the funnies and reads Nancy. That's horrible, he says.

Nancy throwing Sluggo in the mud for the one billionth time, and you don't think it's funny?

He hands the comics back to me. I can always trick people into reading Nancy.

Waves of heat warble over the parking lot pavement, and staring through the distortion gives the impression of disguised movement, as if the cells of the pavement and a few cars have deatomized and are in the process of recomposing. We sit for a decent time, the wait longer than expected. I don't mind, and sit relaxed, watching the woozy illusion of heat movement.

Pel stands up and starts walking toward the door. I get up and follow. Pel stands at the door, holding it open for me, as the hostess is announcing over the intercom, Sayer, party of two, Sayer, party of two. I stop dead in the doorway. Pel walks past me to the hostess stand. I stand there for a second then follow him in. The hostess leads us to our table and we sit down. Pel puts his head in the menu.

That was a pretty good trick, I say.

What, he says, face still in menu.

How'd you know they were about to call my name?

He smiles with no teeth showing, kind of cutting his eyes at me over the menu. I just felt it.

Just felt it, I repeat.

We eat in silence, my stomach shrunken, knotted. The food comes and I eat only two of my four steak and biscuits. Can you read minds, I ask.

Pel looks up from his bowl of beans and laughs.

We finish eating and Pel pays since I got the gas earlier, and then we're on the road again. Pel lights a doobie, I a cigarette. The Clash play on the tape deck, and Pel bangs the steering wheel in time with the drums. I'm looking out the window for something to see.

I can't shake that trip, I say, my voice shaky and pitiful.

What do you mean?

I don't know. I just keep having weird things happen to me. Weird dreams and premonitions. It's like every single thing has significance.

Everything does have significance.

But it's paralyzing. Every single moment becomes a free choice versus fate decision.

I imagine that life's a river and I'm just a leaf on the water. I only go where the river takes me.

But if you're on the river, you no longer have free choice, the river dictates.

You have to choose to fall in the river.

We drive in silence. Pel lights another doobie. This is Marietta, he says, last chance for a smoke.

I take the joint and smoke before I have a chance to give this moment cosmic implications. And right away the THC in my system revs up again with this second round. I'm stoned as a bat. I think I've probably made a mistake coming on this trip with Pel. I look out the window and try to rise into a sky that is no sky.

Is this the same weed we smoked earlier?

Why?

Because I'm fucking torqued.

This is some weed I got from Trick. Does a little dance on your head, doesn't it?

I light a cigarette, but no good. My heart's racing very fast. A shadow breathes on my neck.

This shit's not laced is it?

Pel laughs. Why do you ask that?

I'm slightly losing my mind.

Pel laughs. Been there done that.

Downtown Atlanta appears in all its paved glory, risen like a hideous metallic phoenix from Sherman's ashes and I'm already claustrophobic. The traffic's bad, has been bad since Marietta, the city spreading like spilled milk on an endless table, twenty Knoxvilles strung together with fastfood strip mall twine. At the Georgia Tech exit, traffic's bumper to bumper. And you can have it, have it all as far as I'm concerned. It takes us thirty minutes to find a parking place behind the Varsity, famous Atlanta drive-in. Pel pulls two Cokes from the cooler and we get out of the car. He tosses a can to me, which I try to one-hand, and botch. Good hands, Pel says, as I reach to pick up the dented can, rolling unevenly and spewing fizz on the sidewalk. I go ahead and pop it and about half the soda bubbles up. I polish off the other half and start to put the can back in the car before Pel says I should keep it to hold water in. It's much too hot to be drinking Cokes all day, good thinking by Pel.

There is no sun, no visible sun, the day thick and surreal with haze. I'm sweating immediately and my sunglasses fog with humidity. It's four-thirty, an hour and a half until Okeye. Pel starts walking toward the Varsity and I follow. We pass the restaurant and hit the sidewalk, which is filled with all manner of black folks, businessmen and women in suits, people dressed in robes and bright skullcaps, homeless people pushing grocery carts filled with aluminum cans, black men bringing food to the cars parked at the Varsity, young kids rapping, breaking in circles, taking time about in the middle.

We sit on a wall in front of the Varsity and watch people go by. It's scorching. The only place to sit on the wall is beside some trashcans nearly full. Yellowjackets swarm about half-slurped Coke cans and discarded Varsity chili dogs that lie tooth-marked, broiling in the bin. I get up away from the trash and stand on the curb.

The street leading to the stadium has been closed off and policemen direct the pedestrian traffic through the congested cars. A mounted policeman, wearing aviator glasses, attempts to keep his steely composure while his horse unleashes a torrent that splashes the wheel of a new white Lincoln Continental. The urine flows down the street toward Grant Field, picking up a small green leaf and carrying it like a yellow river to wherever this road must end.

My face feels greasy from the heat and humidity and not shaving. I wipe the crease of my nose on either side with my shirt, leaving an oil spot. I wish I'd waited for a tissue. People in the street are shoulder to shoulder, but mannerly, smiling for the most part, happy to be out of work early. Old ladies wear high heels and wide-brimmed floral hats, many men wear ties even in the heat.

Two white kids in dreadlocks and tiedyes kick a hackysack. They look stupid. I think this and am immediately sick of myself. An old man walks by, crippled, dragging his right foot, sweating profusely, a piece of bread crumb stuck in his grey beard. Why does God allow handicaps and disease and humiliating bread crumbs in beards? The old man, past me now, stops and turns around. He smiles, and then keeps walking.

Pel is sitting next to the trashcans. I watch him watch a yellowjacket land on his knee. He watches it until it flies off, never having made a move to disengage it. The pot was very strong. I watch the crippled man walk down the hill and I'm sure he'll trip and fall. Something in my mind is saying that I'll make him fall, just by thinking it, that I secretly want him to fall, his old yellow teeth smashing the concrete and the blood on the pavement and passersby not even stopping to help. I will kick him in the head when he's down on the ground, right in the ear, as hard as I can. But I don't want him to fall. I don't want him to fall.

There's rats here, a teenage black girl says, stopping in front of me and looking down at my feet.

What? I ask, looking down, stepping back to look. She's looking beyond my feet now, as if the rat's already gone. She keeps walking with her two friends. What?

She looks over her shoulder. She doesn't look alarmed. There's rats here. Are you a rat?

I watch her walk off toward the stadium. She looks once more over her shoulder and then is swallowed in the crowd. I look over at Pel, his black ponytail long and greasy now on his back, his pointed nose and black stubble thin and shining with sweat, and from my angle I see behind his glasses, dark eyes narrow sweeping the street.

I point at my Coke can and then toward the Varsity to show Pel I'm going to fill it with water. He gives a slow nod and turns his Coke sideways to show he's not yet opened it. I start walking. This is a test. Everyone hates the rat, but he is nonetheless one of God's creatures. The rat is sneaky, dirty, a liar. A rat will rat you out. The Bible says to love everyone, not to judge. I didn't see a rat. Why would a girl say that? Maybe there was a rat I didn't see. Wouldn't a girl be scared of a rat?

How's Trick, someone asks behind me, right in my ear, the breath hot on my neck.

I turn quickly, the shadow behind me quicker still. A man peels away, the man who spoke, lost now in the crowd. How's Trick? I heard it clearly. Maybe he said, how's tricks.

I get to the bathroom and the water from the sink is cold on my face. Maybe it's hot. Cold. It's cold. It is definitely cold. Why did I think it was hot? It's cold. The water on my face is cold and it feels good.

I stay at the sink a long time, splashing my face and looking in the mirror. My eyes are wide, nostrils flared, face flushed and splotchy. I don't look like myself. People are waiting behind me. I didn't realize. Excuse me, I say, backing up, water dripping off my face and hair.

No sweat, the man says. He smiles and shows a gold front tooth. I look around the bathroom. It's trashed. Paper towels everywhere, dirty water on the floor. Someone has thrown up in one of the stalls.

Hot out there, Gold Tooth says, splashing water on his face. He has two huge sweat frisbees under his arms. Hot as hell, he says. He finishes up, wiping his face with paper towels, and turns around to see me still standing there. You all right son? You need me to get you some help?

I consider the question. He's talking about paramedics. I must look like I'm suffering from heat prostration. Maybe shock.

I'm okay, I say. Just hot.

Okay man, but be careful out there. Drink you lots of water.

Thank you.

I want to stay in the bathroom. I've met a nice person. It smells very bad. It's dirty. A rat would like it here. I walk out of the bathroom quickly, bumping into an old man in a suit and Panama hat. Excuse me, I say, putting a hand on his back to steady him. He looks at me strangely and keeps on into the bathroom. The restaurant is teeming with people, hot, sweaty people, the sour sweet pungent smell of too many people in too small an area. I've forgotten to fill my water can.

I wait in line at the water fountain. I'm dying of thirst. I fill the can and drain it while standing against the wall. I get back in line, fill again, and again drain the water. I'm still thirsty. I fill the water can a third time, and try to drink, but my stomach will hold no more. I may throw up. I move as if in a dream through people, first to one side of the crowded restaurant, then the other. I'm looking for clues, for someone to tell me the right thing to do.

I walk back outside where it's hotter but there's more room to breathe. I take off my shirt. I walk a few steps and then put it back on. I consider walking back inside. I look on the ground for rats, look on the ground for my fleeing sanity. I take my shirt off again. I walk forward. I count the steps. Seven. That's a good number. I stand on seven steps and look around. Most of the crowd is heading for Grant Field. I look to the trashcans on the corner. Pel's gone. I stand on seven for a long time. No one speaks to me. No one gives a clue.

I walk seven steps to the trash cans. I stand by the trash. I am a rat. Lord have mercy on the rat. Lord I will stand here if you want me to be a rat.

Say, Pel yells from across the street. I remain where I am. I don't want to move from seven steps. Pel comes over to where I'm standing.

I was checking out those T-shirts. Where've you been?

Chasing my sanity.

He laughs. It's a brand new day for Say. A brand new day.

We walk down the hill, past the Varsity, and toward the stadium. Going down the hill hurts my knee. Pel walks quickly through the crowd, darting through small spaces in the mass of humanity, taking advantage of his quickness and slight build to move faster than the general pace of the crowd. My leg prevents me from keeping up. I monitor Pel's movement ahead by his swinging ponytail. Every now and then he turns to see how far back I am, and then, finding a clearing away from the crowd, he waits for me. Let's go Say.

I can't walk that fast on my knee.

Oh yeah. I keep forgetting about your knee.

He hands me my ticket and when we get to our gate, we go in. I follow Pel to our seats, which are located on about the thirty yard line. The speaker's platform is in the endzone, and is decorated with several ANC and American flags. This same endzone is where Uncle Clay first came to national prominence by throwing the only touchdown in a 6-0 victory over Coach Bobby Dodd's mighty Georgia Tech Rambling Wreck. The game was notable for the combined thirty-two punts and quickkicks. Uncle Clay did the kicking too. He made Life magazine that week. Cover of Sports Illustrated too.

The crowd is nearly all black, with smatterings of white college students and hippies and professorial types about. I am still on the outskirts of sanity. A shadow is behind me. Behind the shadow, a large woman fans herself with a Martin Luther King fan. I smile at her. Hot, honey, she says, as dollops of sweat run down the canyon separating her breasts. I turn back around and feel the fan on the back of my head.

The stadium fills. A minister comes on and asks the crowd to join hands for the Lord's Prayer. I grab Pel's hand on one side, and a young woman's on the other. My hands are sweaty and squeamish. The prayer begins and I bow my head and join the crowd in reciting. The lady behind me speaks loudly, nearly singing the words. I look up at Pel, who's looking straight ahead. I squeeze his hand a little. It is a cool hand, and dry. He continues to look straight ahead.

After the prayer, the mayor of Atlanta comes out and talks about Martin Luther King and his time in Atlanta. Then more speakers, politicians, some white, all uninspired, and I remember the heat again. Even Pel has a trickle working down the side of his face, and he rarely sweats. I grab his water can and leave to get us some water. I walk up the stairs and then down the long ramp into the bowels of the stadium. Grant Field is old and dirty here beneath the stands, but cool, cavelike. My eyes have difficulty adjusting to the darkness. Water drips from a pipe and hits me on the top of the head. I look up and another drop hits me in the eye. I move. Where is that water coming from?

I see a man forty feet ahead go into a bathroom. The door is open when I get there, and I take three steps in.

This is the women's room, an old lady says into the mirror. She's washing her hose in the sink.

Oh I'm sorry, I say to her reflection, and turn quickly to leave. I thought I saw a man walk in here.

I didn't see a man, she says, but I'm already out the door.

Humility. I lack humility. I know so much, so I walk into the ladies' bathroom. I deserved that. There are many tests and many reminders. I walk quickly.

There's the men's room. I check the door again. Men. I check again. Not women. Men. Men. I go in. Beige grey lifeless old men's piss smell. Rats lurk ready to scurry. I am the rat, not Pel. That was the test to see if I would blame Pel for what I am, when it was Pel who found me when I was stuck on seven steps and praying for help. Pel is a prophet. You should love all men, follow all brothers. Beware of false prophets who come to you in sheep's clothing.

I'm standing at the urinal, a large troughlike basin with water spraying out of tiny holes. I set down the water cans and unzip my pants. I can't go. I feel someone standing behind me. I'm straining to go.

Hey brother, that's where you wash your hands.

What?

That ain't the urinal. Piss back there, he says, nodding his head to a long corridor I hadn't seen.

Oh, I say. I zip my pants and pick up the water cans and stick them under the spraying holes.

No man, you don't want to drink that water. That's dirty water. That's piss water.

Oh. I look around for a trashcan to throw my cans away. I don't know piss from water. I look for a trashcan, but see none. I have eyes to see, but cannot see. I'm looking for trash. Trash is all over the floor. Water and piss are the same. I am looking for a trashcan, not trash, I'm looking for a place to throw trash. Water is water, piss is piss, they are not the same.

You all right man?

I don't know. Do you see a trashcan?

Right there, he says, pointing behind me where I hadn't looked. The trashcan is under the paper towel bin where it should be. I'd never have thought to look there.

Do you have to go to the bathroom?

I think. I think that I need to stop thinking and remember if I have to go to the bathroom or not. This man is trying to help me. I look at him. He's smiling a little strangely at me, as if I were a child frightened of nothing at all. He's younger than I, maybe nineteen. He's about my size exactly. He thinks he's looking at a very crazy white man. Yes, I have to go to the bathroom, I say.

Right up there. He points with his arm, and shakes his head affirmatively.

Thank you.

I walk up the long corridor, dark save a lone bulb high in the ceiling. It is an odd place for the toilets. You can't really see back here from the door. That trough did look like a urinal more than a sink. I almost pissed in the sink.

When I come out of the bathroom, the young guy's waiting. Come on, he says, I'll get you some water.

I follow him further around the stadium. He stops at a concession stand and says, Denise, how bout giving this man some water. A black girl about his age, who's smiling and very pretty, grabs a small cup from under the shelf, fills it with water, and hands it to me.

Thank you.

You're welcome.

I drain the water fast and it tastes so good on my burnt throat.

Hit him again, my friend says. This man's dehydrated.

Denise does. And this time I drink more slowly, savoring the cool good water. She fills and I drink four more times.

Let me give you some money, I say, reaching for my wallet.

You don't owe me anything, she says. I look at her friend, my friend. Take some money, I say, handing over a ten dollar bill.

No man, he says, smiling at me again as if I were a sweet child. Water's free.

Water's free, I repeat, trying to smile, too tired, smiling tired with my eyes I think. Thanks man. Thank you Denise. Remembering Pel, I ask if I could have one more cup for my friend. Denise fills the cup again and I turn to leave.

Stay out of the heat, he says.

Thank you, I say, looking back over my shoulder, and start back from whence I came, carrying a cup of that good sweet water for Pel.

I walk past the women's bathroom, yes, there it is on the door, Women. I get to Gate 23, which I think is my gate, but I've lost my ticket stub. I walk in past the usher and stand on tiptoes to see Pel's ponytail, but I see only the backs of black heads and no Pel. I walk down to Gate 24, and repeat the tiptoeing look down rows and rows, aisle by aisle, and I notice all the pretty colors the ladies wear, and I look to the field where I see a black man speaking, presumably Okeye, but the sound is not good or perhaps I just have difficulty with the accent, but looking around the football field, I see hightop cleats kicking high punts, higher than the lights, the brown leather solitary as a bird against the yellow sky and then back down again and the rush of jerseys, three-quarter-sleeve jerseys, thick cotton, and there is my father's father in the stands, hello my grandfather, smiling at his boy Clay, the two-step punt, not three, quicker release that way, both his boys two-step punters, both tailbacks on his Huntland High team, I can't punt a lick, and man I miss my Grandsay, I could never hit a straight golf ball with Dad, but with him, straight and long off the tee. And he's saying, you look faster this year.

I think I'm just playing with slower kids.

No, you're just faster.

And my dad not as fast as Uncle Clay, can't turn the corner as well on 37 Sweep, can't burn that angle like Clay, and how straight, slow-legged I am, and Grandsay leaning against the hood of his car in our driveway at the old house watching two-on-two touch football, thinking, I was too tough on him, too tough, should have never compared him to Clay, and Jason, I'm telling you, you look faster to me. You're really starting to burn that angle.

I turn around and walk toward the car. Though it remains very hot, I'm glad to be outside away from the crowd. Here on the street a few stragglers. Many have slight limps or awkward gaits, older men for the most part, loose ramshackle small men who turn up from nowhere wherever there is a gathering of people. Do they look for loose change or lost brothers, these shuffling city nomads? Many are homeless, pushing stolen grocery carts with all manner of trash and necessities, or pulling large plastic bags filled with aluminum cans. A few young turks dart about, swinging their heads from side to side as if the next side alley or passerby could mean a great deal of money. Two old men sit under a tree listening to a baseball game on the radio. I walk past and consider joining them under the tree. Who's winning? I say.

Who's playing? the man wearing a Braves cap says to me.

I don't know.

What you care who's winning then?

I laugh. Just making conversation.

I see.

I walk on up the hill. Braves down 3-2 in the top of the fifth, he says to my back. I wave. They playing Pittsburgh, he hollers.

Go Bucs, I say, and keep walking.

I'm still woozy. My eyes will not stop seeing, my ears hearing. Let those with ears hear. I hear only myself. I cannot rid myself of myself. If I could stop listening to myself, I could hear what I am to hear.

A blind man sweeps the walk in front of the Varsity with hard, smooth strokes, left to right, hot dog wrappers and Coke cups and leaves flying steadily off his broom into the road. I stand in the road and watch him, curious to see if he misses a spot. He doesn't. He finishes one square, toeing the line in the sidewalk as a mark, and rests on his broom, looking up at the sky as if to see what could be causing this heat. He's between forty and seventy years of age.

Can I give you a break? I ask from the street.

You're not a broom thief are you? This broom belongs to the Varsity, he says. He continues to look up the walk, though I'm to his side.

No sir, I say, coming around in front of him. Just thought I might give you a break.

Well, all right. I suppose I could set awhile.

I walk up gingerly, clearing my throat when I'm in front of him. He hands me the broom, and walks to the small grassy mound that separates the Varsity parking lot from the sidewalk. I start sweeping.

Left to right, he says. Trash goes in the street.

I continue to sweep left to right.

Long steps, long strokes. What your lady going to say you give her them little short strokes?

I widen my sweep, and pick up the tempo. The trash flies. No lady, I say, I sweep alone. I look at him. He's smiling a little, sitting on the knoll with his thin legs sticking out of his pants, his socks not covering much of his ankle. His socks are brown, his pants grey. I think he could have done worse.

A young man with no lady. Saddest thing in the world. And helping an old blind man with his work. You're working for God's commission.

I continue sweeping.

Am I right?

I stop sweeping and regard him there on the ground. A yellowjacket has landed on his ankle, but he pays it no mind. He smiles broadly now. I don't know that I know what you mean, I say.

You don't?

What do you mean by commission?

Reward. Grace.

I don't think grace is earned. Grace is a gift, I say, the words coming out fast, high-pitched.

A gift you say?

Who cleans up the trash in the street, I ask, changing the subject with a crowbar.

The city. All I got to do is keep the sidewalk clean. No trash allowed on the sidewalk is how I earn my commission.

From the Varsity?

He smiles. From the Varsity.

I continue sweeping, moving up the sidewalk square by square until he's about seven feet behind me. The yellowjacket now sits on his shoulder like a small bird. Do you live around here, I ask, turning over my shoulder to see.

No. I live down at the bottom of a hill. On one side I got the Baptist Church, on the other the graveyard.

I don't say anything.

You believe that?

I don't know. I guess.

All my life. Church on one side, boneyard on the other. Lots of comings and goings. A man with eyes could see plenty.

I look at him to see if he can see, to see if he's looking at me through his dark glasses. But he continues to face out toward the street, smiling at the accumulating trash.

I turn around to face him as I sweep, moving backwards up the hill. My broom has slowed again, short choppy jabs at the walk. Won't the sidewalk just get dirty again when the people come out of the stadium?

Yes.

Then why sweep it now?

Cause now's when I sweep. Maybe people will see this clean sidewalk and decide they don't want to dirty it up. I'm not saying they will or they won't. Fred pays me to sweep the sidewalk at seven o'clock. That's when I sweep. You're chopping at it again. I think you've made your commission for the day, helping an old blind man with his work.

I'm not working for a commission. I want a commission, I'll talk to your man Fred.

Now you're talking. Don't let a cross cross you up. A cross is supposed to get you across. There's all kinds of crosses. Crisscrosses, doublecrosses. Backcross leftcross rightcross. A cross is supposed to get you across. You remember that.

How do you know the difference?

Make sure. Don't let a cross cross you up.

I don't know that I follow you.

You're trying to follow me?

I look at him. He stands up and walks up to where I'm standing. Let me have that broom, he says. I can see my sunglasses in his, see my arm handing him the broom. He sweeps, long and smooth, his face looking straight up the hill.

Are you trying to tell me something?

No sir. Nosiree. I never try to tell anybody anything.

It sure sounded like it.

Maybe it did. I'm getting old. I try not to tell folks too much. It's a sure way to get them not to listen to you.

A loud roar comes from the stadium. Well, I say, I guess I'm gonna go on. Crowd'll be letting out soon.

All right. I appreciate you sweeping.

It was nothing.

Hot out. I needed the break.

You take care, I say, picking up my cup of water and walking away toward the Varsity.

Same to you, he says, looking to his left at me. The sun shines off his glasses. I walk, the swish, swish, swish steady at my back, in my ears.

I get to the car and sit on the hood to wait. It's too hot. I pour half the cup of water on my head, and the rest on the hood. The water steams. My head feels cool. I sit down and wait. What I take to be a hooker walks by. She wears lime green lycra shorts that are much too tight, and a lacey kind of Kmart Madonna number that doesn't cover much of her spilling breasts. She sees me. Hey honey.

Hello, I say, with tape on my glasses, protractor protruding from pocket.

Are you looking for a party? She smiles as she rubs her hand on her thigh.

I don't think so. I'm waiting for my friend.

Your little friend can come to my party, she says. Her hand brushes her breast. You want to buy me a drink?

I don't think so, I say, and wonder if I should give her money.

Your loss honey, she says, swinging again through the parking lot, moving through the cars, laughing out loud for no apparent reason, turning to look at me and shake a finger, naughty boy, laughing, big ass falling out of green shorts, ice cream out of a bowl, garish those high-heeled pumps, high calves flexed, toned, pretty good legs, where does she sleep at night? Where does she eat breakfast? I remember all the money in my pocket and feel guilty. I should have given her some. It wouldn't have done any good. Maybe it would have done some good.

Another long noise from the stadium, and soon people start filling the streets. I watch them. I'm looking for the man with the limp. Perhaps I think he can walk normally now. After awhile, Pel walks up. He has his shirt tied around his head like a sheik. Say Say Say. You get lost?

Yep.

Couldn't find this, he says, waving my ticket stub in front of his face.

Where was it?

Under your seat. I saw it after you'd been gone about an hour. You hear any of the speech?

Not really. How was it?

It was good. What'd you do?

Oh, just kind of walked around. Walked in the ladies' bathroom.

Say just don't know where he's going sometimes.

No Say don't.

We get in the car and wait in traffic, which breaks about ten miles out of downtown. The breeze through the window is still hot, but feels good on my face. The sun sets to our left and rear. It's the first time I've seen it clearly all day. We drive on, not speaking. The sky, hazy and colorless all day, musters some pink and dark purple around Dalton. Pretty sky, I say. Yep, says Pel, thinking he saw it first. He puts in the Grateful Dead.

Fuck the Dead, I say, quickly, too loudly.

Well what do you want to hear?

I don't care, but not the Dead.

He turns off the stereo. We drive on, past Chattanooga, Athens, Sweetwater, the wind through the window cool now. My face and arms are sunburned. I don't look at Pel. He's not looking at me. We pass farms now, the faint sweet sour smell of manure in the air, the cool wind smell of distant shit, and I'm listening, like one slinking in the dark, for the far cackle of a midnight crow.

If for no reason than I doubt my friend.

At my mother's house, it's see you Say, yeah see you. I walk up from the bottom of the driveway. The house is dark, no light on in Mom's bedroom. The garage door is down, so I go around back. Pookie's out. I consider lying on my back by the pool and looking at the sky. But now the air is still and it wouldn't be much good for looking. I go on in the back door to the kitchen. The door creaks and makes me kind of sad. I'm sad already, the door creaking going into this run-down house, and my mother living here where she doesn't want to live, and me on the couch, the creak announcing my reentry into the house, my jinx come home to roost, and Mom's nice dining room table and no dining room, just this open space off this small kitchen, and the nice candelabras, and nobody ever eats there, except our halfass fake family Christmas, and nobody knowing how to act, and Tom's girls getting Mom a present, us never getting Tom jack, and why in God's name does she insist on putting fresh flowers on that table?

I go to the refrigerator knowing there'll be no Cokes, knowing all I'll see is buttermilk and pineapple prune juice and maybe some bottled English pea soda, and I open the door thinking, you had money why didn't you buy some Cokes, and there they are, eight cold ones, shiny and new, and a six-pack of beer and some Gatorade, you sorry doubting negative thinking sack of shit.

I grab a Coke and two beers and head downstairs. I take off my shoes and sit on the couch to watch television, popping the Coke as soon as the set starts to hum in the quiet of the den, yes Mom, I owe you, the little Coke is good. I light a cigarette and go to the bookshelf and grab the Bible I've been reading. I flip through it, set it back down. I try the television. News and talk shows. Lame movies. A couple of televangelists with puffed-up hair. Weather. The time.

I turn it off. You never see guys like Reverend Madden on television. Always some clown who looks like he's trying to trick old ladies out of money. And Chapman got rid of Reverend Madden after my senior year. It was ridiculous. A few seniors had been suspended for a week for drinking on a political science trip to Washington. No school, no extracurriculars, etcetera. They'd missed the whole regional basketball tournament that week, the final of which was Saturday night. So early Saturday morning, Mr. Dickey, our headmaster, made a point of calling every kid at home and telling them that the suspension included the weekend, that they weren't to attend that night's game. Here the basketball team is in its first ever final, the first in school history, and he's trying to keep our fans out of the game. Of course none of their dads were on the Chapman board, donating a lot of money to the school. Well, they showed up anyway, seven of them, four boys and three girls. The Chapman Seven. I'm in the lay-up line when they walk past Mr. Dickey at his sentry post, past our coach trying to pull his head out of his ass, and into the upper corner of the student section which is cheering like crazy for them. Not too long after, here comes Reverend Madden, walking slowly, past the headmaster who is doing his best impression of an intimidating stare, past coach and his futile extrication attempts, through the cheering students cheering him on and up to sit with the Chapman Seven. He sat there the whole game. Three months later he was shown the door.

I turn the TV back on, flip channels, turn it off again. Watch the blank screen for awhile. I'm sitting up with my eyes closed when I hear light footsteps on the stairs. It's my mother tiptoeing, running her hand along the wall. She stands there at the bottom of the stairs wearing an old robe, looking both older and younger than she is. You just get in kiddo?

Not too long ago. Did I wake you?

No. I was up.

Not a lot of sleeping going on this house.

Not a lot.

She sits down in the chair next to the couch. How was your speech?

Okay. Pretty good.

How's Pel?

I don't know. Different.

She nods her head. It hasn't been an easy year, she says, and I realize she's come down to talk to me, to look to me for comfort, and I feel a little guilty about it always being me, my problems, help me with my problems, me.

She picks up the Bible on the coffee table, turns it in her hand, starts to say something, wants to say something. Sets it down again. I'm going to help you get an apartment, she says. I've got a little stock I can sell. I want to get you settled somewhere, at least for a little while. You'll feel better in your own place.

I don't say anything.

I'm not going to be here much longer. I'm getting out.

I figured. Tom's been talking to me a little bit about it.

He has? What's he said?

Nothing really. I just don't think he'll be surprised if you leave.

Well don't say anything. I still don't know where I'm going. I'd like to get out of Knoxville.

That would be a move.

There's nothing in Knoxville for a fifty-year-old single woman. All the men my age want thirty-year-olds. She smiles, showing a few crow's feet around the eyes.

There's not shit in Knoxville.

Oh there's plenty of shit, she says, and laughs again.

I'm worried about Tom, I say.

I am too. He's a nice man. I just don't know what else I can do. Neither one of us is getting it going. Maybe he'll shape up if I leave.

Maybe, I say, crushing out my cigarette. I hope so. He's been good for you.

I know he has. When your father and I were first divorced, I had a real tough time. That was another tough time. Dead broke. Couldn't meet any nice men. You remember. I was dating Jimmy Rust.

Shortcake?

Yeah. Shortcake. Well he wasn't the nicest man.

No I never liked that short son of a bitch.

No. Pete didn't either. So that was it for awhile after Shortcake. And then Tom came along. And he was so fun. So funny and sweet. Would sneak over at six in the morning on a Sunday and wash my car. Wait on the porch for me to wake up and then cook us a big country breakfast.

I nod.

Oh we had a blast those first two years. Used to go to Gatlinburg every other weekend and go dancing at the Ramada.

I smile.

She stands up to leave. Well I guess I better hit the hay. Got a busy day tomorrow. And honey, you know I'm always there if you need to talk.

I know, I say, the eternal five-year-old, the all-time mama's boy.

And then my mother is walking up the stairs to share a bed with a man whom she'll soon leave, to lie in bed and hear the deep breaths of a man whose life is slipping away, and down the hall, down the stairs, the faint hum of a television, her first son with his beer and the word of God that saves or forestalls or pacifies for a few hours the beating quiet, the restless dark.

July

I'm in the pool working my knee. I lean against a wall and push my leg slowly against the water. I do this again and again until my thigh burns. I'm two days off of crutches, nine since the operation. The swelling has gone out of my knee for the most part, only four small scars in the shape of a diamond show where Dr. Brimswick went in with his nimble arthroscope. I was in the hospital for a total of five hours. For this I was charged four thousand dollars. Four thousand dollars after Dr. Brimswick waived his fee.

I should be able to jog a little in another two weeks, and play basketball by October. Right now my leg is a stick, a white, hairless, egg bone of a stick. They charged me two hundred dollars to shave my leg at the hospital.

Tom's headaches are worse. He's not sleeping, and drinking twice as much. I avoid him when I can.

I get out of the pool and walk through the high grass to the kitchen. I'm not taking the Percodans anymore. The first week was pretty bad, but since then the pain is mostly from working the knee, working out the soreness, a good kind of pain. Tom takes my Percodans now, but they don't seem to help. I finally just gave them to him, so he wouldn't have to ask. The phone rings and rings in the morning. Nobody calling with good news.

Now my mother makes bland, useless statements about the yard, how it looks so bad no one will ever see the house, how the realtor won't even show the house the yard looks so bad, the house needs painting, the gazebo needs painting, the basement has a leak, and yes she's had reason to complain, but what now, we've worked that glorified pasture of a yard all summer, and not one potential buyer came by. Some fat-ass realtor came over and recommended just enough improvements to insure they lose money on the house. And Mom will have them done. She will get out. Tom can sit in the kitchen all day long and try to drink his headaches away, but my mother is getting out.

In the kitchen, the quickly accumulating hospital bill reminders are stacked on the windowsill over the sink. I was to have called them last week, according to my mother, to figure out a means of payment. I light a Mike Dorendo sponsored Camel light and call St. Mary's Hospital. As the phone rings I tally what money I have left. Two hundred dollars. I can go another month without work.

Hello St. Mary's Hospital, a voice says to me, ready to help, ready to say, listen Jason, we understand, forget the bill, we just want you to get better.

The nice lady transfers me to accounts where a woman answers with her dukes up. I give her my account number. She tells me what I owe.

Yes that's what I'm calling about. My bill seems a little high. You charged me twelve hundred dollars for a hospital room I was in for less than an hour.

That's the rate. I don't have anything to do with it.

But don't you think that's a little high? I say, as Tom walks into the kitchen. I mean I could have stood on one leg for that long. I could have got my mom to hold my leg up while I waited for the doctor.

Tom laughs. The lady in accounts does not. As I said, I have nothing to do with the rates.

Well how about letting me talk to someone who does.

She clicks to hold without a word. I look at Tom. I'm going to rip this guy a new ass, I say.

He shakes his head up and down yeah.

James Kincaid, a smooth, disembodied, administratively unerring voice drones into the phone.

Mr. Kincaid, Jason Sayer. I'd like to talk about my bill if I might.

Yes. What can I do for you?

Well, I say, looking at Tom, you can tell me why it's so high to begin with.

It's not high. Those are the standard hospital rates for the surgery you had performed.

You charged me nearly a thousand an hour. I'm paying for this myself. Is there no way you can reduce the bill, considering an insurance company's not handling my account?

The rates are standard. We don't adjust for the insurance company or the individual.

And you don't think four thousand dollars for four hours in a hospital is exorbitant?

Not at all.

I turn the dial to maximum hostility, saying, good God, I would have limped for the rest of my life if I knew you were going to charge me what you did.

That was your prerogative.

My prerogative? To limp for the rest of my life? How do you sleep at night?

I sleep fine.

I bet you do, I say, and you've just been slightly less than a complete pain in the ass. Then I slam down the phone, beaten as usual by the nerveless composure of the terminally competent. I have wild visions of stalking one James Kincaid to the ends of the world and kicking him over and over in his right kneecap to see how he reacts, to see how composed he is when a little stress is administered to the control group.

Tom looks at me and nearly smiles. His eyes are tired. He sits at the table like he's resigned to pain. Tom never went to Australia. He spent a little time in Europe in the service. I assume he screwed some women over there. Women like him. I've been wondering lately if it's a curse or a blessing to have a little smile, a grin, to have always about you the residue of boyhood.

He waits for me to say something. I hate a smug asshole, I say.

Yep, he says, too tired to smile.

Hell, if I knew they were going to charge me four thousand dollars, I'd have just cut the damn thing off. Where the hell am I going to get that kind of money?

He looks at me. You ever thought of getting a job? he asks. And saying this, his tone is hard to determine. I know he's worked his whole life, this is the first time ever, even as a very young man, he's had no money in his pocket.

That's a thought.

I'm serious. Have you ever considered working for a living, making money to pay your bills?

Yes, I've considered it, I say, looking him in the eyes.

He holds my gaze. I'm thinking, it's none of your damn business. Who are you to talk about me working? I wonder quickly if I could take him, if I really had to, could I beat his ass.

Tom lights a cigarette. I stand in my wet shorts, my raw shaved skinny leg knobby beneath me. I study the small white hairs beginning to grow on my leg. Tom would pound me into the ground. I turn and limp down the stairs.

Back in my lair I light a cigarette. Mom wouldn't talk to Tom's kids like that. I take off my shorts and sit on the couch and smoke. My Playboys call to me. Tom's not happy and seeing my jobless ass moping around the house isn't making him feel any better. Tough luck. Mom's been paying the bills around here. Then the siren call proves too much and I tire of tallying emotional debts.

From the bathroom, the salacious click of naked heels, naked fire-ladies, naked sheiks, naked nurses and librarians, naked tennis players, naked damsels in distress, naked cavewomen and cheerleaders and clowns, naked sky divers and cyborgs and aliens from the future and before I know it my fingers are reaching for the phone to call the one girl I figure might actually sleep with me, good old Penny Jackson, who has red hair and a good body and lives in Lenoir City, out in the country, with her father who can't work because of a bad back and about fourteen grandparents and whichever wormdoggy brother is home on leave. And is it her insistence on looking in my eyes while she does all manner of naked gymnastics, a stare both stimulating and unnerving in a pornographic way, that makes me want to and not want to give her a call? Half a synapse later, I'm dialing.

A grandmother answers, as I knew she would.

May I speak to Penny please.

Yes, she says. May I ask who's calling?

Yes ma'am. This is Jason Sayer.

Oh, yes. I'll put Penny on, she says, daintily, impressed by my fine manners, anxious to meet the young squire who will escort the debutante this evening.

What are you doing, young Penny says, girlishly, yet with a certain bravado.

Just seeing what you're up to.

I'm fixing to go to the church with my grandmother.

On Tuesday?

We clean it every other week. I make twenty-five dollars for about an hour's work.

That's a good deal.

Hell yeah.

Well, I was really calling to see if you might want to meet me for a drink later on this evening. But it sounds like you're busy.

I can meet you.

Really? Good. About nine-thirty at Spinners?

How about nine?

Fine. Good.

Looking forward to it.

Me too.

I hang up, and the only pertinent question is whether or not I can make it to nine o'clock without chopping down some serious timber.

At Spinners I get a booth in the bar area. Spinners is just like every other chain restaurant in the world. The only advantage to this place is that

I won't see any of my friends here. This is West Knoxville, the homogeneous zone. The alternative club has their meetings downtown.

My waitress comes by wearing a bow tie and starched white shirt and a button with her name on it. Betsy. Betsy is cute and efficient. An enthusiastic member of Team Spinners. Though she is obviously twenty to thirty years my junior, she asks to see my driver's license. The Spinners corporation will not be sued for underage drinking on Betsy's watch.

She checks the discombobulated face on the license, compares it to the ironic one in front of her. Like are you kin to that football guy by the stadium?

I am indeed.

Huh?

I am kin to him.

Really?

Really.

She hands the license back, searches valiantly through a memory bank clogged with salad dressings, desserts, specials of the day, for some tidbit or another about the football guy by the stadium. Comes up painfully empty. Winces at the missed opportunity to complete my Spinners experience.

Before your time, I say.

Yeah, she says. Yeah.

Half a scotch and five minutes later I'm Cary Grant sipping bubbly on a yacht just off the coast of Monte Carlo. Fake English accent and all. Then Penny walks in the door the way you'd like a woman to walk in a door when you haven't seen one in awhile and aren't sure when you're going to see one again. She takes her time making her way to the booth, smiling at a couple of older gentlemen, gentlemen you bet, who have turned to watch her pass. She sits down across from me with a hello, how you doing, we'll be screwing later, look on her face, just as Betsy comes by for round two.

What are you drinking, I ask.

Bourbon and Coke. Jack and Coke, she corrects herself.

Betsy trots off, twitching her nose at my hyperdilated eyes and Penny's cutoff jeans. Yes please.

I light a cigarette. We've been doing this on and off since I was twenty and barbacking at the Quality Inn, where young Penny worked in the gift shop. It took me the entire summer to seduce her. She made me work for it. At twenty, I had no idea there were such things as slumps, but that was before AIDS, in the last stellar, slutty, incontinent years, the disco craze meeting the early Reagan years, before my hands started to shake. She works now as a receptionist at a law firm and talks of moving to California. She never speaks of her dad or any of her family, other than she's proud of her brothers in the service. She makes her own car payments on a car that's always in the shop. She pays her own way.

How'd you get here, I ask.

My grandmom dropped me off.

What'd you'd tell her?

That I was meeting you.

Do you need to be in early?

Nope.

That's good.

She smiles at me and then at Betsy who brings her Jack and Coke, and I feel for a moment like Matt Dillon flirting with Miss Kitty, a minimum of words, a quiet understanding that as soon as I shoot these bad guys and you close the bar and I get Festus to quit humping my leg, you and I are going to ride each other until we break.

Penny Jackson has a way with men. My scotch tastes good. I'm about to do something I'll feel guilty for. But at this moment I am very much looking forward to it.

When good old Jody McDowell walks by. An obvious signal to close my eyes and become invisible. But too late. He's spotted me and is on his way over, acting as if he's not a blatant stalker at large. This one-horse town, this one-horse town. I casually put out my cigarette.

Jason Sayer. How're you doing?

Fine, Jody. What are you up to?

Meeting some friends for dinner, he says, smiling. He's not stopped smiling since he saw me, and his well-groomed, smiling, Christian, for-giving face makes me quite uncomfortable.

We just got back from a retreat in Colorado. Actually we got back a couple of weeks ago, and this is kind of a reunion.

Really, I say, daunted as hell. Oh, this is Penny. She reaches out to shake Jody's hand. He smiles at her too, and I move past daunted to flat-out flustered.

What've you been up to this summer?

Just messing around really, I say, wanting very much for him to leave me to my drink and concubine, and hoping very much that Beth is not one of the friends due to attend the big two-week reunion. Maybe it's a dif-ferent church retreat in Colorado, I think, at about the same time Beth is walking in the door with another girl. She sees me, waves, and keeps walking on into the restaurant.

Didn't you live in Colorado for awhile or something? You and Pel?
Yeah.

Man, that's awesome. I loved that place. Didn't you just have a blast?
Yeah, it was fun. It's pretty country.

I'll say, he says, and man he is taunting me with all this sincerity, paying me back for blowing him off that day at Starnes Cafeteria.

Nice to meet you, he says to Penny, and then to me, let's get together sometime. I'm in the book.

All right. Sounds good. I'll talk to you later.

He puts his hand on my shoulder to say goodbye, and then we are alone, Penny and I, with Jody's niceness like a pall over my debauchery, and Beth at a table with the church group, her halfass wave hanging in the air.

I excuse myself to go to the bathroom. Not smoothly I might add, nearly smashing into dear Betsy and her tray of fried cheese. Compliments of the house Mr. Sayer. You are this week's king of cheese. I steady Betsy, her tray, look at Penny, who is nonplussed, smiling into her Jack and Coke. Two more drinks please Betsy, I say, cool as curry.

In the bathroom I mull over lies to tell anyone who might ask me anything. I consider calling the police and requesting a restraining order on one Jody McDowell. I contemplate whether my knee will encumber the naked aerobics routine I've choreographed for Penny Jackson. I try to formulate a Beth plan. Approach the church group cautiously and say in a friendly voice . . .

Finally I decide just to ride it out, finish this drink, head home and take care of business. Beth's not my girlfriend.

I come out of the bathroom head held high, ready to storm the Bastille, and nearly knock Beth over as she rounds the corner.

Hey, I say, and I can't help it, I've got this grin on my face that I get sometimes when I'm nervous and a bit dull-witted. The grin means to charm, but is a foolproof engenderer of open female hostility.

Hello Jason, she says, school marm extraordinaire.

I had my knee operation, I say, heading full bore into neutral waters.

I heard that.

You did.

Yes.

And we stand there in silence. I'm grinning like an idiot because I'm embarrassed and glad to see her and have absolutely nothing to say. Finally she cracks, out of pure embarrassment for me. You are such an asshole, she says.

I know, I say, it's unbelievable.

So you got your knee fixed.

Yes.

And you got you a little date.

Now about that, I start, but she's waving me off, shaking her head no she doesn't want to hear it.

Can I come down to the pool, I say, for some rehab. Are you still life-guarding?

You can come down.

You're sure it's okay? I can use my mom's pool but she doesn't like me swimming without adult supervision.

You can use the pool. I won't let you drown.

But I'm still in the doghouse.

Oh yeah. Big-time.

I get back to the table and Penny gives me a look like I've been gone for a long enough time. Not a big one like she's giving me a guilt trip, just to let me know that was long enough. My fresh drink is on the table and I take a big swig. Then I light a cigarette. When Beth comes out of the bathroom, I look away and toward the bar with a quick nervous twitch that cracks a couple of vertebrae in my neck.

I've still got the postcard you sent me, Penny says. The Great Barrier Reef.

She smiles, grabs a cigarette out of my pack and lights it.

I was missing you about then, I say.

Weren't getting any, were you?

In my mother's basement we watch Blaze, the movie about Edward Long, the governor of Louisiana, and his love affair with a stripper and her heart of gold, and drink beer that becomes increasingly warm since I don't want to hustle upstairs to the refrigerator every ten minutes and talk to Mom and Tom who are up watching television in their den.

Afterwards, after the bathroom sink and Penny's head banging against the mirror, with my Playboy Bunnies and Penthouse Pets beating on the doors of the cupboard, howling in jealousy, wanting to get out and show their naked long legs in their high-heeled shoes, riding their naked motorcycles and horses, walking their sudsy naked dogs, naked hoses spraying naked water on naked cars, naked pool balls and pompoms and toolboxes and laser guns, me hollering, hush up in there, you two-dimensional, glossy-assed prick teases, I got a live one here, after that, we lie on the floor of the orange shag carpeted den, stretched out on Pete's old NFL sleeping bag, the one he used to get in headfirst and slide blindly down the stairs of our old house. I smoke a cigarette and wonder what Penny's grandmother must be thinking now, whether she's up, unable to sleep, and why it is I never take Penny out to dinner.

That church y'all clean, is that where you go?

My grandmom does. I go sometimes.

You like it?

Okay. Why?

I don't know. I was just wondering. I've been thinking about stuff like that lately.

That's good, she says, and backs up against me closer, we are lying sideways, and kind of settles in, moving just a little, slowly. I lie still, listening for a train to sound, but none does. I listen to hear Tom snoring, or the chirp of a cricket, but there is no sound but our breathing. Slowly, and without faces, the silent movement of ghosts.

My mother and I are in the kitchen wondering where Tom is when he calls. Just bought us a goddam riding mower, he says, need someone to follow me home.

You're going to drive the mower home?

Well hell yes.

It's nearly dark out. That's two miles you're talking.

Let me talk to your mother.

She can't convince him not to drive the mower home. It's got goddam headlights, he tells her. He says he'll call Jackie, and hangs up.

And we talk, Mom and I, about how she must get out of the house, Tom is irrational, he's not getting better. Because he's sinking is no reason for her to sink as well. A riding lawnmower. How much does a riding lawnmower cost? What is he thinking buying a riding lawnmower and not even knowing how he's going to meet his half of the house payment?

I better go down there, I say. If Jackie's not there, he's liable to ride that mower home by himself.

And I drive to the Kmart wondering how a grown man lets himself go like that, lets the drink get him so bad, and I'm mad that he's put my mother in this situation, mad when I get to the Kmart.

Tom's standing outside in the parking lot next to his red mower, and next to him is a confused-looking salesman who's glad to see me.

What say, Jason, Tom says. He's smiling. A little wildly, a little too broadly. But there is no doubt. He's happy with his mower.

Hey Tom.

How you like it?

It's a good-looking mower.

We can do that back yard in half an hour.

I ask him if he got hold of Jackie, if Jackie is coming with his truck, but he doesn't hear me. He's standing back from his mower to get a better look at it, about as liquored up as you'd ever need to be in public.

You going to follow me home?

It's too dark Tom. That's a long way to travel on a lawnmower.

Bout a mile. She's got headlights.

He points out the headlights to me. The salesman looks scared, as if he might be held responsible for whatever pending calamity awaits.

I don't think it's legal, I say. Some cop might pull us over.

Shit. Once you get off the Pike, it's back roads all the way. Cops. Shit.

Maybe it'd be best to wait till tomorrow to pick it up, the salesman says. He is perhaps regretting this sale.

We'll get Jackie's truck, I say. We'll pick it up first thing in the morning.

All right, he says, and starts walking to my car, passing his own car on the way, looking now and again over his shoulder at the mower, which he's left in the parking lot with the salesman and me.

We'll be by tomorrow, I say, and hurry off before Tom changes his mind.

Tom's in my car watching the salesman push the mower through the parking lot when I get in. That's a hell of a mower, he says.

It sure is, I say. And Tom's smiling on the way home, the lights from the fast-food restaurants shining on his face as we pass.

The next day, around five, Mom calls and asks for Tom.

He's not in, I say. He and Jackie dropped the mower off around noon and I haven't seen them since.

Have him call when he gets in. I'm running late.

All right, anything else?

Did he say anything about going to the doctor?

No ma'am.

Okay, she says, I'll see you later.

About five-thirty, I go out to inspect the new lawnmower. It's a huge red monster, not quite as large as a VW Bug. I sit down on the thick leather seat and test the steering wheel and locate the gear settings. I finger the key and think about cranking it but fear being bucked off and chased around the yard. I glance around the blade area for the foot amputation center but can't locate it. Then I dismount and head down to see Beth and to do a few laps.

At the pool, Beth's giving a swim lesson to Paul. It's hot as hell out still, so he'll have to come up with another excuse this time. An older man in a Speedo swims laps, steady and unhurried, his large mouth gasping air and slurping and spitting out water with every stroke, unselfconscious as old guys are. Beth sees me and waves, as she backs up backs up, carrot in front of a donkey, just out of reach of Paul's slapping shovels, his gagging wrenching pinched face. On occasion he actually puts his face in the water and one could fairly describe what he's doing as swimming.

There's no one in the deep end so I do my laps down there horizontally. About every fourth one I have to keep my eyes open so as not to smash into the old guy. I do laps for about twenty minutes, then tread water ten more, working my legs hard, getting the good burn in my thighs and around my knee. Then I've had it.

I get out of the pool and dry off. Paul and his mother have gone, but the Swimming Machine chugs on. Beth's changed into cutoffs and walks around the pool folding chairs. She's got her hair in a ponytail and wears a baseball cap, which can look too cute on some girls, but she's tomboy enough to pull it off. She can hum a baseball. I point at the swimmer and nod my head in approval.

Every day, Beth says, a full hour.

I nod my head. Johnny Weismuller lives.

I help her fold chairs for awhile. Then I spray down the concrete while she checks the chemicals in the pool. I watch the swimmer as I spray, every stroke the same length, every lap the same speed, patient and steady turning of head for huge-mouthed gulping of oxygen, same arm in front of same arm, movement of water and movement in water, the hard clean hiss of power hose on concrete, last heat of the day, beginning of honeysuckle, end of chlorine, that mixing of night and day smells that is the first hint of dusk, and now the swimmer finishes his laps and trudges thick-thighed and tired-shouldered up the stairs of the shallow end, older than I thought, maybe seventy, chest sunken with age, but otherwise good to go, breathing deep and steady as he ascends the stairs, as if he swims still.

Good swim, I say.

He nods. Flexes a bicep. Then he puts on sandals and walks without towel or shorts or shirt past Beth, who says, goodnight Mr. Glassman, and he nods, and then on out into the parking lot and up the hill toward home or perhaps the bicycling portion of his triathlon.

Paul's swimming better, I say to Beth across the pool.

I guess so. At least he's trying.

Yeah it looks like it.

Beth nods, keeps screwing with the chemicals. She has one leg under her and the other spread out and it's a good leg, brown and strong. And she's got her back to me, giving me the full back treatment, some solid body language. As an experiment, purely for scientific reasons, I shoot the hose in a high arc across the pool in her direction. The spray lands softly in the pool, a good three feet from her back. She blanks me. Full bore I power hose three feet to the left of that imperturbable back, the water skipping off the concrete like a hot grounder. Don't, she says.

And I don't. For a second. But I'm afraid I've spent too many days by the pool with Cousin Butch, and before the left side of my brain can intervene, I've pretty much soaked a shoulder, a hip, and a good portion of extended leg.

You asshole, she says, jumping up to face me, statue in motion, stasis overwhelmed, madder than I hoped.

Sorry, I say, Belushi having just smashed the sensitive guy's guitar.

No you're not.

I know.

Then she goes back to her chemicals and I to my spraying. Every now and then I look over at her to see if she's really mad, but it's impossible to tell. Backs are hard to read. When I finish, I carry the hose to the storage house. Then I walk over to Beth, thinking maybe I ought to apologize. What I do instead is grab her from behind, underneath the shoulders, and act like I'm going to throw her in the pool.

She grabs my leg, hard, the one just operated on.

The knee, the knee, I say.

You're going in with me, she says, doubling her grip on my leg, wrapping a calf around an ankle to insure maximum torque.

The knee, I say, letting go of her shoulders and kind of slumping down sideways in a failed attempt to alleviate pressure.

Oh shit, she says, letting go of my leg, too quickly, for I'm off-balance and fall over her legs and onto the concrete.

In a situation like this, sprawled on the ground, clutching a leg, face gargoyled, in the immediate afterthroes of a most infirm and graceless moment, a man can either laugh in a good-natured show of self-deprecation and high threshold of pain, or he can choose not to laugh, and say, in effect, that he accepts his pain and humiliation with silent and proud resignation. I, on the other hand, opt for the fake cry, the Cowardly Lion.

Afterwards, of course, is better. All hail the banana peel. We sit in foldout chairs by the pool and watch the night come on. Beth tells me about life at the community center, about her trip to Colorado. She had a good time in Colorado. She hiked a lot. She went white water rafting and was scared to death. She rode mountain bikes. She'd never seen such a huge sky nor so many stars. I sit there and listen. It's nice to hear her talk. It makes me miss Colorado. Pel and I had a great time out there.

She starts telling about some guy who fell over when they were white water rafting and how it really did look bad for awhile until he caught on to a rock, and lightning bugs have begun to float through the chain link fence and over the diving board, and a dull glow from the light in the deep end frightens away whatever cave fish might be in the pool. The honey-suckle is strong now, too heavy, headache inducing, and the air is heavy with water and crickets and frogs. The sky is too low. If you were to lie on one side with your eye nearer the ground closed, you would feel like you were swimming in sky. Pink heat lightning in the distance. Innocuous thunder. Dogs sleepy with suburbia halfheartedly barking at a moon that isn't there. Beside me the quiet voice of a girl, the squeak of a chair, and that indescribable feeling, that knowledge of life and death, that is sitting in a wet swimsuit at the end of a summer day.

I'm sorry about that night.

I know.

And we sit in the heavy night, looking out over the pool and behind the pool to the dark trees that run along the train track. Every now and then our legs brush, and her thigh is warm on mine. It's shocking how warm. Radioactive. She's been nude sunbathing up at the power plant again. My leg, on the other hand, is plastic and came with the bathing suit. My leg, to be perfectly honest, was just exhumed from a Scottish bog.

Your leg's cold. Are you cold?

No, I say, for some reason, because I am.

She looks over at me. She's got her cap turned backward now and part of her ponytail has come loose. A long strand of blonde hair falls across one eye. I saw Bobsmith yesterday, she says.

Really.

He asked about you, how your operation went.

I don't say anything.

You're not going to tell me anything are you.

No. There's nothing to tell.

Well you've gotten weird and so have they.

That's true, I say. That is true.

Is it drugs?

Some of it is.

She looks down, nods. Why do you hang out with those guys at all?

I don't know. I've known them a long time. I've known Pel since before you started school. When we were still running from girl germs.

She smiles a little. Then I hear paws trotting down the parking lot and the thin clink of dog tags, and I say, I think that's my dog. I stand up to look and there she is, the French tacky herself, quick feet trotting, her proper lady's walk now, tail lofted over back like an elaborate duster, ass high in the air, down the sidewalk and through the open gate to the swimming pool where she stands before us with her black tongue out and tiny men in barrels cascading down her saliva falls.

You little tart, I say, going over to stroke her neck.

That's your dog?

Yeah, hell yeah, best dog in the world.

She's down here every day. This one lady brings her toy poodle down and your dog just drives him crazy prancing around the fence outside.

That's her. She's a little vixen.

And Beth and I talk about Pookie for awhile and it's good and neutral that way, no talk of my friends, or of Pel. After awhile I walk her to her car. Thanks for letting me swim, I say.

Sure, she says.

Hey, Tom's daughter's getting married later on this month.

Who?

My mom's boyfriend's daughter. My common-law stepsister.

Beth laughs.

Would you want to go?

Okay. When is it?

Last Saturday in July.

Yeah I can go, she says. That'll be fun.

She offers to drive me home, but I decline, preferring to walk. Then she gets in her car and drives away. I stand in the empty parking lot and call for Pookie a couple of times, but she's long gone. Then I walk home, feeling more tired than it seems I ought to.

When I get there, the back door is open and Mom sits at the kitchen table drinking a glass of wine. Before I'm all the way in the kitchen she asks if I've seen Tom.

No ma'am. I left him a note when you called and I've been gone since.

She nods, takes a sip from her wine. I start to ask her if she's seen the mower, but don't. Do you want some wine, she asks, there's some in the fridge.

I grab a glass and sit down at the table, still in my wet swimsuit, and feel a little queasy. I drink wine and make small talk about my nonexistent life, though my operation and convalescence give me at least one topic of conversation. Mom talks about work and what Pete's up to and a lot about all that needs to be done for Rachel's wedding. And in the dimly lit kitchen, with the hum of the refrigerator and moths popping against the window and every now and then the crack and rumble of the icemaker, we wait for the slam of a car door without ever mentioning why it is we wait.

Just after eleven we hear the garage door open and, a long minute after that, hear it close again. Then the door from the garage to the den and the panting paws of Pookie up the stairs. She looks at Mom, at me, then nudges open the screen door and stands there, ass in kitchen, torso and face on the steps, lapping water from her dish very loudly.

Good gosh, Mom says laughing.

I laugh with her.

Tom's knee pops on the stairs and we look toward the stairs and then we're both watching when he walks in the kitchen. Look at her, he says, pointing at Pookie. Keeps me out half the night then wants to eat in the kitchen. Pookie, hearing her name, looks up, smiles at Tom, then walks on out into the yard, letting the screen door slam behind her.

I smile. Tom is smiling. Mom has her head down as if looking for something in her glass of wine, but what it is is she has a worried look on her face and not the facility to take it off.

What you up to Jason? Been swimming?

Yessir.

How's the water?

It's good, I say, and start to explain where I went swimming, then don't.

Is it, he says, smiling like he's maybe never been swimming, or as if the pool's brand new and he hasn't yet had a chance to try it. I think I'll have a swim, he says. Been hot as hell all day. He turns to go toward their bedroom, then stops. You see that mower?

Yessir. It's a fine-looking mowing machine.

He smiles, looks over at Mom to see if she understands our complicity in this mower business. They catch eyes for just a second and then he looks back over at me, smiling even more. We, after all, are the mowers of lawn, and the look he gives, a kind of sweet-faced rebel schoolboy look, tells me, and my mother, why it was he bought the riding mower. Yes indeed, he says, looking out the window, perhaps he says it to the window, that is a mowing machine.

We can hear him back in the bedroom changing into his swim trunks. He's singing an old Freddy Fender song, Wasted Days and Wasted Nights, and laughing every now and then at the lyrics or something else that strikes him funny. I look over at my mother and grin, which maybe prompts her. Tom, she says.

She means, or thinks she means, to yell his name or say it pretty loudly, but she doesn't. I reach over and touch her hand, shaking my head no.

Tom comes through the kitchen in his swimsuit. He's rubbing his hands together, hyperbolic mad scientist. This is going to be good, he says. Then he's out the door, and before the screen door slam has fully registered in our ears, there's a loud splash of the cannonball tidal wave variety. Mom stands up and rinses out her wineglass. She places it in the dishwasher. Goodnight, she says, heading off to bed.

Ask him tomorrow.

She nods and then is gone.

I get up and turn off the light and start to head downstairs. Then I think I ought to go outside. Instead I light a cigarette and pour myself another glass of wine from the box in the refrigerator and sit back down at the table in the dark kitchen. Through the window, a few fuzzy stars, the tops of brooding trees. I close my useless eyes. Outside, it's splashes and barks, the mad running of a dog, the full clear laugh of a man.

Pete's in town for a visit. He's in town to provide moral support. What the doctor told Tom was that he had cancer of the brain and lungs. It looks bad. He's already started chemotherapy. He's tired from the radiation and pretty irritable. The whole thing is embarrassing to him, people asking how he feels, having to sleep all the time, having a scorched bald head.

At dinner it's hard to look and not to look at Tom. The top of his head is a reddish purple from the burn. He doesn't wear a hat. I gave him a baseball cap I had, a new one that I liked, but he doesn't wear it. I think maybe since it's new and not broken in, it hurts the burn.

Pete doesn't know what to say here at dinner. Mom has candles lit on the table, and the lights turned low, to insure we'll all feel pressured to make this meal a success. There is a direct correlation to how much my mother wants a family meal to succeed and the likelihood of that actually happening. Call it an inverse proportion. Pete's accustomed to being able to make things a little better. I'm accustomed to eating as fast as I can before something happens. I can feel Pete wanting to say something, anything. Mom is driving him crazy, chatting away about some Chapman classmate of his whose extravagant wedding was all the talk earlier in the summer. Tom doesn't listen to her, but Pete thinks this drivel must be irritating to a man dying of cancer, if for no other reason than it's irritating to two men who are not. I'm thinking that if we were all at the kitchen table, maybe even with me standing up and eating at the sink, rather than in this halfassed dining room, with the tablecloth and flowers and good silver production that is an undefeated jinx, things would proceed in an unmannerly but relaxed fashion.

Really? Pete says with barely concealed lack of interest. Mom has been quoting sausage ball prices. Tom, Pete says, what do you think about Tennessee this fall? They going to have a quarterback?

Tom smiles a little. He pushes his plate away, having taken only a couple of bites of the homemade chicken pot pie his sister-in-law from Niota dropped by. He doesn't eat more than a few bites a day. The chemotherapy burns his tongue and steals his appetite. Can't say as I know, he says. He gets up from the table, leaving his plate behind, and reaches under the sink for his big bottle of Dickel.

That all you going to eat Tom? Mom asks.

I'm not hungry.

You've got to keep eating. You've got to keep your strength up.

Janey, he says, looking up from the precise pouring of bourbon into glass, I can't eat if I can't eat. I'm just not hungry.

His tone is not as sharp as it is matter-of-fact, but Mom's feelings are hurt nonetheless. Okay, she says with a theatrical wave of her hand.

Pete stands up and takes his plate to the sink before he says something smart to our mother. I can see him set his jaw, saying to himself, I'm not going to say anything, this is not my place, not my life.

This is my life. Through the open back door I hear a train whistle, thick and sweet with departure. Tom walks back to the bedroom and turns on the television too loud. Pat Sajak gives dollar values on the wheel. I can picture Tom, lying on the bed with his shoes on, sipping on his drink, softly rubbing the top of his bare burned head. What does a man think in such a situation? Does he not think of selling all he owns and hopping a train to Vanna White, to plead for just one night, just one, of mindless, beautiful sex? Does he not think of killing Pat Sajak for no particular reason? Perhaps he thinks of nothing but the lying down, the sipping of bourbon, the moment when his lover comes in the room to rub his tired feet.

Pete comes back to the table and sits down. He's exasperated by his own inability, by the dysfunction, the rundown spectacle of those who share his blood, who share a roof with the mother who brought him into this world. Surely there's been a mistake. He was a baby switched at birth. Do these people not see that life can be solved, that the solving is related to the knowing, the acceptance, that all is fucked, and what you need to do, what you have to do, is just ride it out and work hard and not be a loser? Everyone should have to take statistics. Statistics are facts. A certain number of people will be hit by cars this year, a certain number of toads born. And the liberation, for those who know the facts of numbers, is that the car crash victims and the toads born are not more or less loved by God or destiny, but merely and beautifully the victims or benefactors of faceless probability. Pete is thinking right now of the believe it or not story of the man who had a flat tire on the interstate and missed the plane that crashed and how this man will interpret this as a sign from God that he is special or blessed or meant to do God's work, when in fact all it means is that one out of every ninety thousand miles on the road a person experiences a flat tire, and it is just the caprice of statistical probability that this particular flat tire kept this particular man off of a plane that crashed, an event that is also inextricably tied to actuarial math. Though it is not likely, a coin can land on heads a hundred times in a row.

You shouldn't get on him about eating, Pete says.

She knows that now, I say, and Pete looks over at me a little shocked. It's been a good while since I've corrected him.

I wasn't talking to you, he says, looking me in the eye. He's about as big as I am now and in better shape.

I was talking to you.

Mom stands up and goes to the sink and starts washing dishes. Pete and I are still looking at one another.

You don't want any of me, I say.

Fuck you.

No, fuck you.

If you think I'm afraid of you.

I know you're not. Now fuck off.

Boys shut up! my mother screams, and a plate crashes into the side of the sink. She's yet to look at us when she pulls her hand out of the sink to look at a bleeding finger.

Shit Mom, Pete says, rising to look at her hand. She stares at it until Pete puts his hand on her shoulder. Get away, she says, just get away, and she walks out of the kitchen, a few small drops of blood falling on the floor.

I don't look at Pete, but follow her into the hall bathroom. You okay, I say, are you going to need stitches?

Get out of here, she says. She has her hand wrapped in a towel, and she puts her face in the towel. I said to get out of here.

When I walk back to the kitchen, Pete's on his hands and knees with paper towels, cleaning up the water and the drops of blood. He looks up and gives a holy shit, we're dumbasses, look. I shake my head yes, holy shit, and empty the sink to pick up the pieces of the broken plate.

I'm watching Tom mow the grass from the kitchen sink window. Rachel's wedding is closing in and the house has turned into a beehive of frenzied and frenetic chore doing. The women buzz around, hands flying in the making of lists, the dialing of phones, talking quickly and succinctly to each other and to themselves, looking around every corner for a worker bee not pulling his weight. Only now, when we are without supervision, can I stand in the kitchen and drink a glass of water in the quietude of blissful malingering.

Tom zings along at a rapid pace, determined to finish the back yard in thirty minutes flat. Sticks and dust fly around the bare parts of the yard. Tom doesn't bother to pick anything up. We need rain badly. He has the mower set too low, and the yard doesn't need mowing. More and more bare patches pop up with every row and big rips in the grass where he's tried to force the mower up the hill. Soon there will be no grass left to mow. Perhaps that is his goal.

I'm watching him now to see when he'll tip the mower over. He insists on mowing the hill, though I've offered to use the weed eater. His face sets, faintly maniacal, as he starts on the first row of the hill that is at a one hundred and twenty degree angle. I'm near the phone so I'll be able to immediately call 911.

He's found himself a hat he likes, a floppy blue jean number, like J.J. used to wear on Good Times. I don't know where he got it, but it looks comfortable. He's been sleeping a lot and doesn't have much to say. He's tired of relatives coming in to see him, tired of saying he feels fine when he doesn't. He'll be glad when this wedding is over.

I light a cigarette. I'm planning on quitting. Watching a man die from cancer will make you think. Tom makes the first turn on the hill, and a wheel catches, spinning up grass and dirt. Tom keeps the pedal down, the grass flies. The mower doesn't move. He stands in the seat like a boy coasting on a bike and rocks the mower back and forth, the engine reving, ready to explode in motion and catapult Tom backward. He rocks and rocks and I'm on my way out to push, when he finally rocks it free, and spinning out a new trench, again is on his way. Our back yard takes on the appearance of a monster truck rally and Tom looks glad to be in motion again.

As the hill steepens, Tom has to lean nearly ninety degrees to balance the mower. His J.J. hat, poised to fall at any moment, can't hide the small red splotches on his neck, the burns. Sweat pours from his face, gaunt with the passing minute. He grips the wheel tightly. I glance at the phone, then back at Tom, a wild, determined, glorious look on his face, defying the laws of gravity, willing the mower on.

He begins the fourth row of the hill, five remain. Here the hill is steepest. Surely he will go for the weedeater. But the mower has its own volition. Tom leans to his left, shoulder nearly scraping the ground, teeth clenched, he will mow this goddam hill he will, and then the telltale jerk, almost imperceptible, and then the slow motion of gravity proving too much, J.J. hat flailing backwards, and mower and Tom down the hill at ninety miles an hour, rocky ride bronco busting through shrubs, runaway train, watch out! and into the pool.

But only two wheels. Tom holds fast, as one suspended, the screech of metal against concrete in his ears, the mower wedged, his head purple and splotched and naked in the hot sun, but the mower has not drowned. He sits in shock, the ride over, only one shrub dead, and welcome back to this world of slow motion reality. He looks around, a boy not sure whether to put the apple in his pocket, is the storekeeper away, has anyone seen this intent, this show of will, this failure, this potential?

When he pulls himself off the mower, I walk outside. He looks at me, an alien, a shadow-propelled entity that counts itself among the living. Ghost speak in this hot haze, the thing yet alive, the ride, a transparency between the thing done and the hot wordless stillness now. Thick are the trees in their green waiting for wind to give them speech. But listen, can you not hear the hard screech eternal, the scrape? And the pool does ripple still, lapping, pressing against containment. Somewhere rain falls.

You all right?

Oh yeah.

Thought you were going to take a swim.

Yeah. Uhhm. Yeah.

He goes and picks up his hat and slaps it against his knee. Then he shakes it, pretty hard, shaking some sense into it after that crazy stunt it just pulled behind the wheel. I take off my shirt and get in the pool.

We can push it out, I say.

I get under the mower and push, but all the weight's up front, and with my knee it's hard to push. Tom takes off his shoes and shirt and gets in the pool with me. He wears his hat.

We each grab a wheel and push, me on one leg, Tom with arms and chest grown thin, dissolving before my eyes. One two three, and she's out. Tom climbs out of the pool and walks toward the house, leaving his shirt and shoes. I'll weedeat it, I yell to his back.

All right, he says, not looking back.

I swim a few laps. When I'm finished, I go to the garage and fill the weedeater with a mixture of oil and gasoline, then go back to the hill to finish. Overhead there is no sun visible, though it's hot out, and light. The haze thick like running in dreams, no sun, no sky, no opposing moon or darkness, generality, a vague notion of heat that drugs those of the city, and makes a cacophony of the mechanical drone, the high-pitched whine. The dry grass soon dead flies. Mosquitoes float unseen.

Jackie and Tom are upstairs laughing about something I bet isn't funny. I assume Tom is laughing though I don't hear him. Jackie laughs too loud, wanting too much to make his friend feel better. Nervous hilarity. I pass by them quickly, heading for the shower. I've done my work for the day. The gazebo is painted. South Fork looks like its old self again.

Downstairs the phone rings and rings and Tom doesn't answer. I pick up on about the fortieth ring, convinced by the caller's persistence that it's a girl for me.

Hello.

Hey Jason, Tom's sister Bobbie says. And if she's not smacking gum into the phone, she should be.

Hey Bobbie.

What you doing? You found a job yet?

No.

Just gonna sit by the pool all summer. Wish I could afford to do that.

She laughs though she's not kidding. If I do get a job she won't have a damn thing to talk about.

Do you want to talk to Tom? I ask, sharply, with precision, intending to offend.

Curt in yet? she asks, spunky as the day is long, impossible to be tactless with the Queen of Chewing Gum.

No. I didn't know he was coming in.

He is.

So I gather.

What?

I'll have Curt call when he gets in.

All right. Tell Sweet I'm on my way to carry him for his treatment.

I'll do it. And I'll let you know the very instant I get a job.

I'll be waiting. And she hangs up. Still undefeated. Still the Champ. And I vaguely consider a browse through the classifieds.

Curt's car is built for gaining the attention of sixteen-year-old girls in Rome, Georgia, where he lives with his mother and stepfather, and he's eager to see how it draws in the relatively big city of Knoxville. I've agreed to go on an early afternoon semi-cruise, in lieu of perusing the job market. Bobbie's razzing little more than bird droppings on a drowning man's head.

That's loud, I say, feeling the bass of a rap song boom through my back, up through my neck and head and out my eyes.

Got third in the WIMZ Crank It Up Contest.

Congratulations.

He turns down the music, sings a couple of words, makes a few popping and spitting sounds to give the full ambience of the melody I'm soon to be missing. Curt's a good kid. Plays football and baseball, a member of the honor society and student government. No visible signs of teenage angst. A throwback kind of kid who likes girls and cars and his parents and thinks my mother is the greatest. He's Tom's youngest child.

We get on the Pike and head toward campus. It's hot out. We have the windows down. I'm the copilot to a sixteen-year-old with a new license and a new car. Curt waves at every girl, leans out the window, tries to get them to pull over and talk. I am hoping that none do. I am seventy-five. Curt is my youngest grandson.

We drive down the Strip, past the bars I began patronizing when I was Curt's age. We drive through campus to Neyland Stadium, huge and hulking, and consider sneaking in, but that would mean hopping a fence, and I'm not up to it with my leg. Neyland Stadium, 95,000 packed straight up in a two-tiered bowl that looms over the field like the biggest of brothers.

I hear the yells of the stadium, hear the cheers for my Uncle Clay, hear them booing Clay, the redneck bastards, when he was carried off the field with broken ribs. And my father has two young sons now and Clay dead, and my mother what can she say, new little house, a two-year-old, a five-year-old, and Clay dead and Dad doesn't talk about it, sets his jaw, tells his father one Fourth of July, I am five and can remember this, my father saying to Grandsay at the house in Sewanee, yes Daddy, if there is a Heaven, and I don't think there is, but if there is a Heaven, then Clay is there. I agree with you on that.

And my grandfather walks us out to the car, my mother and grandmother not wanting to cry in front of the boys, but this is no way to end a visit, and the sadness now in Grandsay's eyes as he thinks about his second son who couldn't turn the corner like Clay, who needs to be told something now, for things not said then, but only a handshake will come, and can a handshake say yes Clay was a good one, and you're a good one, better than I knew, I see you now as a man, and understand your early defiance, your defiance now of me and God and those who do not see your goodness. Don't forget your goodness. You have sons now and I hope you raise them perfect, but it's not easy, you'll see, and sometimes you won't see their goodness, their strength, but maybe you will, I hope you will.

And in that drive home from Sewanee, with no talking, and the headlights of passing cars shining in our silent car, I remembered them booing Clay with his broken ribs, remember like I was alive then, remember it in my blood.

And Grandsay is telling me, you look faster this year Jason. You're getting faster every year.

We drive on, up to Henley Street, past the Sunsphere, the symbol of a World's Fair whose theme was energy, a golden golf ball on a tee, Knoxville's monument of height and progress, three hundred feet high and sunk in a ditch. Three hundred feet of hot damn we made it over the mountain jubilation reduced to chinning the Holiday Inn on the hill, waiting patiently for some hillbilly giant to smack it into oblivion with a two iron.

I talk Curt out of visiting a girl he knows out in Carter. Cute girl, long-legged, says, where's it at? Curt brings these girls by the pool to torture me. Used to make a living off those girls. Where's it at? Where's my bikini bottom to for at?

We drive home on the interstate and I imagine what it must have been like when Mom and Tom first started dating. Heading up to the Smokies for a weekend alone. Catching a nice buzz at the Gatlinburg Ramada then dancing in the hotel disco, really shaking it, Tom's shirt maybe unbuttoned a little farther than usual, Mom maybe showing a little cleavage, the hotel DJ saying, now we're really rocking it folks, and afterwards, after a few drinks and a lot more dancing, giggly and sweaty in the elevator, Tom winking at an old lady who's trying to turn up her nose, and then into the room that overlooks the lights of the small city, and behind the lights the mountains that seem to swallow up whatever waits down in the valley, they begin, Mom and Tom, to jump up and down on the bed in their underwear, yelling, no kids, no kids, no kids.

Boy, Dad's sick, Curt says.

Yeah. He's pretty sick.

I'm afraid he's not going to get well. Rachel says it's bad.

You can't ever tell. We just got to see what this chemotherapy does.

You still smoke?

Yeah, some.

You ought to stop.

I will.

I sure am glad he met your mom. Janey's been good for him. I thought she was going to leave last Christmas when he was drinking so bad. I told her she ought to. I'm going to miss her.

She's not going anywhere.

Curt drives, not saying anything more. A small bird flies in front of our car, but Curt doesn't have to brake. He shuffles through his tapes, looking for something I'll like, then figures what's on is all right.

We're gonna be bad this year, he says.

Football?

Yeah. I'm going to try and play linebacker. Not enough action at corner. I like to hit, he says smiling.

I bet you do. I'll come see you play next year.

All right. I'm serious. We're going to be bad.

We drive on toward home, not stepbrothers, but sons of unmarried middle-aged lovers. We've shared a few awkward Christmas Eves and some days by the pool, and I will never see him play football, and when he's my age, he'll remember me as a minor character, glib and likable, a bit shaky perhaps. He'll not have a father anymore, and I could tell him now that his father is a good man, but he knows that. I could tell him to just keep going, keep doing what he's doing, the student government and the enthusiasm and all, but he knows that too. He'll answer the Christmas cards Mom will send, will include a little note about how he's doing, ask about Pete and me. And there are those who can skate through a fake family Christmas Eve, handing out presents to near stepbrothers, changing the Christmas records on the stereo, helping your dad's girlfriend clean up the house while her boys are out with their friends as soon as the presents are opened and the minimal amount of fake family small talk has been exchanged, and there are those who cannot, and there's not one thing I could ever tell this kid about life.

At home again, Curt sits by the pool and listens to Mom tell about her awful day at the florist. I sit by the pool as well, but don't listen. Tom walks out and sidearms a Little Debbie oatmeal cake that Curt one hands like a Frisbee just over Pookie's lunging mouth. Curt opens the package and splits the cake with the dog, who, ever the Southern belle, chomps it down with one bite and looks to Curt for the other half.

We can't feed her tomorrow, Tom says, she's getting spayed Wednesday.

Pookie looks at Tom. Tom looks at Pookie.

You heard me. We get you fixed, you can cat around the neighborhood all you want. You can hump your little butt off.

Tom! my mother says, but she's laughing, who's kidding who, and Curt's laughing, and Pookie's slinking toward a hole in the fence.

Not long after, I head down to the community center for some laps. It's late when I get there and only Beth and the Swimming Machine are around. I swim laps vertically alongside old Weismuller, but half the time I'm country boy swimming with my head out of the water and the other half I'm breaststroking or Man from Atlantis. Very rarely do I execute the proper Australian crawl, and when I do I get about half the pool in my mouth. What water I don't swallow is sealed with hot wax in my ears and will be sloshing around next to my brain for the next week. Grizzled diviners will pour down from the hills to follow me around with wildly shaking sticks.

I finish my laps and do some treading. Then my underwater resistance exercises. When I'm through I walk over to Beth, who's finished her closing up chores and is waiting, impatiently, to go home. You look ready to go, I say.

Getting there. Soon as Mr. Glassman finishes up.

You want to get a beer later?

I would but I've got plans.

Plans? You're not allowed to have plans.

Oh I'm not, she says, and I wait for her to tell me what she's doing, but she doesn't.

Behind me the swimmer swims on, steady splash after steady splash. We're still on for the wedding aren't we?

Sure.

Mine and yours?

No, she says, shaking her head.

I'm on the couch watching television, worrying about Pookie who's out in the garage sleeping off her operation. I check on her every hour. We made a little pallet for her in the garage where she'd be cool. She lies curled in a ball on the floor. She doesn't whine or cry out, but I'm worried about her.

I go to check on her and she's out of water. I get her dish and fill it with water and when I come back she tries to stand up to drink but doesn't have the strength. I put the water dish right under her face and she drinks daintily, laboriously, small laps of water followed by long pauses. I pat her head while she drinks, and talk to her, hey baby, hey baby, pookie pookie pookie pookie, you'll be all right, you'll be fine, don't try to get up, you need to rest, just rest.

Inside again, the house is ninety degrees because the cancer or the chemo one keeps Tom cold. I undress and make up the couch and lie on top of the covers. Peripheral light from the television shines on the family pictures behind and to the side of the television, pictures of young Tom with his young kids, and I have to make a concerted effort not to look.

On my way over to Pel's I have to wait for a train to pass. When I woke up, Tom was long gone and I figured I should make my escape too. I'm going over to Pel's because Mom and Rachel are losing their minds about this wedding and I don't have anywhere else to go. The yard looks as good as it can considering we haven't had any rain and Tom mows it every half hour. I've planted flowers around the mailbox, remulched the bed of shrubs along the house. I've trimmed hedges and clipped branches and cleaned gutters. Tom and I have painted the shutters and the pool chairs and the chain link fence that keeps us prisoner. We've cleaned out the garage. We're tired of yardwork and of each other and the planning of the wedding. We are most tired of the tireless women and their tireless planning.

Bobsmith's reading the sports page when I walk in. Sweet smell of cannabis in the air. Pel comes out from the kitchen and we talk about baseball. We're talking about baseball when Angie comes out of the bathroom in Pel's robe. Hey, she says to me.

Hey.

She walks through the den combing her wet dark hair and into Pel's room. I watch her all the way, then turn to mouth the word, bastard, to Pel, whose eyebrows are scraping the ceiling, who smiles with just the corners of his mouth as he makes the bong gurgle. I love Angie, I say silently, pointing my thumb toward the bedroom as if he needs reminding of the pseudo bohemian delight contained within.

I sit in the back of the car, bicycle-made-for-three veteran, while we drive Angie to her apartment. When she gets out, I hop in the front seat.

See you tonight, she says to Pel. See you Jason.

I watch her walk away, her cutoff shorts with the frayed edges, the little striped hippie bracelet around her ankle. She shakes out her clean brown hair and waves back at us. Pel does the toodle-oo. I just watch.

You suck, I say.

Pel puts the car in drive. She's open game, he says. Ask her out.

Naw man. Not now. You ruined it.

That's dumb, he says, smiling.

It's not dumb.

So you want to be in love?

Probably. I definitely want them to be in love with me.

That's selfish.

Do you love Angie?

Sure.

But you don't date her.

I love a lot of people. Monogamy is an outdated tradition. Marriage is bullshit.

So you wouldn't care if I slept with Angie tonight?

No. You're both friends of mine.

Bullshit, I say. Bullshit.

Back at Pel's I work Bobsmith over in darts. I can finally put a little pressure on my knee, which you need to lean toward the board and throw well. Trick comes in, still in his suit from work. What's up Say? How you been? How's the knee?

Getting better. Be ready to play ball soon.

Excellent. And am I to understand you've been getting some other exercise of late?

What?

You haven't had any visitors lately have you? Any young lady friends?

What makes you say that?

Oh, a little bird told me, he says, and sits down on the couch to load the bong.

What's this Say? Bobsmith asks.

Nothing.

Penny Jackson isn't catting around these days is she, says Pel.

Penny saved is a penny earned, Trick says, laughing smoke through his nose.

Penny for your thoughts Say.

They're old jokes. I laugh but don't fess up. I go outside to smoke a cigarette on the porch. A few grey clouds move in the distance. We're finally going to get some rain. You can smell it in the air. A cool breeze blows.

You sticking with the cigarettes these days? Trick asks, coming out to the porch.

Mostly. I'm getting too weird when I smoke dope.

Still?

Yes.

How so?

I see things. I think bad things about my friends.

About me? Trick asks. He's smiling.

Yes.

What kind of things, he says. He's taken off his jacket and tie.

I don't know. I don't think I want to say.

The wind blows harder, knocking small dead branches off the tree in the front yard. Electric air and movie sky, fast clouds moving against a facsimile blue, grey coming in from the mountains. Dog tags on the road, a thin jingle, hollow and spare, then a wiener dog trotting at walkrace speed. He looks over at us, stops, keeps going.

Birds keep flying in front of my car, I say.

Do you hit them? I hit one yesterday.

No. I always brake first.

I didn't brake. It shouldn't have flown out in front of me.

They don't know.

No one knows. What do you know?

Nothing.

You're not holding out on me?

Trick smiles and then stops. Inside someone has put on Jethro Tull. A few big drops of rain fall on the sidewalk.

Why consider the mote in thy brother's eye, but consider not the beam in thy own eye, Trick says.

I'm doing that aren't I? Man that's bad. I'm sorry. I'm doing that. I'm sorry.

Don't worry about it. Everybody does it.

I know, but you shouldn't. I should know better. I'm sorry Trick. I really am. That's shitty of me.

The prophet is never honored in his own town, he says. Take it from your favorite religion major.

Reverend Madden liked that saying too.

The old wrestler himself.

You remember that?

Sure. I was an impressionable young man. Pure of heart, pure of mind.

You were. Seriously. You're kidding, but you were.

And then I met a certain young man wise in the ways of the world.

I laugh. Early ripe, early rot, you know.

Now now, let's not be too hard on ourselves. Man has instincts that supercede all societal conditioning to the contrary.

I should've never let you guys go off to college by yourself.

Couldn't agree more my friend. Couldn't agree more.

Then he stands, smiling, to head inside. He holds the door open for me, saying, come inside, come inside. Good samaritans await. I have told them of your coming. Brother Pel expects you for dinner.

I start in, then stop. My mom's cooking supper, I say. I better get on home.

Now that's a good family boy for you. That's the kind of principes non homines man that Chapman High can be proud of.

Principes non homines you say.

You know the motto, he says, stepping into the house. Leaders not men old boy. Leaders not men.

At home I'm locked out of the house. For some reason Tom locks all the doors now and has the garage door opener connected so I can't just pull the door up. Pookie whimpers inside. Despite our work the house looks old and sick in the rain, an old lady wearing too much makeup. Out back the gazebo fake-smiles in white and soon tadpoles will be hatching in the pool. The huge riding lawnmower red and waterbead shiny waits at the gate, the damp underneath a nice resting place for snakes, the seat a high perch for squirrels. In the rearview the For Sale sign naked and forlorn.

I'm reclining in my car when Tom pulls up. I get out and run to the garage and I'm standing beside his car when he opens the door.

Shit, he says, jumping like he's seen a ghost.

Sorry, I say. I was out in the car. I was locked out.

I never saw you.

Sorry.

Hey let's go get us a drink, Tom says, still sitting in the car. They'll have us working in the rain if we stick around here.

All right, I say, and walk around the front of the car. I pat Pookie on the head. She stands up and licks my hand and then sits down again. When we pull out, she doesn't try to follow.

We drive out of the neighborhood with a George Jones song playing on the country radio station. Tom sings along. He's got a nice voice, reedy, surprisingly soft. You're a good singer Tom, I say.

Naw, he laughs. My brothers and sisters are though. All of them sang in the church choir. I'm the only one in the family can't sing.

And now Tom's stopped singing and I wish I hadn't said anything.

At the small strip mall that houses the Lasso, we park and I get out and start to run for the door because of the rain, then remember Tom and wait. It takes a second for him to get out of the car, but once up he walks quickly.

Inside, he wipes his boots on the mat. A former UT lineman works the door. A big man. No trouble at the Lasso. Raining like hell, he says to Tom.

Tom steps back to better size him up, looking up at him as if he reckons a beer bottle to the head might do the trick. He smiles. Like a cow pissing on a flat rock.

We sit at a high small drink table along the glass window that looks out on the Pike. Cars and concrete and rain. Fast-food joints across the way. A waitress comes to take our order. She's around forty and has bleached hair. She wears black dress pants, a white shirt, and a bow tie. She has a nice figure. Round hips, womanly.

Hey there Sweet.

Well hey Corrine, Tom says, putting his arm around her waist. She winks at me.

You're looking good, she says, rubbing the top of his head.

Hell I feel good. Y'all got any liquor back there?

We might. If you're good.

We'd best leave then.

Corrine looks at me and winks again. A good one too. Not too Mae West. One of those Sweet's a mess isn't he winks that has a little bit of go ahead and look son, I'm a full grown woman.

Sweet wants Dickel and water, she says. What can I get you hon?

Just a beer.

She walks to the bar and we watch. Those hips roll. Tom shakes his head as if in pain. Lordy, he says.

Lordy, I agree.

Later, Tom buys drinks for some ladies at another table, and then goes and sits with them. I stay at our own table despite an invitation to join. I order another beer and when Corrine comes back she asks how Tom's doing.

Okay. He's hanging in there.

Good. You let me know if he needs anything. Somebody to take him to the doctor or anything. I've known Sweet a long time.

She smiles at me, an odd smile. Maybe I have an odd look on my face.

Are you Janey's boy?

Yes ma'am.

You favor her. She's a pretty woman. She's been good for Sweet. For Tom I mean.

And saying this, correcting herself, her face changes, the wink has gone.

At the other table Tom and the two ladies lean together, joined at the head, so the older man at the next table won't hear what's said, though he wants to. Tom's telling some kind of bawdy story that leaves the blonde with her hands over her ears, and the tall darker one who's smoking and chewing gum, hollering, oh hell, godawmighty, somebody call the police.

Corrine looks over at the laughing table and smiles at Tom. He smiles back, nods a little. And I know that look. He glances over at me with a smile that says, yes your mother's leaving me, if I don't die first, and she's a good woman, she's been good to me, everybody knows that, you can ask anybody that, but you only knew Tom, you never knew Sweet, and Sweet, the women, they all love Sweet.

The rain has stopped when I come outside and a steamy three-quarter moon curves milkily in the sky. The area around the pool is strewn with leaves and sticks from three days of heavy rain. Someone's built a drawbridge over the brown moat in the yard. Rachel exchanges nuptials in four short days so Tom and I have our work cut out getting the yard back in shape by then.

I'm on my way down to Mentors. Mom's given me forty dollars for work done on the wedding planning committee. The forty dollars does however come with an assignment. I am to ask Pel or Bobsmith if either is willing to bartend the reception after Rachel's wedding. Cousin Butch was originally conscripted, but he's finagled an out-of-town interview for a job he doesn't want just to avoid working for three hours. Now Mom is frantic. She knows I'd prefer someone else bartend, and that it won't be my friends' cup of tea. And I've informed her that though Beth and I are just friends, I am nonetheless escorting Pel's ex-girlfriend to the wedding. These things she knows. These things she knows and gives not one damn about. She has cheese balls and doodads and tablecloths and toothpicks and tents and scorched yards turned muddy and dying boyfriends and insane progeny and a young lady who wants a nice wedding on her mind and she needs a bartender and all my friends are bartenders, and I owe her, and though this hasn't officially been designated as a calling in of debts, that's what it is, so I'm on my way, without any kind of plan or angle, to ask Pel or Bobsmith if either would mind joining me for a few nice donkey kicks to the head.

Bobsmith's working at Mentors and I'm drinking free. The band is small-time college cover and Mentors is much too hip for such. Staff and friends of staff keep backs to the band. The waitresses work half speed, sneaking drinks from Bobsmith, complaining about boyfriend problems and their crappy tips.

When he makes his way back down to me I go ahead and fire the question. Hey Bobsmith, you want to make some extra money this Saturday?

Doing what, he says, a sly smile working for such a proposition from a moneymaking machine like myself.

Tom's daughter's getting married. Mom needs someone to tend bar from about seven to ten. It'll be real low-key. Mostly wine and beer, some highballs. Fifty bucks cash for three hours. You can throw a tip jar out if you want to.

Oh man I'd do it, but I'm opening. I got to be here at three.

I kind of figured. What about Jimbo?

He's on at six.

I nod.

Pel might do it. He won't need to be down here until late.

Yeah I thought that might be my best bet.

Beth's going with you isn't she?

Yeah.

Bobsmith shrugs. He broke up with her.

Can you think of anyone else?

No, not really.

Well think on it.

I will, he says, then he's pouring me another scotch, and I'm on my way to the bathroom with a good old fashioned shadow on my back.

When I come back, Pel and Jimbo and Angie are down where I'm sitting, and I'm conscious of walking, which makes my legs get stiff, which makes me walk funny, and then I stop the nonsense and just walk naturally. Angie sits on a stool in jeans with the knees torn out. She's changed after work to go out. She sits with her legs open like a boy, which can look bad sometime, but she just looks unaffected and a bit tomboyish and still pretty, and she probably knows that's just the way she looks, but she looks great anyway, pretty girls acting unaffected is an affectation, but catching them makes them unaffected again somehow, and I stop thinking for a second and say, hey Angie.

Hey Jason. I thought you were going to ignore me all night.

And I have nothing glib to say.

Uh. I have nothing glib to say, I say. Hello. How are you doing?

Great. You and Pel going to the Endzone?

Yeah.

Do you care if I tag along?

Actually I do, I start, and then I just say, no I'm kidding, that's great.

And I am one pathetic conversationalist.

We go, Pel and I in my car, Angie in another, down to the Strip, where the Endzone has dollar longnecks on Tuesday. The bar is not too crowded which is good. The only bad thing is there's not enough people to sweat and smoke away the smell of twenty years of urine and vomit and testosterone and stale beer. It's kind of a meathead bar. Lots of guys in coaching shorts and tanktops and turf shoes. Lots of burr haircuts and 300 Bench Club T-shirts. We used to pop down here in high school and take turns asking huge college guys to dance to AC/DC songs just to see if we could get away with it. Cute as pie we were. Tonight there are maybe five girls in the bar, all of whom are hiding an ostrich egg in the Dollyesque mammothicity that is their hair, and at least thirty guys.

Pel goes to the bar and orders three beers, though Angie has yet to show.

It's a boner gauntlet in here, I say.

You've got yours strapped on, don't you?

I'm a one-man boner phalanx, I say. I'm Testosterone Man. I just pissed on the bar to mark my territory.

Angie sits between us and talks to Pel about bands and different concerts they've seen. I watch the Braves get pounded by the Mets on a television over the bar. With every Met hit, the young guy next to me cusses. Shit. Fuck. Hoping, I think, to entrap the bartender into a conversation. The ploy doesn't work, and being a veteran conversation dodger myself, I get up and head down to the poolroom to look at the old pictures they keep of former Tennessee players. I immediately spot the one I'm looking for. It's of Uncle Clay and Grandsay after a game, both dressed in square-shouldered, narrow-waisted suits, and sporting thin ties. I think it's Clay's junior year. Grandsay looks young and proud.

It used to make me feel guilty when I was younger, drinking in a bar with a picture of my grandfather in it. He wasn't too serious, but he didn't do a lot of jacking around either. When I was younger he used to ask, if you have two pieces of pie, and one is your favorite and the other is not your favorite, which do you eat first?

I save my favorite piece for last.

You do?

Yessir. Which one do you do?

I eat my best piece first. That way I'm always eating my best piece.

When I get back to the bar, Angie's off somewhere and Pel's watching the ball game. The Braves fan has attached himself to a table full of baseball caps.

Checking out those pictures?

Yeah.

I always liked that one of your grandfather.

Yeah. Me too.

Still make you feel guilty?

Nah.

He turns back to the ball game and I'm glad he remembered Grandsay's picture. He knew him too. We used to spend a couple of weeks at his house each summer. I got a favor to ask, I say.

All right.

Tom's daughter's getting married Saturday and we need a bartender from seven to ten. Fifty bucks cash.

Sure, he says.

It'll be easy. We're having it at Mom's house. You'll definitely be out by ten if you have to work.

I'm there.

I order more beers. Before you say yes for sure, you probably ought to know Beth's going to be there.

He nods. That's all right. That's cool.

Thanks, I say, you're helping us out. Mom was going nuts. Then Angie comes back and I've got nothing to say that wouldn't be third wheel, jokester, tears of a clown, so I excuse myself to walk around the bar and think some insanity or another.

I watch a couple of guys play pool for awhile and think that it's pretty cool that Pel still remembers my grandfather's picture. And I start to feel bad because I've been crazy and not much fun, and probably jealous of Pel because he's not crazy and he's still fun and he's hot with girls and I wonder if I'm the one who's changed and not him.

Later, Pel rides home with Angie, and I drive home by myself. So I don't get pulled over, I drive slowly and go the back way on Lyons View, past Cherokee Country Club and Lakeshore Mental Hospital, where lightning bugs are floating through the wrought iron fence. Then I'm driving over the railroad tracks and all the way home it's been quiet out, and cool with the windows open after the rain, with the smell of honeysuckle along the road and the steady hum of crickets, steady until you don't hear it anymore, until Knoxville doesn't seem such a bad place to be.

When I get to the house, I park out in front, in the road, so as not to wake my mother and Tom. The garage door is open and I don't see Pookie, so I go around back, and there she is, coming up to me at a slow trot, moving stiffly but with more energy than before, shaking and rolling her head back and forth. I can hardly pet her for her licking my hand, and she can hardly lick my hand for me petting her. We talk for awhile, and then I take off my socks and shoes, and my jeans and shirt, and I'm in the pool, diving as quietly as I can, and that water is cold and good and there aren't as many leaves and sticks as I'd thought and I swim underneath, incognito, the frog man on a secret mission, Aquaman diving deep to save the trapped submarine, to the far end of the pool, working my knee hard as I go, and then back, my wind better than it should be, then back again, and when I come up the air is humming with stars and the sky navy blue, not black, and I may be the only person alive.

Inside I sit on the couch and smoke cigarettes and watch the preview guide on the television with the volume off. Then I go upstairs quietly, silently open the refrigerator, and take the last piece of lemon ice box pie. Back downstairs I eat slowly, with relish, without guilt about taking the last piece, because my mother made the pie especially for me.

I wake up shadowed. I lie on the couch and try to shake it. I tell myself, Pete's asleep on the floor beside you. Mom and Tom and Curt are upstairs. Pookie's in the back yard. This is nothing but your own paranoia. It's just the acid. You're not well yet. You are not yet well.

I force myself off the couch and head upstairs, fat-faced with sleep and bad dreams. I come in the kitchen and outside Tom's friends from the tent company are finishing up the last corner. Half-price tent just taken down this morning from a reception at Cherokee Country Club the night before. Good hustle on that one Tom. I'm surprised not to see Tom or Curt or Mom or anyone else I know, but they're probably on a last-minute jaunt to Mexico to kidnap a mariachi band for the reception.

It's hot outside, but not too humid, a light haze day. About as good as you could hope for in July. The yard looks okay considering we've had no rain, and the pool is blue blue blue and smelling of chlorine. I sit down with my legs in the water and fight the urge to jerk around and see what's behind me. If I turn around to see what's behind me, it will still be behind me, and I'll be a dog chasing my own tail.

In front of me, across the pool, tables have been set up for a buffet line. Behind the tables, up the hill, the tent. To my left the gazebo, where I've set up the bar for Pel. Behind me a shadow. Behind the shadow, female voices just coming into the kitchen. Who's that out there, a woman yells in a loud voice. Is that Rip Van Winkle?

I laugh but don't turn around. It's Bobbie, Tom's sister. Oh she's a pill. She is a pill. I've worked all week on this yard and the first time she sees me I'm sitting by the pool. I wave to confirm that yes, she's hilarious. Then flop into the water as if I've been shot in the neck.

Beth and I walk in the church and there's that feeling of being somewhere unfamiliar. Whispered voices down the hall. It's Rachel and her bridesmaids and her mother. I'd forgotten about her mother. Have fun at the reception Tom. Rachel sees me and waves, then goes into a double finger-cross, shaking her head and smiling that this day may come off. She sees Beth and throws an eyebrow wiggle at me.

We walk down the aisle to our seats. We're late and up front Mom has turned full around and is in full beaming mode. I of course am a bit conscious of walking, with all this beaming going on, then realize no one's looking at me, they're all looking at Beth, and right myself and walk a little less like Dr. Frankenstein's favorite and make it to the pew without incident.

Seated, listening to the organ, I tell myself this isn't too bad, though it's too quiet and hot. The organ plays and people sit quietly. There's nothing to look at but silent people and pews and a large wooden cross behind the pulpit. Unnerving peacefulness. I look across the aisle to the groom's side to change the direction of my mind because I don't want to look at the cross, I'm afraid if I look it's going to come crashing to the floor, so I'm looking across the aisle to see something normal, a kid playing in his seat or an old lady all dressed up, and instead my eyes come to rest on a man with a prosthetic leg. His socks are too short. And I'm looking at his plastic leg, wondering why in the world wouldn't he buy socks that were long enough, when he turns and smiles and I hold his glance long enough to give him a weak smile back but I'm sure he knows I was looking at his leg. And the organ music begins to sound chintzy or old-fashioned and I'm the kind of person who notices prosthetic legs at weddings. I notice men wearing plaid jackets and ties instead of suits. I look down at my shoes, if I look up I'll see something else, I'll notice something else no one should notice at a wedding, and I'm looking at my shoes, my shoes on the thread-bare cheap red carpet, and my shoes I haven't polished them, they don't look so hot, who are you, look at your shoes, it's a wedding and you haven't polished your shoes, and I'm looking at my shoes when Beth leans over and whispers that the flowers look nice.

I'm looking at my shoes.

And Beth says, your mother is so pretty.

I look up and the groomsmen and Devon are filing in from the back of the church. Rachel's brother Taylor is a groomsman, all older brother cocky smiles. Curt is a groomsman too, the last one out. He takes his position on the first step and looks at his mother. Then at mine. Then he spots me and it's a wink without winking, a piece of cake, this groomsman business. Devon's dad is best man, looking like a man, like a dad, holding back a smile. And Devon's ramrod straight, looking down the aisle. He's got his shoulders back, waiting for a good woman to walk down the aisle.

Then the bridesmaids with their bouquets, looking pretty and embarrassed, and Jolie, Rachel's sister, is a bridesmaid, and then the Wedding March, and we all stand to see Rachel, who's smiling and beautiful, she's glancing side to side as she walks to smile at people she knows, and she is a beautiful bride, and there's Tom, taking it slow, he's done this before, looking tall and just a bit self-conscious, get me out of this tux self-conscious, and then they're in front of the minister and Tom's peeled off to sit next to Mom and we all may be seated to witness this union and to ponder our private and unprompted flights from composure.

Beth and I are on our way to the reception. I was hot in that church, I say.

Yeah you were a little fidgety.

It was a nice wedding though.

It was.

We drive down the Pike and I've got a pretty solid dread going about the reception, the Pel and Beth thing, Tom's teetotaling brothers, my own desire to drink a lot and fall into the pool.

Did you see that man with the fake leg, Beth asks.

Yeah. You did too?

How could you miss it?

I don't know. I didn't think anybody else would notice.

How could you miss it? I don't think he was wearing socks.

I laugh. She's laughing.

He better not show up with a parrot on his shoulder, she says.

And what a girl, I think, what a girl.

Beth's up on the hill, under the tent, dancing with Curt, who's bruised my ribs with a hundred elbowing, she's cute, she's cute comments. It's dark in the corners of the yard and along the fence, but tiki-style lanterns leading from the house to the tent illuminate most of the proceedings. The DJ is in full disco form now after the obligatory Tennessee Waltz and Rocky Top and a few other tunes for the older folks. Now it's Devon and Rachel and friends and a few of the stalwarts out for the first real set of hard boogie.

I'm down near the gazebo where the bar is, having just gutted my way through a conversation with Tom's brother Dale about what it is exactly I do not do. Dale looks not too much like Tom. He's smaller and slow to smile and pretty big on eye contact, of the boring a hole through your skull variety. And the whole time I'm breathing my scotch breath everywhere and he's blowing back baby aspirin over Kool-Aid, and he's not trying to be nosy, just making conversation, and I can be glib and I can be earnest but I cannot answer a certain line of questioning, so by the time he walks off I've pretty much worn him down with a combination of pathetic truth and exaggerated failure and am calling for a mano a mano dirty joke contest with Jackie.

I walk over toward the bar, where Pete is talking to Pel and his assistant Trick. How Pel roped Trick into this I don't know, other than it's early in the evening and nothing goes on before ten anyway. They look like they're having a decent time, and are, as I would probably be in the same situation, stoned as monkeys.

I'm talking about nothing with Pete and Trick and Pel when Jackie comes up. He holds his cup out to Pel. Play it again Sam.

I cringe, more so because Trick has cut his eyes at Pel and then at me. How you boys doing tonight, Jackie says.

Doing fine, Pete says, taking the initiative, though Jackie has asked the question with a swiveled head as if we should all answer. Fine, I say. Pel nods. Extremely well, says Trick.

All right, good to hear, but godawmighty why ain't y'all after some of that trim?

We laugh unenthusiastically. Pel hands over a bourbon and Coke and we wait for Jackie to leave. Instead he hollers at Tom who's standing by the pool talking to Devon's father. Hey Sweet, get your ass over here a second. Tom laughs, puts up half a hand to say he'll be back and walks over towards us smiling.

These fellows ain't queer are they?

I don't think so, Tom says, giving Pete and me a look like, yeah, he's drunk. Then, just because he's a compadre and isn't going to let Jackie stand there solo in front of four college boys who think he's drunk, he says, I don't think they're queer Jackie. Then again, I ain't fixing to do no toe touches round the bar neither.

Jackie's laughing. We all are, all I suppose for different reasons. How you boys doing, Tom says. He looks at Trick and Pel, then takes the bottle of whiskey Pel was reaching for and pours himself a drink. He sets the bottle down without looking at Pel then he has his arm around Jackie's shoulder and is leading him up toward the tent for a little dancing.

Pel and Trick look to me with the beginnings of grins on their faces, like I'm going to say something smart to get the ball rolling. But I'm not. And Pete's body language has gotten tighter, he's got his shoulders back and is looking away from the three of us like whatever might be said he doesn't want to be a part of. But the grins are gone as quickly as they appeared. You need a drink Say? Pel asks.

Yeah, I say, and up on the hill a new song has started and Jackie's bolted onto the dance floor just as Beth is thanking Curt for being her dance partner. She nods at something Jackie says. Laughs overexuberantly to compensate for not thinking what he said was funny, then begins a half-hearted twist to a song too fast to be twisted to, all the while looking to the gazebo for help.

You want to smoke one Say? Pel asks.

I consider the proposal, consider that I should probably help Beth out. Yeah, I say.

Pete?

No thanks.

I got to be quick Pel, I say.

We'll be quick.

Walking away I can tell Pete's not wild about me going off to smoke. Not that he's against it in principle. Just in light of my recent insanity.

Which is a good point and one I should have considered before I started behind Pel, through the gate, and around the front yard to the side of the house where we can't be seen. Pel lights the tater, drags, hands it to me. While I'm hitting it, Dale and his wife cut through the yard toward their car, talking in quiet tones.

It was nice, Dale's wife says.

It was. It was a nice wedding.

I pass the joint back over while Dale's opening the car door for his wife. He closes the door softly, too softly because it doesn't catch, and he has to close it again, more firmly this time, and then he walks around to his side of the car slowly, pausing by the trunk, head down like he'd like to be alone for a minute, like he's talked out and has a long ride home ahead and will it be worse to talk or not to talk on the way to Niota about the wedding, about how his brother Sweet is holding up.

You ought to come down to the club tonight, Pel says. Good band playing. Kind of electric bluegrass.

I don't know when I'm going to get done here. Put me down though, I say, watching Dale start down the road, I might make it down.

Should I put down one or two?

I don't know.

Pel hands it back over to me. She looks good, he says.

Eah.

You in love Say?

I look at him, he's smiling. He takes the joint and holds the lit end towards his mouth. Shotgun Say?

Been awhile.

Like riding a bike.

He places the lit end in his mouth and I'm on the opposite end as he blows a stream of smoke that hits my throat dry and harsh and knocks my head away and I come up coughing and choking.

Did you get a hit Say, he asks, laughing.

Bent over, incapable of speech, I flip him a one-winged, asthmatic bird.

When I'm able to stand straight again, Pel offers the doob but I wave him off. He takes a hit off my scotch. I light a cigarette though my lungs are on fire. Pookie trots up, gingerly. Hey girl, I say. She sniffs once at my outstretched hand and trots off again, toward the road.

From the back yard, muffled disco music and thin light easing around the back corner of the house. On the street a line of cars, mailboxes. The

For Sale sign stowed away for the weekend. Pel reaches for my cigarette and takes a drag. Along the house smell of fresh dirt and grey flowers. How will watering Pel's flowers heal me?

You ready to head back in Say?

Yeah.

Then we're heading down the front walk. At the corner of the house, Pel stops. He bends down to look. You plant these flowers?

Yes.

They look nice.

In the back Pel slides around the bar and pours me a drink. Then he pours himself a Coke. Under the tent Curt and Beth are talking. It's a slow, bad, new country song and Rachel and Devon are dancing, and my mother and Tom. All the faces, under the white lights of the tent, against the back-drop of the dark trees, look ghostly. Peals of pantomimed laughter. Tom's head slick with sweat.

Under the gazebo it's Trick, Pel and me. Aren't you going to dance with your bride, Trick asks.

What?

Aren't you going to dance with the bride?

I don't know.

Beth's looking hot, he says, looking over at Pel.

Yeah, I say.

He nods his head, smiles. I look over at Pel. He's watching the dancers.

Trick says, at the wedding at Cana, Christ changed the water into wine.

Yes, I know.

Pretty good trick.

Pel looks at the boxes of wine on the ground and says, we've got enough to last the night I think.

Trick laughs. Up on the hill Beth and Curt turn to wave as if I were the topic of conversation. I wave back but when they start down the hill, I about-face and head toward the house. Inside, in the kitchen, it's bright and some of Tom's relatives are talking at the table. How you doing, I say, plowing on through without waiting for an answer, and downstairs to the bathroom, which is occupied, then out to the garage. I want to go outside but can't open the doors because of cars in the driveway. I stand in the dark garage and chug my drink, but it's no good, and come back inside and back up the stairs, quick nod to the same people I saw sixty seconds before, then outside, letting the screen door slam before I remember not to, and toward the gazebo.

Beth's fidgety and Trick is smiling and Pel's facing the tent. Pete walks up. Looks at the group. At my nervous ass. Begins singing quite badly to a funky rhythm of his own devising, moving his shoulders in arrhythmic white boy fashion, shaking his head loose neck style, fat rich guy dancing with his young wife's new breasts at Cherokee Country Club,

Ja son
duh duh dum
Ja son
duh duh dum
A lawn mason
duh duh dum
The lawn mason
duh duh dum
Oh Jaaaay hey hey hey hey
Buzzing all the way
Ja son
duh duh dum

Head tilted, lost in soul man rapture, he sways to the beat, every now and then screeching my name in a tortured falsetto. Beth's laughing. I've covered my ears in horror and am begging for another set of hands for these beleaguered eyes.

Good God, Trick says, laughing.

Pel smiles.

Pete looks at me, still doing his cement-foot shuffle. His smile is a strange one, kind of welcome back stoner. Then he looks toward Pel and

Trick, stops dancing. He's looking at Pel and not saying anything and he's not smiling anymore either. He turns to me, you ready for a drink big brother?

Yeah, I say.

He sets his glass down and grabs mine. Pel has the bottle ready to pour, but Pete takes it out of his hand. I got it, he says, squaring his shoulders and staring at Pel. I'll pour for my brother if you don't mind.

Then Beth takes me by the arm and leads me up to the tent. The lights hit me and I'm self-conscious and stiff-legged, robot on the dance floor. All around me sweaty drunken people. Mom gives a big thumbs-up around Jackie's back, because I've got a date, because we've pulled off this reception. I smile weakly but pick up the pace. I'm still dancing mummy style, but at a faster tempo. Beth taps me on the chest and points with her head for me to turn around and look. I dance her around so I'm facing where she wants me to be facing and it's the one-legged guy cutting the rug, a kind of half twist move, leaning heavily on his good leg, letting the plastic one spin where it may. I hop around quickly so Beth is again facing him. I make a face, good gosh.

All night, she says. I've danced with him twice.

Then Brick House by the Commodores comes on and a lot of people hurry onto the floor. I start out slow then get a little sweat going, start sloshing the old drink around. Pete comes out with Bobbie and they dance next to us, Bobbie with hands in the air like she just don't care, shaking a pretty good rack, Pete looking over and smiling. Word to your mother, he says, Jimmy to Donny Osmond, and then he's dipping down, rocking his head back and forth eye level at Bobbie, the brick house of the dance floor, and Beth's throwing her hips around and I'm getting low, putting pressure on the knee, getting low, cobra on the recoil, until I'm all the way down and holding, rocking, appreciating the view.

Beth and I dance to a few more songs then head down for more drinks. Pel and Trick are on the other side of the bar on their way out. Mom hands

Pel an envelope with his money in it. Thanks again Pel. You came through in a pinch.

He waves her off. No problem.

Well I appreciate it, Mom says, then she's off toward the house.

See you Say, Trick says.

All right, I'll see you.

Come down to the bar if y'all get out of here, Pel says. I'll put you on the list.

All right.

Beth nods, looks up to the tent.

A smile works at the corners of Pel's mouth. Bye Beth.

Bye.

It was good seeing you.

It was good seeing you too.

Then Pel and Trick are walking loose-armed through the yard, nice spacing between them, and Pel tosses his keys, a light jangle, you're driving Trick, and Trick left-hands the keys over his shoulder, no break in stride, and they're through the gate and Beth and I are heading to the gazebo, where Pete and Curt now man the bar.

At the community center, Beth has a hard time with the lock on the pool gate, but eventually gets it to turn. The gate opens with a rusty screech. Beth walks in while I'm still looking feverishly from corner to corner, behind bushes and trees, for a night watchman. Come on chicken, she whispers, motioning with her hands.

Are you sure about this?

No. Now come on, she says, and not waiting to see if I follow, she goes into the dressing room to change.

I walk around the pool to the deep end. I've changed into jeans and have cutoffs on underneath. I take off my shoes and dip a foot in the water. It feels good. I take off my jeans and shirt. It's quiet and dark, no lights on anywhere and just a sliver of moon. The pool is black glass. I stand over it and look. No reflection and no reflection of anything in it. Then I'm smooth in the water like an eel, barely a ripple, and with eyes open underneath I'm swimming in night, that feeling of sky gone liquid. I come up in a rush for air at the shallow end as Beth's coming out of the dressing room. I didn't see you, she says.

I don't say anything.

Is it cold?

No, it's good.

Then she's walking slowly down the steps, ankles, thighs, waist, too cold that way, and a shallow dive all the way in. I start for the deep end, this time swimming with my head out of the water. I'm swimming silently and behind me the nearly inaudible ripple of Beth in the shallow end. I get to the diving board and hoist myself out of the water with a half chin-up and stay that way, looking across the water at Beth. It's kind of a posed move, the diving board chin-up biceps flex, and I catch myself and drop all the way in and blow bubbles until I'm at the bottom, and I stay there, thinking, but not too clearly, and looking up at nothing and side to side at nothing, and where is my hand that's in front of my face, and closed eyes and open eyes the same, until how can you tell what water feels like if that's all you feel and tiny chisels are chipping away at the inside of my skull, and still I hold on, dormant gills reopening on my neck, until that's it and I push off the bottom hard and can I make the top and where is the top and gasping break the surface and nearly knock into Beth and wolfing air and the dry echo of breaking the surface and the sudden wet echo of the black trees, remember again what water feels like.

Beth's treading water and makes way for me to swim to the edge. The night has gone loud with breathing and the steady gulp and click of the plastic drain door being flipped. You all right, Beth says, laughing. I was coming to check on you.

I nod yes, mouth agape.

Are you sure?

Yes.

Then she's swimming again toward the shallow end and not too far down the track, the faint whistle of a train.

We've been talking about nothing. We're in the shallow end, hands pushing through the water, equatored at the waist. It is a night without details. I'm talking to Beth but would like to notice something. She's standing in the shallow end pushing water with the palm of her hand. I'm doing the same in an idiotic mimicry. We're talking about swimming. Her hair is wet, and off her face, and her face is less hard to see than before. She watches her hand push through the water. Behind her the community center a block of nothing. Chain link fence, asphalt, plastic chairs. I've walked toward her in the corner. She's not looking, looking at her hand in water, still trees, black pool. Her wet hair, in the corner of the pool, and she's looking at me, crazy man, and no trains and no nothing, everything the same color trees sky pool, and I'm still a little drunk, and her hand half out of water pushing water, small waves heading toward walls, and when she looks up at me again, the touch of legs in water.

And then I'm away. She closes in on herself, shoulders narrowed, hands on forearms. I come close again, slowly, and I'm looking at her and her arms are back in the water, and I've pushed up close, arms out of the water, palms shown but shoulders looming, and her hair wet and when legs touch again in the corner we are halved by water and the touch of lips, ghost kiss, the brush, and then moving forward for the proper, thighs more thickly brushed, pressed, and pressed, shoulders and hands cornered, and she's looked to the side and we're cornered and I'm thinking, give me your eyes, give me your eyes, because my eyes have gone all steely and sexy and drunk and sincere and I can have your eyes and I'm thinking, give me your eyes, get your eyes looking at mine, and then I'm backing away a bit, hands up, nothing but the knee touch, and it's an old move, the press into the light touch followed by the fake breakaway, and Beth is looking at me and I'm looking, eagle's viewpoint, at the pool and the community center and at me in the corner being someone who is not me, who I do not want to be.

I lean over and kiss her, a full one, no tricks. I lean against her, my elbows steadying on the asphalt. I kiss her soft on the mouth. I back away, just slightly. Are you ready to go?

Yes.

I kiss her again. And it's a nice one, friendly, but we all know that trick, the sexy friendly one, and it's all there, the you should have waited, threadbare loyalty to Pel, but what it is, what it really is, is me.

August

I'm in the kitchen after mowing the lawn when Tom and Rachel come back from his treatment. He goes straight to his room. Rachel comes into the kitchen. She shakes her head to show a long day.

Boy I could go for a beer, she says.

Hot out there.

She opens the refrigerator and takes out the jug of water. No alcohol for the expectant mother.

How's your dad?

Mean as a snake, she says. She wipes perspiration from her forehead and drinks the water. She looks pretty, is not yet starting to show.

I need to sit down, she says. She sits. Lawn looks good. How you like that new mower?

Good. It's fun. A lot better than pushing.

Dad wanted to mow. He's too tired to even sit.

Yeah this weather's hard on him.

I light a cigarette.

God, I want one, she says. No, I don't. Daddy cussed the doctor today. Doctor tried to tell him to quit smoking. And that he didn't need to be drinking. Daddy's like, what the hell for? I'm dying. I can do whatever I damn well want to. I was so embarrassed. The doctor tried to make a joke out of it, but Dad just kept on cussing, ranting and raving about being a grown man and doing what he wants to do.

I don't say anything. I take a couple more drags on my cigarette and put it out.

Then he gets on me for driving too fast. And he drives like a bat out of hell.

Sick people get cautious about different things, I say. He never used to lock the doors to the house, but now he does most every night.

Well it's his own damn fault. We all told him he was going to kill himself. He just kept on. He just, you know. All this is just wearing me out.

I don't know what to say. What she's thinking is that her father will never see his grandchild and that it's not fair of him to die. She's a good woman. Tom raised some good kids.

I know he appreciates you being around, I say. He's got a bunch of people that want to take him to his treatment, but he always tells them you're going to.

He just doesn't want to put anybody out.

Nah. It's not that. Me and Jackie aren't doing anything most days. And Bobbie's available. He wants you to take him.

Rachel looks out the kitchen window. A breeze lifts the leaves and pushes thin clouds on the sky. How's Pookie feeling?

Better I think.

I think I'll go check on her. She pushes herself up from the table with an exaggerated grunt, then smiles at me, at the ridiculousness of her condition, of our condition, human animals conscious of being alive and of dying. I don't want to get fat! she screams in a Bride of Frankenstein voice. Then she walks out to play with the dog.

I'm downstairs on the couch when Mom walks in. She asks me why the For Sale sign is in the middle of the road. Before I can answer and take credit for mowing, she tells me she's worked out an arrangement with St. Mary's Hospital to pay for my surgery, that she's paid the first installment of one hundred dollars that from this day forth will be my monthly payment on running and playing basketball again. I hate it when she comes in chop chopping right off the bat.

Thanks, I say, turning down the volume on the television.

Well I figured you weren't going to handle it.

It's bullshit. It's too much money. I wasn't there two hours.

It doesn't matter Jason, she says, and boy does it irritate me when people call me Jason for emphasis. That's what they charge, that's what you've got to pay.

So she's wearing her taking care of business suit, which always calls for a little ingratitude on my part. Call it a ritual. She's exasperated with me, which I know, but unless I act like her irresponsible cross to bear, she won't get her money's worth for the kind gesture. Then she looks so tired, and I'm too old for this, and she's all right, old Janey, one of those former cheerleader types who don't discover they're tough until late, and I start thinking that a lot of these old gals, my mom, Pel's, Trick's, they haven't had it so easy since the big stick left, since the big belt was put away, and I say, you're the best Janey. I appreciate it.

Which surprises the hell out of her. Her natural inclination is to say, oh, it's nothing. But these are tough times, and this is a tough Janey.

Okay, she says. I'm glad we got it worked out. The lawn looks good. You need to trim around the mailbox and the sidewalk.

Okay, I say. And I get up and walk to the garage to get the weedeater, as Mom walks upstairs to talk to Rachel, to compare notes with another woman who knows what it's like to deal with incompetents, with men.

We order pizza for dinner. Rachel doesn't stay and Tom doesn't join us. I drink a couple of beers with dinner and Mom has one. Tom's relatives start calling and I go downstairs. About ten, Cousin Butch comes by to get me and we drive toward a bar we haven't decided on yet. We never want to go to the same place. Butch wants to go to Spinners but I veto that, which of course makes him insistent on going. He drives to Spinners and parks the car, saying, come on Cousin Spud, my favorite yuppie, time for your Corona. Then he walks in the bar.

Butch doesn't come out. He'll have at least one beer and see if there's any women he knows. I get out and sit on the hood of his car and smoke a cigarette. In a minute, from the back of the building, I hear the heavy squeak of a Dempster Dumpster sliding door and what I reckon is a couple of busboys talking in low tones as they haul out the trash. Those doors are always hard to pull and when you finally yank them open the smell of the Dumpster hits you like a shovel full of shit, and you can't get those bags in fast enough. Usually the bags are heavy with bottles and spilled beer and you can't just fling them in by holding them at the top because there's holes in the bag from broken glass, and if that baby splits it won't be the manager out there cleaning it up. So you have to grab it at the bottom, and you get stale beer and strawberry daiquiri goo on your hands, but that's okay, just keep it off the old button-down because you've only got one wear out of it and you don't want to have to get up early and wash it in the morning, and if you can just keep it halfway clean you can go out right after work without going home first and changing, because if you don't go out right after work you're going to miss it, something, you're going to miss something good.

The door is yanked shut and the guys are talking, still in low voices, laughing a little. The trash isn't so bad when someone's helping you. And maybe they're smoking one or the bartender has slipped them a beer. But not at Spinners. Probably not at good old corporate drug testing Spinners. So they're probably smoking cigaretes, milking the clock a little. Those dirty glasses aren't going anywhere.

After awhile it's quiet again. Behind the restaurant the faceless drone of the interstate. Then slowing. Just a car every so often. Then quiet. A shadowy parking lot. No cars coming or going, no people. Shadowed. Like a double of oneself not seen but in dreams, in parts of the brain unused. I get off the hood shaking my neck and head, shaking it off.

A car's lights spill on my face as I'm doing my twitching routine. I grind out my cigarette. The car pulls in across the parking lot and two couples get out. They look to be around thirty. They look like two recently married couples who just moved into a new subdivision called Pine Breath. Both guys wear clean faded jeans and white running shoes and I would be proud to have either represent me in a court of law. I look like I've just smoked a doobie, like maybe I just got kicked out of the bar. I look like a guy standing by himself in a parking lot who's put out his cigarette before he was ready just so he'd have something to do and not be a guy standing in a parking lot doing nothing except thinking a lot of craziness. How you doing, I say.

Fine, one of the guys says, wrapping an arm around his tall and radiant wife. She smiles, in my direction, but she's smiling because she lives in Pine Breath with a sane and normal guy and not some lonely lunatic like myself.

After about thirty minutes Butch comes out and I get into his car without speaking. He gets in and smiles. Have fun Spud?

Yep. Better than I would have had in there.

There were some girls in there, he says, still not starting the car.

I don't give a shit.

I want to go back in.

Go ahead. I'll walk home.

Poor little Spud, Butch says starting the car, so scared of the pretty girls.

I don't say anything. I've waited on him and it wasn't that cute, and he knows he's on my nerves and doesn't say anything more. You want to try O'Doyle's? he asks.

Yeah, that's good.

We drive down the Pike though it would be quicker to take the interstate. But this way Butch can insure that he's not missing the naked coed contest down on the Strip. Not much traffic and we're on the green light cycle. The first light we hit at Papermill was yellow but since then six straight greens. We're catching the green lights, Butch says, as we hit another at Volunteer Boulevard.

Seven straight.

We go on down the Strip, nothing much going on. A group of four coeds crosses in front of us on their way to the Orange Club, and they look good, but too young, and then a couple of frat boys with baseball caps pulled low as if shielding some great mystery, inscrutable are they, Sam

Spade in a Vols cap, and Butch has hit ten consecutive greens and runs a yellow on Vine Avenue to make eleven straight, or at least eleven straight nonreds, and we pull into the Old City and park, feeling, as we should, a bit lucky. Good hustle on that yellow Butch, I say.

Eleven straight. You got to want it Cousin Spud.

Then we're walking through the Old City, feeling antiquarian as can be, and into O'Doyle's, where the first person I see, of course, is good old Jody McDowell sitting down to a double Coke and ice. Next to him, in an interesting development, is Beth. I duck quickly into the bathroom while Butch heads down to the far end of the bar. In the bathroom I don't have to go so I wash my hands and look at myself in the mirror. Nothing I haven't seen before.

I come out of the bathroom hoping they don't see me. But Jody does. What's up Jason?

Not much. How you doing Beth?

Fine.

I nod my head, try to think of something to say. Well, I say, I'm going to check on my cousin. Make sure he doesn't drink all the beer in the bar.

Jody smiles. Beth says, see you later Jason.

We drink a couple of beers and Butch flirts with the bartender. Every now and then I can't help it and glance down at Beth. She seems like she's having a good time. I think about sending them a round of drinks, then figure it's not that cool to send someone a Coke or a glass of water, and I can't tell if Beth's drinking or not. It could just be an appetizer and virgin daiquiri night, so I don't do anything.

The rest of the bar is mostly bring a guy get in free night, but there are a few available women around. None of whom I know. None of whom I have any illusions of talking to. Someone has put on an Elton John tape to torture me. I curse O'Doyle's to Butch. I curse the music and the dearth of women. Butch has heard it all before and ignores me. Isn't that Pel's ex-girlfriend, he asks.

Yeah.

Didn't you have the hots for her when she was in high school?

Yeah, I say, kind of.

Butch is in the bathroom when I try to order another round. But the bar is crowded, especially where we are, so I head back toward the middle where the cash registers are, always the easiest place to buy a drink. I'm trying to get the bartender's attention when Jody calls my name. I look over and he's sitting alone.

Yeah Jody.

Come here a second.

I look to see if the bartender's about to take my order, but she's still at the well making drinks, so I go over to see what Jody wants. A bit impatiently.

What's up Jody.

He's facing me now in his stool, his back to the bar. The crowd is to my back and I'm blocking the aisle, but if I sit down there's no looking back.

Are you all right, he asks.

Yeah, why.

Are you sure?

Yes.

He nods his head.

Why?

I don't know. I just had a funny feeling when you walked in. You looked like, I don't know.

Like what?

Like something was bothering you. Like you had a shadow behind you or something.

What did you say?

I said you looked like you had a shadow behind you.

Did you see something behind me, I say, I say it fast. Did you see something?

I don't know. I felt something.

I'm asking you what in the fuck did you see?

I didn't say I saw anything. I just felt something when you walked in.

But why did you say shadow, I say, right up in Jody's face.

I don't know why. That's just what I felt. Are you all right man? Do you want to talk?

I'm standing there looking at Jody thinking so many things at once that I'm not thinking anything at all when Beth walks up. Oh, she says, were y'all talking?

I don't say anything. Neither does Jody. I move out of her way so she can sit down.

I better go, I say.

Be careful, Jody says.

I nod and start to walk off.

Give me a call sometime.

I nod again. Then I'm back at the end of the bar and Butch has a beer waiting and I drink it slowly, with a fast heart.

Tom and I are in his Lincoln on our way to the hospital for his chemotherapy. I'm driving. Tom has his window down though the air is on. It's the dog days and the hot air swallows up whatever cool there is and stays on your skin and in your lungs. We're listening to the FM country station and with every new song Tom lights a new cigarette with a half-smoked one and throws the burning butt out the window.

That girl you brought to the wedding was nice.

Yeah she is, I say. Real nice.

Good-looking.

Yeah, that too.

The DJ comes on and starts babbling about the upcoming Tennessee football season, just filling time, showing the good folks out there that he's with the home team, that his blood, as they say, runs orange. Tom turns off the radio. We drive in silence, Tom looking out the window at the withered grass along the interstate, billboards, exit ramps crowded with cars. That girl, she got any sense?

Yeah, she's smart.

Hell I didn't ask if she was smart. I asked if she had sense. You know the difference?

Yes. I think so.

Better learn if you don't.

She's got sense.

Tom nods his head, eyes squinting off in the distance through yellow haze, west to Niota, to some farm girl never forgotten. She looked like it.

I'm awakened at some time in the morning by a man's voice coming into the house from the garage. The overhead light comes on and I look over my shoulder with baby rat's eyes, pink and naked and pained, not fully aware I've thrown off most of my covers during the night.

Oh excuse me there son, says Skip Dugan, the realtor. I was just going to show the house to the Baileys.

Who are in their mid sixties and look disconcerted to see a naked young man sleeping on the couch in what is probably the middle of the day.

Excuse me, I say, sitting up on the couch and pulling the covers over my chest. I wasn't expecting you. Give me a minute and I'll clean this place up.

Skip Dugan laughs a skippish little laugh and starts up the stairs with the Baileys. Mrs. Bailey pauses and says, well we should have called to warn you. You probably had a late night.

It's no problem. I need to be getting up anyway.

We won't be long, she says, and you can tell by the way she says it that she wouldn't want strangers seeing her ass first thing in the morning. The Skipper could care less.

When I come outside Tom's throwing chlorine bars in the pool. I watch him throw about three of them in, shocking the pool. The pool has looked better and it's looked worse. It is now only slightly green and has the approximate viscosity of a melted split pea milkshake. I still swim in it, if that says anything.

Tom has looked better. The weight comes off fast. His head sweats under his hat, and it's water weight that won't be replaced. He walks painfully around the sides of the pool, his bones loose in the skin, the weight of the skin on his face looking as if it will pull out his eyes. Mom says it hurts for him to lie down and it hurts for him to walk. His skin hurts to be touched harder than a tickle, but the doctor said cancer patients need to be touched, that the need for human touch is magnified when one is dying from cancer.

Tom curses at the pool and I laugh. This damn thing, he says.

How's she looking?

Like shit. Old pools need too much damn work. Doesn't drain worth a shit. Water won't circulate. Looks like piss. Soon as I get it clean, it'll rain again, and grass and mud and sticks and shit'll get all in there.

It doesn't look that bad.

Naw, hell, I know it. By God it's a lot of trouble though.

This shock will probably do it.

I suppose. That damn realtor still in there?

Afraid so. They wake you?

Naw. I was up. I just don't like the way they bust in on you.

I was butt naked downstairs when he brought them in.

No, he says. He looks up from the pool, wanting to smile.

Yes. I was dead asleep with my ass hanging off the couch. I didn't know what was going on.

He laughs, pretty hard, then he starts coughing. Then he's laughing and coughing and trying to say something. Finally. Shot em the moon, did you?

Full moon. Glowing in the dark moon.

I thought I heard Pookie howling, he says. He looks back to the pool. Laughing has tired him. Laughing and dying and fucking and drinking, raising kids, working, loving a lot of folks, all things to wear a person out. And working on an old pool that probably ought to be filled in and forgotten about.

I reckon they're done upstairs, he says, and starts for the house, slowly, walking on the grass with quicksand legs. He gets to the back door and turns halfway to me. If you think about it, he says, check the pool this evening. If it hasn't cleared off any, throw a couple more of them bars in.

All right.

Just if you think of it.

I will. I ain't going anywhere.

He turns all the way around. Shot em the moon did you?

Pookie comes in the back gate as I'm filling the mower with gas. Pookie and I could graze the lawn faster, but Mom and her fixation will hear nothing of it.

Since her operation, Pookie looks wilder than ever, burrs and twigs caught in her matted hair, muddy paws, dried saliva along the edges of her mouth. To a stranger she would look dangerous. She plays harder than before, snapping jaws precariously close to hands, showing teeth more often. She'll rarely just sit and allow herself to be petted.

I put the gas cap back on the mower and place the gas can under the gazebo. Pookie stalks me as I walk, hunched down on her belly and scooting along with her back legs. When I turn around, she rises to all fours, but is still low to the ground, ready to spring. Hey Pookie.

She feints for my leg.

No.

She crouches again. I walk past her and sit in a chair by the pool. She watches me.

Come here.

She continues to crouch, but understands I'm not going for the rough stuff. She walks over and I pet around her neck. She doesn't roll her head like she used to. I spot a tick on the back of her head and start to pull it out. She snaps at me, just missing my hand. I smack her. Pretty hard on the side. Don't do that Pookie.

She shows her teeth.

I grab her by the collar and push her head down and smack her again, not as hard, but she's by god not going to bite me. And I will, by god, get that tick. She squirms while I hold her, but not her hardest. If she really wanted to get free she could. I get the tick, and careful to get all of it, to get the head, I yank it free. I let Pookie up and show her what I was doing. Do you see this, I say, holding the bloated brown tick, legs writhing, in front of her face. I throw it on the ground and squash it. Dark purple blood stains the concrete. Then I walk over to the mower and get on. Pookie moves from the pool to the shade of the gazebo and watches me mow with her tongue hanging out.

While I mow I think about Jody McDowell. I pass under a tree and it's cool and a shadow comes on me. I come back into the light but the shadow remains. And I'm shadowed and Jody used the word shadow and I've gone over it a million times and I'm about to go for a million and one when I'm doused with an ice cold bucket of water.

You looked hot, Curt says, laughing.

I put the mower in neutral. I didn't know he was coming to town. Pretty funny Curt, I say.

I thought you saw me for sure. I was in the gazebo, then Pookie started barking. I thought you'd see me for sure.

He's still laughing. I'll get you, I say. You wait. When you least expect it.

You're getting too old. I'm young and fast, he says, shuffle-footing and jabbing the air around me.

My knee's better, Curt. I'm getting strong again. Take your licks now while you still can.

I will, he says, laughing, cocky, two-a-days start Monday, and Curt plans on kicking some ass. He runs back to the house, just to run, and then stops to wrestle with Pookie, both of them on the ground, both tough, playing hard.

I put the mower back in drive. The shadow has gone and my back is cool, and I can't help smiling at Curt and at my silly ass so serious.

When it's time to mow the hill, I start up high and cut a strip just where the hill starts to angle. At the end of that strip I make a tight turn, close to the fence, and then circle back to the hill and then down at a wide angle. I'm thinking this circular method of cutting will lessen my weedeating.

I come around to the middle top part of the hill and have to lean far to the left to keep the mower balanced. I circle back around, notice Pookie barking at a squirrel halfway up a tree, the squirrel pausing just out of paw reach, waving its tail. Pookie's barking like a madwoman, and starting the descent I notice I'm going too fast and lean as far as I can to the left. I hit the brakes, but no brakes on this thin grass and Mr. Gravity's on my back and I'm fast down the hill, Pookie barking, the mower turning over, and I push off the mower hard with one leg then I'm rolling over covering my head thinking blade peeking out of the corner of rolling eyes as the mower skids, flips over onto the seat, legs and elbows scraping against concrete, hands over head, rolling eyes seeing the mower skip in front onto the concrete, the scrape of metal like toenails being ripped, and stopping, upside down, next to the pool.

And I have stopped, next to the pool, and wrong side up the blade is still turning, though the engine's cut off.

You okay, Curt asks above me.

Uhhm.

Did you hit your head? Are you cut?

No. I don't think so.

I'm looking at the mower overturned. The blade turns still, wedges of grass stuck to the side, scraping sound in the air.

I stand up and test my knee. A bit sore from landing but not bad. Red scrapes on elbows and chest and cheek. No breaks. No concussion. No apparent need for stitches. The mower is likely dead.

Shit.

I heard you scream.

I screamed?

Yeah. What happened?

Got going too fast. Wasn't paying attention. Help me push her over.

Red paint marks streak the concrete. I didn't hear myself scream. I thought people only screamed in movies.

I pick grass and small rocks out of the cuts on my elbow. Curt takes off his shirt and wipes bits of concrete off my face. He has a frightened look. And I suppose I do too.

See if I left any toes in that blade.

No kidding, he says, glad to laugh.

The blade turns slowly enough for Curt to stop it with his hand. We get on the side of the mower and push it upright. About half its paint is gone.

Your dad's going to be pissed.

Nah, Curt says, sitting down on the mower to see if it'll start. It does.

Good as new. Just scratched up a bit. It'll be all right. I can paint it.

I'm going to go tell your dad.

He's asleep. It's no big deal. We'll tell him when he wakes up.

Okay. God I'm an idiot. I'm going to get the weedeater. That's what I should have done to begin with.

I'll do it, Curt says, hopping off the mower and starting toward the garage. Go clean up. I'll finish up here.

I walk toward the house with Pookie trotting along. I brush-stroke her head but don't stop and she runs in front of me like she used to, blocking my way. Go on, I say, pushing past her and she stops and watches me go in. I let the screen door slam, forgetting that Tom's asleep, and the flat smack lingers in my ears as I walk down the steps to the bathroom.

Back from visiting Tom in the hospital, I walk into an empty house that smells of sitting water. Five days of rain have flooded the garage and now water seeps into the den. I walk on soggy carpet that makes a squishing sound and retains a footprint when walked upon and is yet another problem for my mother to worry about in her delusional quest to sell this house. The stagnant marshy odor, though indicative of a fertile breeding ground for crickets and mosquitos, small frogs and snapping turtles, smells of slow rotting death, and where I once felt the electricity and manic paranoia of darkness approaching, I feel now only unromantic decay.

I go upstairs where at least it's dry and there are windows where I can watch the rain fall without much conviction from a grey sky grey for years. It feels like late afternoon but is only a little after two.

At the hospital, the sick were still sick, the dying still dying. I moved about awkwardly, hoping for errands, for the chance to get a newspaper for Mom, a Coke for Rachel. Tom's brother Dale and I sat in the hall and he talked to me, in a voice just above a whisper, about what a rascal Tom was as a youngster, how their mother doted on him, how he never liked going to church unless it was to hunt Easter eggs or for the egg tosses and three-legged races on field day. And sometimes he liked the revivals because there were more people, people from all over and new girls and it was easy to slip off, and saying this, Dale nearly smiles, looking at me so I see that though he may have been born at night, it wasn't last night.

We tried for years and years to get him to sing with us in the choir. He just never would.

Tom says he can't sing.

He can sing, Dale says, leaning over, neck out, eyes locked in to make sure I understand what he means. He can sing. Sweet sings good. Don't ever let him tell you different.

And in the hospital room, Bobbie and the other sisters laugh and cry and talk loudly about that crazy Sweet. They put cool wet rags on Tom's head, make him eat his jello. Women know Tom and know Sweet and know death. We men talk primarily in whispers, pace the halls, one step ahead of nothing, neither laughing nor crying, lest we be considered coconspirators in the matter.

Tom's oldest son Taylor doesn't handle this well. He's come from Birmingham in a hurry, moving fast to shake the dead. He talks to Tom for a few minutes, his eyes moving quickly about, taking in flowers and cards, the view out the window of asphalt and cars. Sweat beads on his forehead. Old aunts and uncles offer guest rooms, insist, and Taylor tries to smile, though his face shows he can smell the dust and mothballs, the closets that hold photo albums of long lost dead and dying. His face shows they don't run the air at night, that there's no beer in the refrigerator, no cable TV, the living room couches are covered with plastic, bric-a-brac from the Grand Old Opry, and he says quickly, me and Curt are staying with Rachel. Then adds, breathing more normally, it's closer.

In the hall he asks me furtively, though no one is near, can you believe this shit?

I smile to show I understand the claustrophobia. Taylor's three years older than I am and we've never had much to say to each other.

I'm sorry about your dad.

Yeah thanks. But man I can't stand it, seeing him so drugged up half the time he doesn't know who's here and who's not. Goddam I hate hospitals.

I know, I say, and then there's nothing more to say, we're just standing there looking at the walls, jerking our heads at everyone walking by just to have something to look at. I pull the keys from my pocket to show I'm leaving, say hang in there, then go in the room to say goodbye to everyone. As I'm leaving the room, Mom says, Jason, will you stop by the grocery store and pick up some detergent?

No, hell no, I say. And Tom laughs. And that was what I was trying to do.

On the kitchen table there's a note, in Jackie's handwriting, for me to call Barry Paige, my old buddy from West Trails, at his parents' house. When I call, his mother says he's moved back to town to start a new job. She doesn't know where he is. He has, she fears, a case of ants in the pants.

I hang up and grab a beer and sit down at the kitchen table to watch the rain fall. I'm considering heading down to Ray and Starr's for a few days in the morning and think about driving down a day early, but this rain, this palpable grey inertia, keeps me fastened to the chair. I'm on my third beer when Jackie walks through the back yard toward the door. He walks slowly and his eyes frown at the rain. The rain mats his hair and pushes the part down the middle more tightly to his head. He opens the door and wipes his boots on the mat outside. Pookie stands up and shakes water on him. Jackie ignores her and comes on in.

Pookie didn't think you were wet enough.

Jackie starts. No lights are on in the kitchen and he didn't see me. He smiles. Shew, he says. Pookie smells like a wet dog. Like two wet dogs.

She ain't got sense to get out of the rain, I say.

Jackie rubs a small hand through his hair to dry his head. It's a cold rain for summer. Can't say I got much sense either, he says. If we had any sense we'd be building an ark. You ever seen rain like this?

I don't know, I'd have to think.

God it's depressing, he says. He takes a cigarette out of his pocket and offers me one, which I take, then he lights first mine, then his own. He looks out the window at the rain falling on the pool, the leaves swirling slowly in the water, the ramshackle gazebo, the tracks of mud on the hill leading to the pool where I wrecked the mower.

Yard looks good, he says. He laughs. He'd left that word depressing in the air too long.

Doesn't it though.

Godawmighty.

He looks back at me and smiles that round-eyed third grader with a Playboy smile, and I think for a moment he's going to say something I don't want him to say. Maybe he sees my face screw up, but his changes also. A serious face. More chin. The face of an adult. It suits him.

You been by the hospital? he asks.

Just got back.

Sweet raising hell on them nurses?

Not too much. He's doing all right. Pretty drugged up, but he's hanging in there. They're hoping he can come home for a day or two later on this week.

I need to get up there.

He puts out his cigarette. Lot of folks up there?

Yeah. About everybody. Jolie's going to come in tomorrow. And Taylor just got in. And most of his brothers and sisters.

Taylor still up there? Jackie asks. He smiles and shakes his head. Not histrionically.

Yeah.

You know he's the only one stayed with Sweet after the divorce. He was the oldest and when their mom moved he just wouldn't go. He was on the high school team and all. They just lived like two bachelors. Sweet taught him how to cook. Shit, Friday night, Taylor'd be sneaking a girl in the back door while Sweet was sneaking one in the front.

I laugh.

I'm serious.

I know you are.

Taylor's all right, he says, and waits for me to respond.

Yeah.

Jackie lights another cigarette. Offers me one. I decline.

I always thought, Jackie says, that the only problem Taylor had was that he thought he had to be as tough as his old man. And man he used to get in fights. Wouldn't nobody mess with him in Niota. Mean I'm telling you. He's not near as big as Sweet. You know him. He's not five nine, but I'm telling you he's tough. Thing is he always wanted to be like Sweet. But he's just like his mother. They're like twins. Sweet'll tell you. Taylor thinks he acts the most like Sweet. The rest of the kids don't hardly drink. I don't guess Curt cares nothing about carrying on. But Taylor and Jolie are like their mother, I'm talking the way you are, not the way you act, and Rachel and Curt are like Sweet.

I can see that.

Jackie goes to the bathroom and I think that he'll probably never see Tom in the hospital. He might go once or twice when no one else is up there, but he won't stay long. Too hard for Waylon to see Willie like that, knowing they've drunk the same water.

He comes back from the bathroom. That mower down in the garage? he asks.

Yeah. Why you going to mow?

Sweet's going to trade it out to me for some money I loaned him. I was thinking about loading it up today. I don't know why. I was just wanting something to do.

You know I turned it over?

He laughs. Sweet told me something about it. Said you were out there doing wheelies.

It was funny I guess. Scared the hell out of me though.

I never knew until just the other day about Sweet putting it in the pool. Godawmighty, it's lucky one of y'all didn't get killed.

I know it. I scratched that mower up pretty bad. You seen it?

Yeah. Naw. It's all right. I'll just pick it up later on. Y'all might need it when Sweet gets out of the hospital.

I look at him to see what he means.

I don't need it, he says. I got a mower. I'll just pick it up later on.

All right. You want a drink?

Naw. I'm going to get on. I was just stopping by to see if anybody was home.

He starts out the door. We'll see you later, I say.

Yeah. Tell them I'll be coming up there pretty soon.

I'll do it.

The screen door slams and Jackie's back in the rain, head down, walking faster than before, and I try to think of some joke I could have told him before he left.

Mom's still at the hospital when Bobsmith calls to see if I want to go downtown to see a band. I don't, but I don't want to stay in this mildewed dark house either.

I was thinking about heading down to my grandparents' tonight.

Wait till the morning. Get a fresh start.

I got ten dollars to my name.

I got you covered. I think we can get in free at the Grotto and Pel's down at Mentors. I got money.

I don't know man. The Grotto?

Good band. What else are you going to do?

Nothing. Maybe brood a little.

Could be some girls out tonight.

Girls you say?

Bobsmith and I walk through the Old City toward Mentors. The misty rain has stopped now, but every bar is dark and quiet and tumbleweed swept, Mentors no exception. A jazz band plays and there are maybe twenty people sitting at tables, probably friends of the band, which is local and composed of middle-aged guys with regular jobs. They're pretty good.

We walk past three waitresses smoking cigarettes at the wait station. They don't smile at us. They're making no money and want to get off, and I assume Pel's given them grief earlier in the night for complaining. They conspicuously don't look at us. We walk past and sit at the far end of the bar.

Bobsmith goes over to check on the waitresses, to give them the Uncle Bobsmith shoulder to cry on. I'm the only one at the bar. Though at any moment a gaggle of college girls will be hitting the door. Drunk ones. Just kicked out of the sorority for incorrigible nymphomania. I order a scotch from Sammy, a new guy, and while I'm ordering, Angie comes out from the back with an order of food. She smiles hello to me. It doesn't look as if she's been complaining. She moves past the other waitresses who are gesturing with their cigarettes about the futility of the night's work, riffling through checks to show the paucity of customers, and Bobsmith is nodding his head, he knows, he knows, not listening at all, smiling at Angie who has winked as she walked by. I watch her walk, graceful through the tables too close together, shoulders square even as she holds the tray of food. Heads at tables smile up at her. The sax player checks to see if she's watching before beginning a solo. She places the food on the table and walks back to the bar, where she stops next to Bobsmith and looks as if she will pinch him, then decides better of it as one of the waitresses points back to the kitchen about some order of food they screwed up earlier in the evening. Angie nods, feigning agreement. She is, after all, one of the gals.

Pel comes out from the kitchen and sits at the bar next to me. Then some of the cooks and dishdogs from the kitchen come out and it's doo rag city. Jimbo comes down the steps and sees me and kind of grins. Penny Jackson comes in just behind him, and I'm glad to see her, immediately thinking of a rendezvous. Then I realize, though it's incomprehensible, that she's with Jimbo. She sees me and smiles. A matter-of-fact smile.

Jimbo talks to Pel and Penny goes to the bathroom. Jimbo's trying to suppress a shiteating grin. He looks over at Bobsmith and then finally back at me. What say, Say?

I smile and shake my head. Not a lot.

He wants to small-talk. He's feeling good about things, about being Trick's philandering protégé. I'm hard pressed not to tell him he looks like a milkman in a tiedye. But I'm jealous. And that is surprising.

Penny comes back from the bathroom and waits at the other end of the bar. Jimbo sits her down at a table near the stage then comes back to talk to Pel. He's showing everyone he's in no hurry to talk to her. She'll wait. Bobsmith turns and gives a sour gumball look.

Fuck it. I don't care.

I wasn't sure if I should've told you.

It's no big deal. I don't have any claim. Is that how Trick knew last month?

Yeah. Jimbo's a clown.

I don't say anything. I shouldn't care. He knew her from Lenoir City and always liked her when she worked at the Quality Inn. Do you remember when I used to be able to get women?

Yeah, he laughs.

How'd you put up with me?

He laughs again. Aw Say, you weren't that bad. A little cocky.

He motions Sammy for another round.

I got to get out of Knoxville. I want to chase women, but I don't want to chase women. I can't do it anymore. I can't be asshole enough. That's the only reason I used to do good, because I was such a jerk.

Bobsmith laughs. You're not going to be one of those people who complains about Knoxville all the time but never leaves are you?

No. I'll leave. I'm yesterday's news. It ain't my town anymore.

No, he says, it's not. And then the drinks come. And then Trick walks in.

Well well well, Trick says.

Well, well. Don't tell me you don't have a date?

She's working late. I'm on my way there now. Thought I'd stop in for a quick one.

Here or there?

Now now.

Trick circles the bar greeting everyone. Then he goes back to the kitchen with Pel, I assume to catch a buzz. Jimbo leaves Penny Jackson at the table and goes to the kitchen as well. Penny waves at me, a bit self-consciously, but more, it seems, because she sits at a table by herself in a roomful of ponytailed guys and waitresses with crewcuts, all strangers wearing black or some variation of tiedye. Penny has on tight jeans and a white halter top. I wave back and think about asking her to dump Jimbo and hook up with me later. But she wouldn't. Then I think that at least Jimbo's taking her out on the town, something I haven't done in a long while.

I walk over to her, not knowing what I'm going to say, just wanting to mess with Jimbo a bit. Fancy seeing you here, I say, with probably too much of a smartass look on my face, and I try to temper it a little. I'm fairly drunk.

Yep, it's a small world. This is my first time down here.

You like it?

I'm not dressed right.

Yeah you are. You look good.

Well, thanks. You do too.

This old thing, I say, pulling on my T-shirt.

Jimbo comes out from the back and looks at us from the bar, then jerks his head back around, looking for someone to talk to. He walks over to Bobsmith.

You like the band? I ask. You like jazz?

Yeah I do. It's different than what I'm used to listening to, but I like it.

Yeah? Good. That's good. And seriously, you look great. You know, you always do.

She smiles.

Well I guess I'll be running along now.

Okay, she says. Bye.

Then I walk to the bathroom.

When I come back, Trick's smiling at the bar. He's the only person I know who can look dressed up in a T-shirt. His T-shirts always look clean and pressed. They aren't pressed, but he looks fastidious somehow. You look fastidious, I say.

This old thing, he says, and I realize I stole that line from him.

I just used that stupid line on Penny Jackson.

Feel free, poetic license. And how is young Penny?

Doing well it seems. Moving up in the world.

Trick orders a beer and tells the bartender to bring me a drink. I gulp the remaining half of my scotch and it burns enough to make my eyes water. Then my new drink comes.

Thanks.

He waves me off.

I'm getting rather hammered. I look over at Jimbo and for a moment I could swear he's sitting in a small cafe in Paris. Perhaps a bistro. So Jimbo and Penny are sitting in a tree, I say. Why didn't you tell me?

I don't know. Do you care?

No. Sort of. I think I care more that I didn't know than anything. That the Shoney's Big Boy thought he was being sly. I don't give a shit. I hope they get married.

Man, it's just chattel. Like borrowing a CD from a friend.

I laugh. Let me borrow a CD tonight.

Go ahead. Be my guest. More than enough for everyone.

Unfortunately your chattel has a say in the matter.

True. But the offer stands.

I'm not like that. I get too jealous.

Can't be getting jealous now Say, Pel says from behind us. He swigs his beer and bums a hit off my cigarette. Penny for your thoughts, Say.

Stick a penny up your ass, I say, which makes Trick laugh, and Pel too, and then the great Jimbo, Penny dilemma is over.

Trick and I talk about my knee, when I'll be able to play basketball again, and I tell him it's going well, I can run on it nearly full speed. I'm still working on that beam in my eye, I say.

He shakes his head, showing it was nothing.

I ran into Jody McDowell a couple of weeks ago.

Good old Jody McDowell. And how is Jody?

Good. He said he saw a shadow behind me.

Calmly, laughing, Trick says, what?

He didn't actually see a shadow, he said he just felt something behind me.

Did you punch him in the nose?

No. I've thought the same thing. Ever since the trip.

Trick laughs. You guys ought to go in halves on a shrink. McDowell doesn't even know you.

I know. That's why it's weird.

He could say that to everybody that walks by, Trick says, and laughs. That could be his little witnessing thing.

Anyway, I say, it made me feel better. Then I start to remind him of some of the strange shit he said while I was tripping, say that maybe I wouldn't have gotten so crazy if he hadn't said that stuff about Christian imagery, about Judas betraying Christ when I found the thirty cents. But I don't.

Good old Jody McDowell, he says. The Prince of Peace. And then Jimbo comes up to say goodbye and give me the sincere shoulder shake, the smiling pat on the back, and Penny is walking out the door to his car.

Trick heads out shortly after for his date. He says goodbye to Pel and

Bobsmith and makes a basketball shooting motion and points to me. I nod my head, blankly, as to a stranger.

After the band's finished and the customers have cleared out, Pel goes behind the bar and pulls a draft for me. Then he lights a pipe and hands it across the bar. The band's still loading out, and there are some people in the bar I don't know, and I suppose I have a nervous look. Everybody's cool, Pel says.

I'm drunk.

This'll sober you up, he says. Then, you don't have to.

Just say no Pel, I say, taking the pipe from him and hitting it hard two times.

Bobsmith comes from the back and hits it a few times.

Did I hear you tell Trick you ran into Jody McDowell, Pel asks.

Yeah.

Hasn't Beth been going out with him, Bobsmith?

Bobsmith nods his head. Yeah, he says, I think so.

Fucking hell, Pel says.

I don't say anything. I take a sip of my beer. I'm thinking this is turning into an unusual night. Is anybody here dating my grandmother?

They laugh.

Nah, Jody's all right. They'd be a good couple.

Right Say, Pel says.

And I'm not in a mood to argue.

I'm Buzz Aldrin by the time Bobsmith and I head up to the Grotto. Pel still has to check out Angie and Sammy and finish closing the bar before he can meet us.

We come out to a cool summer night. The street is empty, just a few desperados wandering about. The sound of water draining and the loud slick swoosh of tires on the interstate. We walk about fifty yards and come up on the Grotto. A good number of people mill about in front of the bar, most of them young, most just off the skateboard circuit, most in black, long hair, shaved heads, ponytails, blah blah blah. I smile at them, give a big loud Jethro, how y'all doing? I nod my head at a bald young woman as we walk up. Howdy miss, I say. In response, she exhales from the recesses of her traumatic childhood and blows smoke into the face of her crewcut friend, whose combat-booted feet are stretched across the sidewalk, blocking my way. Excuse me darling, I say, stepping over, still using my just down from the hills voice. Ain't had much book learning, I yodel, and Bobsmith looks back at me, wondering if I'm going to be a jerk the entire night.

Inside, Bobsmith explains that I'm with him and the doorman waves us in free. It's another of those renovated warehouses. Unfinished wood floors and brick walls stretching up to very high ceilings. Local modern art hangs on the walls. This week the offerings include a large watercolor of ratlike deer jumping over an enormous penis that has been toppled in the woods. Another collection shows a series of clown suicides in black and white. Clown balancing on ball with noose around neck. Clown in dressing room daubing self inflicted gunshot wound for blood to use as facial paint. A child laughing feverishly as a clown sticks a hypodermic in his neck.

It's the Smoky Robinson collection, I say, pointing to the clowns, but it's too loud in the bar, and when Bobsmith says, what? I just wave my hand never mind.

I follow Bobsmith and there, at the bar, is my old friend Barry Paige. He doesn't see me coming and I bump into him hard on purpose. He jerks around fast like he's ready to fight, then sees it's me.

Holy shit. What's up Say? What are you doing here?

I'm leaning on him, the old rope-a-dope, fists up. I'm needing some of your ass.

You're messed up, he says, laughing, pushing me off. You want a drink?

You're messed up, do you want a drink? Hell yeah I want a drink. Get my buddy over there a beer too.

Anybody else?

Nah, I say, going into a wrestling sugarfoot stance. Just two beers for me and my friend. Two apiece.

He buys our beers, one each, and I hand Bobsmith his. He points upstairs and I nod that I'll be up in a second. I pat Barry on the back. I'm damn glad to see him. Who you here with?

He points over to a table where a good-looking twenty-year-old girl sits. She's sitting Indian style in her chair, a sure sign of precociousness or melodramatic tendencies. She's wearing torn jeans and an Earthfest T-shirt and talking to three young guys. The three misunderstoods nod serious heads to whatever she's saying. I'm with her, he says.

Save the baby shoes.

What?

Wee doggies, she's right fancy, I say. She from France?

Good old Barry Paige shakes his patient head.

You're dressed wrong, I say, taking the UT baseball cap off his head. And you're wearing loafers. Good god, can you name one Sylvia Plath poem?

No.

Why don't you run on back to O'Doyle's where you belong?

I will as soon as I can get her away from those fucking poets, or whatever they are.

Save the baby poets, I say, loudly, and Barry's date and the Holdens look up at me.

He hits me in the chest. Shut up.

All right, I say, waving sorry to the young Parisians. All right BP. No more of that. When did you get back in town?

Just a couple of days ago. First National transferred me back up here from Atlanta.

No kidding, I say. I'm really glad to see him. A West Trails Allstar he is. That's great. That's really good. And how's your sister? How's old Joshua Pudge?

He laughs. Man I forgot about that. She's good. Still in school.

Tell her I said hello. Tell her I miss the pudgy one.

I will. But where are you now anyway? I heard you and Pel were in Australia.

That was awhile back. I'm staying with Mom now. Broke as hell. Dateless as hell. You don't want to know.

So nothing else is going on?

Just trying to get the hell out of Knoxville.

You don't like Knoxville?

No man. Fuck Knoxville.

Fuck the Vols?

Hell yeah fuck the Vols. I don't give a shit about the fucking Vols.

What about your Uncle Clay?

What about him? What I feel about him doesn't have a damn thing to do with football.

All right, all right, he says. I can buy that. But what about Cedar Bluff Middle? Fuck Cedar Bluff? Fuck the Giants?

No man, not the Giants.

Fuck West Trails? I thought you were an Allstar?

No not West Trails either. West Trails rules.

He smiles, shakes his head up and down damn right. This is your city. You've had some good times here. Come on man, you were Cedar Bluff student council president.

He's got me. Good old Barry Paige. He's the allstar of allstars. You got me, I say. Go Giants. Go West Trails.

He laughs. Why don't you come on with us over to O'Doyle's. My date's got some cute girlfriends.

I might later. I'm going to go see this band for a minute. Pel's supposed to meet me here.

Is he? Tell him I said hello.

I'll do it.

He sticks out his hand and we shake. Good to see you Say. Give me a call sometime. We'll go hoist a couple and lie about old times.

Sounds good, I say. Go Giants.

Go Giants, he says. Then the old student council president is heading up the stairs to see Captain Black and the Envoys.

Upstairs is much more crowded than I expected, but immediately I spot Bobsmith's bushy head as he slouches against the far wall. I push through a small crowd around the bar and then through a larger one, mostly guys, facing the stage and dancing in the middle of the room. The band has a slinky white boy synthesized funk going. It's a good sound, and I walk up to Bobsmith nodding my head yes, rock and roll.

The room is much like downstairs, but gloomier, and hotter. There are no windows. Only two narrow doors at either end of the large room. I plan my fire escape. Plowing through punkers fast.

A lot of guys have their shirts off, which rubs me wrong at first, until the humidity of the room makes me start to sweat through my own. Thick brick walls trap the body heat, no breeze coming in, no air conditioning, people dancing, fecund sickly sweet smell, breathing in the heat, the band moving now to something with a thicker bounce, the sweaty mangy crowd bouncing, the old wooden floor bending, the futile frenzy of the late summer June bug smashing recklessly into your grandmother's screen door.

And the Captain moans, not love exactly, before love, a summer dog popsickling around the neighborhood. Bobsmith and I bounce around, our beer sloshing out of the bottle. A couple of thin kids start moshing in front of us and one makes as if he'll come at me, but I hunker down between bounces, lowering my shoulder, a drunken stoned moshing shoulder, and he decides better of including me in his dance. I bounce hard, nearly moving into a full two-footed stomp, the knee holding up fine. The floor bounces. I have no evacuation plan for the collapse of the floor. I stomp up and down. I'm having a good time. Bobsmith looks over at me and laughs.

I get some money from him and go to the bar for beer. I've spilled most of mine on the floor. I order and the bartender's quick getting them out of the cooler and she pops them with an opener she keeps in her back pocket. I tip her a couple of bucks on speed and dexterity points. Bobsmith would do the same. I start to walk away, then I see this stack of pamphlets on the far end of the table for something called the Unity Coven. I sidestep down to have a look, one of those car wreck looks, and read on the front page a headline about Jehovah's five-thousand-year-old lie. I stop reading. I'm too drunk. Witches bore the shit out of me. Somewhere along the way something got screwed up and I have nothing to do with it. I assume they are very nice witches. I notice the bartender looking at me. I don't care for the word coven, I say.

Messed up, she says, and something in her voice speaks of high school girl's basketball. Out in the country.

I nod and walk off. I get about halfway across the floor and turn around and walk back to the bar. You play basketball?

In high school, she says.

I nod and put my hands together, still holding the beers, and give a little ball fake. She lifts her elbow, ready to swat my shot. I give her a drunken look, modeled on some irreverent actor, though I can't say who. Then I walk off.

Captain Black is heavy and older, at least forty. He wears a Marlon Brando Wild One biker cap and matching black T-shirt. His gut hangs. He has a Fu Manchu and a round squinty-eyed face and I'd wager some real ugly groupies. He and the Envoys can play though. I've been leaning against the wall listening to music like I've never heard before. I don't hear any antecedents. A strange sound. The set moves, song to song indecipherable. Captain Black sweats through his shirt. He never faces the crowd, giving only half sideviews, hand-covered face, broad back, and he's singing words but I only hear the music, only hear the background, the words seeming background, the music background. I like it. My head feels heavy, but not bad. I'm sweating like a pig. Bobsmith and I bounce without lifting our feet. I take my shirt off and tuck it in my shorts. Bobsmith makes a face at me, a sleepy smile, thick-eyed. He looks old and funny.

I turn around and Pel's standing next to the sound guy. He smiles and points at me, wryly, amused I have my shirt off and that I'm bouncing around with Bobsmith. He comes up and headbutts me, not hard. Captain Black strokes kittens on fire. It's the best band I've ever heard. The mean-faced jelly man rocks. Pel and I stomp together, the song gets faster. I turn around and there's Angie at the back of the bar, standing on a chair. She smiles at me having a good time.

Peter, the bartender from the Old Pub, hops around in front of us and then starts jumping into the brick wall, slamming his shoulder into it. The whole place is going crazy, the old floor will go at any moment. I keep stomping, sweating, Pel and Bobsmith and I smashing into each other.

The song comes to a sudden stop and the Captain walks off the stage. The Envoys follow. I'm screaming at them to play more. Pel hollers. Bobsmith dog-whistles through fingers. I come up behind Pel and put him in a sweaty bear hug, lifting him off his feet. While I have him up in the air, Bobsmith shakes his head like a shaggy dog, throwing sweat over both of us. I put Pel down and look behind me to see Angie, but she's gone. Pel motions for us to head out and we follow. I assume the band's finished for the night.

Downstairs is crowded and no Angie. I look around for Barry Paige but he's long gone. I go outside and sit where the combat boot girl sat earlier and light a cigarette, and in a minute Pel comes out with Peter from the Old Pub and a couple of other guys I've seen around but don't know and a pale girl in dark eye shadow who wears a short cape.

We head down the street and the Old City looks pretty good after the rain, the water shining on the cobbled road, the old-timey streetlights. I think briefly about heading over to O'Doyle's for a minute to see Barry Paige, then figure I'd just be third-wheeling it as usual and keep on behind Pel. We get to Mentors and he unlocks the front door and the whole group of us heads down the dark steps. I have to hold the rail to know where I'm going. We stand in the dark until Pel turns on a light.

No quiet like an empty bar. Especially here underground. The silence moves, brushing against the walls, wanting to get out. I'm never introduced to the guys I don't know and they never look at me. The pale girl keeps her eyes on the floor. A pipe and a sack of potatoes pop up on the bar. Bobsmith talks with the two guys I don't know about a band that's scheduled to appear. A cockroach climbs a bottle of Tia Maria.

Jason, that's a cool name, Peter says, smiling a wide country boy smile through hair that comes down in front of his mouth.

Thanks a lot.

I'm serious, I really like that name. Friday the 13th, man, wicked movie.

It was my parents' favorite.

Jason and the Argonauts.

Pel hands me the pipe. I take a hit and hand it back. Jason and the big buzz quest for pussy, I say.

He laughs. Pel turns the pipe backward in his mouth and starts giving shotguns. I come up for one and get a terrific hit that leaves me coughing and gasping and walking around in circles trying to get my breath. Bob-smith laughs. You get a hit, Say?

I'm talking to Peter, who is not my brother, who is not the rock of the church, about football. What he thinks of the Tennessee coach. He doesn't know jackshit. I'm about to tell him he doesn't know jackshit, when Pel introduces me to the girl in the cape. Say, this is Nettie. Nettie, Say.

It's actually Jason.

I know. I heard you talking to Peter.

I nod. She's gone from staring at the floor to staring at me.

Your last name is Sayer. Did I hear right?

Yes.

So are you related to the statue?

I laugh. It's my uncle.

The hero. Are you a hero too?

Not quite.

Nettie's a graffiti artist, Pel says.

Is that right, I say, more than glad to change the subject.

Yes.

Do you just paint it anywhere?

Yes.

Just regular old graffiti?

Graffiti art.

How are they different?

They're not.

I nod.

Maybe I'll do the hero one day.

Don't do that, I say. There's no need for that.

And she doesn't smile or say anything else, content to stare at me with her blue button eyes. I try to return stares for awhile, but there's no way. After a few moments of this, she says, I like to look at people.

I don't say anything but sort of shake my head, trying to get her to stop.

I like to see how they react.

That's interesting, I say, and I'm off, slow glide, continental drift, toward Bobsmith, nodding my head at her chin as I go.

Back outside, heading down the street to the Grotto, I look over to O'Doyle's but they're closed up. I start to tell Pel that Barry Paige said hello, but he's laughing with Peter about something, so I don't. Twenty or so people hang around the front of the Grotto, two of whom turn out to be Envoys, the bass player and the guitarist. Are they going to play more, I ask Pel.

You want them to play more?

Hell yeah. It's got to be late though, what time is it?

Three-thirty.

Bullshit.

Bullshit.

Bars close at three. They can't play. Isn't it against the law?

Ask them.

Y'all going to play some more?

The bass player looks up slowly. His clear drugged eyes look at mine, cloudy and weighted. You want to hear some more?

Yeah, that'd be good.

The bass player stands up and looks at the guitarist. He wants to hear some more, he says. The guitarist looks at me, starting at my knees, works his way up to my chin, but never makes the eyes. Then he too stands up, and he and the bass player walk inside.

They're going to play, I say to Pel. How they going to play after three o'clock?

You got to want it, Pel says, walking past me and on into the bar. I follow Bobsmith, and the other people on the sidewalk do as well. When we get upstairs, a different bartender is on, and the place has cleared out a good deal, but not nearly as much as I'd anticipated. I look around for Angie, but no go.

Pel stops at the bar and I follow Bobsmith back over to the far wall where we were before. There are probably thirty people up here, maybe thirty more downstairs. Angie's chair is empty. Pel comes over and hands me a beer I don't want. I'm dehydrated and my legs have lost their strength. I take the beer from Pel and go sit in the empty chair at the back. My heart beats fast as it does when I smoke too much, and I'm at that bad time of night when your mind races though your body begs for sleep. My brain is blistered. I'm not having a bad time. I didn't know it was so late, and I wasn't tired until I found out it was so late.

The bass player plays thick offkey chords slowly electric that discombobulate the room. No lights are on the stage. The guitar starts in on one long snake, an antiriff played with fingers underneath strings. I kick over my beer. Strange music plays, different from before. I can hear it but not hear it. I can't organize it. Discordant sound climbs the walls but doesn't make it all the way back to me. Offkey melodic wet snake through an electric fence, strangely sweet, Novocaine wet nervosity, spiders in your hair, eyes behind eyes where the brain gets thick. I have to stand up.

I go over to where Pel and Bobsmith are standing. I shake my head. Weird.

One light comes on over the stage and the drummer comes out and starts in, a drum beat you hear then forget is there. And a minute later the Captain. People start hollering. The people downstairs have come up, the floor is nearly full. Captain Black takes the mike and paces the stage, back and forth, the music getting faster, but still sideways, moving off into the corners, sliding along the ceiling. I like it, but it's different, different from before. We've moved closer to the stage, I'm looking at Pel, his eyes slanted from smoke, laughing at me liking this band, having a good time at the Grotto. Bobsmith, the old man, is behind me to the right, closer to the wall. He looks like he's ready to lean, but not quite sure if he wants to make the move two feet over. Pel and Peter smile at one another. I turn around and there in the back, in Angie's chair, is graffiti Nettie in full stare.

I am that I am.

I look to the stage.

I am that I am.

Pel yells. Everyone yells. Peter up front is jumping up and down and pointing at the stage. A sharp slice of bass hits me in the temple. The Captain walks back and forth across the stage like a preacher. I start to smile, though this is weird, just because I want to smile and not get stoned about this.

I'm not here to save you! he screams out to the crowd. I am that I am and I have not come to save you.

Peter jumps up and down up and down like a monkey. I step back and see out of the corner of my eye, Pel smiling.

I am that I am, says the Captain, crouching down and facing the people who are jumping up all around the stage, reaching out to touch his legs. I say that I am that I am!

Slow motion screams. Twisted faces in side smile screams, and I have begun to hear the drums and then only drums.

THIS IS FOR THE HEAVYWEIGHT CHAMPIONSHIP OF THE WORLD!

Screams that don't stop.

Peter jumping on the backs of people, people screaming, laughing, jumping, raising their fists, Peter looking back still jumping like a monkey, laughing but no laughter.

Bobsmith is behind me.

Pel to my left and we look. I look. And he looks. His eyes empty.

And then the drums and the crowd spreading and I am stepping back, the drums, only drums. The Captain has turned his back and the crowd in haphazard lines takes three steps to the right and bows down. Then three steps left and bow. I step back farther trying to shake my eyes straight and everyone dances onetwothree bow, onetwothree bow, and Bobsmith steps in front of me and bows, and Pel to the side, onetwothree bow, and the crowd bows and the Captain says I am that I am and I have not come to save you and I'm running to my car with graffiti stares and I'm driving on the interstate away.

I'm down at Ray's. I had forgotten. Pulled out of the dream by my dreamself, I have wakened to the first thinning of black creeping outside the shutters. A shadowed Franklin County pennant, Aunt Sarah's. A desk. Old forty-five records placed in a metal rack without dust covers. I turn away from the shutters, where the grey early light has not yet made its way. I'd forgotten where I was. This is the next day after the last day which lasted all the night, through the drive, two hours at a truck stop wide-eyed looking for epiphany in all-night waitresses and men of the road, then down to Ray's when it was day enough and not totally implausible that I would come down without warning and at such an early hour. Then breakfast, errands with Ray, looking at some property up for auction in a few weeks, by the newspaper to see some man Ray wants to put me to work for, lunch, read the paper, television, supper, gin rummy with my grandmother, television, bed, sleep long time coming though I am tired, too tired to sleep, too long on adrenaline, then dreams, then now. I'm at Ray's.

The picture on the far wall just seen through eyes adjusting to the dark. Five round pictures in one frame, a baby, maybe one year, maybe one and a half. The baby wears a white shirt with a wiener dog stitched in grey, but not grey, the picture is in black and white. The baby reads a book, looks seriously at a book, his short chin tucked into his fat neck, a baby frown of concentration. The baby smiles with a tiny plastic football in his hands, his baby teeth laughing at a funny face unseen behind the camera, looking as if at any moment he will run to the funny face. The baby chews on a pipe, perhaps thinking of future lawsuits and child-rearing slander that can be flung in the face of parents who will and must take all responsibility for all failings after baby teeth have fallen. The baby tugs on a man's hat, his grandfather's, that's been placed on the back of his head, this too makes him smile. The baby looks straight ahead, not smiling but bemused, seeing something in his future that could not be said in words even if he had words to use, the knowing before knowing, before things are forgotten, but perhaps this is just a first bravado, for the family, for the funny person, the camera, and I turn away, back to the shutters, where the light, though not exactly light, continues to move unsurely, as if not wanting to intrude on my darkness.

When I wake the second time, it's daylight and the smell of bacon frying up the stairs from the kitchen. My stomach turns. All night I have dreamed of someone cooking, burgers, hot dogs, more burgers, bacon, and I kept eating and eating and as long as I eat, the person continues to cook. The cook cooks as long as I eat, but the cook doesn't eat his own food. It tastes good, and I eat because it tastes good. I eat until I'm sick, and still the cook keeps piling burgers on my plate, seeing how much I will eat.

I don't want bacon this morning. I feel sick to my stomach. I see the dancing, the bowing, they were bowing, but all blurred by lateness of night, drink, drugs, a long drive, sleep deprivation, residual paranoia, post-traumatic stress. Pel's empty eyes. Pel is the cook in my dreams.

Ray starts up the steps. Step. Pause. Step. Pause. And then the shuffle of his slippers on the wood floor. He doesn't pick up his feet when he walks, and I wonder if affectation has become necessity.

He eases the door open and peeks his head around, the five-year-old sent up by an aunt to wake an uncle who drank too much the night before. A sly peeking. Our eyes meet. Eyes too similar. And we smile at our own eyes looking back at us. Morning.

Afternoon, Ray says. He's still in his pajamas. Or else he's been to town already and come back and changed.

Is it that late?

It's nearly two o'clock. We could have sold forty mules by now.

I laugh.

The owner of this place sent me up to see if you was going to be staying another night. And if you was, would you be paying cash or with a check.

My check any good?

You got collateral?

I got a car that's paid for.

That'll do, he says, and shuffles back down the stairs, leaving the door open to say he's ready for me to get up. Which I do, sitting for awhile at the edge of the bed, nearly lying back down, then up with a push. I go to the bathroom and don't look at myself in the mirror, and get in the shower and don't think, or at least not as much as I might.

When I come out, I have to put on the same shorts I've been wearing and I try the shirt, but it's too far gone. I come downstairs barechested and sit down with my orange juice and the newspaper in the same den I've always known. Ray and Starr's den. Same wood paneling, same pictures of fat babies and my young mother and young aunts. Aunt Tippy in her stewardess uniform with the pillbox hat, damn jaunty. My flatheaded brother. The African tapestry of camels, each camel a different color, each smaller right to left. Carved ebony elephants and giraffes on the bookshelf. A crossword dictionary, the same books. The couch I sit on now, reupholstered once, sometime around the midway point of my life. I like the old couch better, I say.

Starr laughs. It's an old joke.

I read the newspaper and everything is where I remember it. I see things that I expect to see. When Ray comes in from the garage he'll let the screen door in the breezeway slam behind him so fast and loud I'll not have heard the initial whine of the door being opened. Starr back from the beauty parlor is a quick squeak stopped midspring, no footsteps, a soft turning on the kitchen door.

Ray comes in dressed for town and asks me to drive him. I have to borrow one of his T-shirts, plain white and much too tight, and when Starr sees me she tells Ray to carry me to Hammer's for some clothes.

Winchester now is warm, but not uncomfortably so. A boy walks back from town lazily, carrying his small paper bag of candy, super balls, army men. He kicks a rock. Smooshes something into the sidewalk. To move faster will only hurry fall and the start of school.

We approach town, where cars travel at a steady speed as if on conveyor belts. We're in the Nissan, not the Cadillac, to better negotiate the maelstrom that is Winchester traffic. I open the sunroof. It cracks me up that Ray has a sunroof. Both cars have cassette players, but all Ray's tapes are eight-tracks stored now in the laundry room. Herb Albert and the Tijuana Brass. Floyd Cramer.

I used to love that Floyd Cramer tape when I was little, I say.

Ray nods, turns down the song on the radio to hear Floyd Cramer in his mind. We cross over the railroad and I miss the old raised bridge that Ray used to ride us over in the back of his truck. Now there's a flat, modern bridge, undoubtedly safer. I miss the old bridge, I say. Do you remember riding me and Pete in the back of the truck?

He smiles, raises his eyebrows.

We would catch air.

What?

It's a ski term. We would fly up in the air.

He nods, and for a moment I think I've made a mistake, bringing up Colorado, which was going on the third year of us not talking, but he says, Pete wouldn't ride on the hump, would he?

He would when he was older.

He nods, seeing Pete huddled next to the cab, gripping the side with both hands, scared and laughing at the same time. I'm all false bravado, yelling, faster, faster. Ray looking over his shoulder, pointing down and behind him at Pete, Pete's shoulders braced, back to back with Ray inside. Ray nodding at me that we're going fast enough.

I head toward his office on the Square, next to Hammer's, but he says to go on around.

Jake Dunlap down at the Ford place is always looking for good workers.

He'd best keep looking.

Ray smiles. We could run by there just the same.

I'd rather not if that's okay.

Well let's ride out toward Belvidere then, he says.

So we ride. Ray turns the channel on the radio, leaving it on the rock station when he points out a miniature donkey in a pasture. The donkey stands by himself near the road, away from the ten or so horses in the field. Ray turns off the radio. I turn it back on and find a jazz station in Huntsville. That's good, he says.

We drive on out into the country, the houses spaced farther and farther apart, separated by brown corn that needs rain and the early tobacco crop. Rangy dogs trot from shade tree to shade tree or listen to their tails thump on wooden front porches. New trucks, old trucks. New barns, old barns. Many satellite dishes. Behind us, Monteagle Mountain forms a low long backwards L around the valley, old mountains these, some of the farthest south of the Cumberlands, greenish purple in the distant haze. I think of my grandmother Sayer up in Sewanee and wonder what she's doing. She stays busy, traveling, keeping things stirred up in the Sewanee Senior Citizens Club. I think of my Grandsay and miss him. I know she misses him.

Sold that farm there three times, Ray says.

Where that barn is?

Yeah.

Good land?

Nah. It's okay. Swampy down behind the barn.

Folks know that when they bought it?

He chuckles. Why sure. I got a good name in this town. Pull on in there.

I pull in the gravel driveway and put the car in park, hoping Ray doesn't ask me to go to the door. Go see what they'll take for this place, Ray says.

No. Come on. No.

Tell them you got somebody out in the car might be interested if the price is right.

You're not interested. You're just screwing around.

Go tell them Ray Crandall's out in the car and wanted to say hello.

Who lives there? Do you know them?

Some old boy. Go on. They're all right.

So I go, sheepishly, laughing, looking once over my shoulder at Ray in the car. He nods his head reassuringly, laughs at my lack of chutzpah. I stiff-knee it up the porch quickly and before I can knock, an old lady is at the screen door. Hello, I say, hammered by the volume of the TV as it hits the quiet country air. I'm Ray Crandall's grandson. He's out in the car.

I wave stupidly at the car, which looks new and foreign sitting in the driveway, more Japanese than I had known. Then a big man with no shirt comes to the old lady's side and looks with detached hostility at the Japanese boy at the door. Put a shirt on, she says, coming out the door, letting it slam behind her.

She's not as old as I thought and moves with a light foot toward the car. How you doing, she says, going around to the passenger side.

Fine, fine, Rays says. You still down at the Utility Board?

No. I'm retired. Three years come Christmas.

I believe I knew that.

I'm standing by the car when the big man comes out. His white T-shirt is too small and strains against his chest. I begin to be embarrassed for noticing until I remember my own muscle-T action.

Jason Sayer, I say, sticking out a hand.

Hey.

I shuffle my feet a bit until he remembers or gets around to shaking my hand. He's looking at Ray. Hey, he says.

Hey there, Ray says, and then to the mother or grandmother, it's impossible to tell, got you a big boy there.

Too big for his britches, she says, not looking at him. Ray laughs. So does the big man. He's heard this routine.

Well, Ray says, I was just taking a ride with my grandson there and was wondering if you might be looking to sell this place.

Oh no, the woman says. We're pretty well settled in. We been here nearly twelve years.

Is that right? Twelve years? Doesn't seem that long.

No it don't.

Well, if you change your mind.

We'll call you first. But like I said, we're pretty well settled.

Ray nods. I'm glad to hear it.

Then I get back in the car and we head again toward Belvidere. After awhile, the tires roll on the road like a wave about to swell. You like that kind of stuff, don't you?

Why sure, Ray says, pointing out a hawk on a fence post. I like to know what's going on.

We ride on through Belvidere, back in time, past old grocery stores and abandoned post offices and roadside vegetable stands and kids hopping around on porches. Ray studies the land, the barns, takes in livestock and tractors and combines, wonders how in the world did we do it with mules? How did we milk, plow, harvest, bale? When did we have the time? And this boy beside me never once saw a colt foaled.

We get to Huntland and Ray turns down the volume on the radio. Used to have some pretty fair football teams over here, he says.

I smile.

Pretty good coach too. Fellow by the name of Sayer. You ever hear of him?

Yessir, I believe I have.

You know I saw your daddy play a couple of times.

No, I didn't.

He could throw that ball.

I heard that.

Used to roll his neck on the sidelines like you did.

I did that?

Just like him. You know, just trying to stay loose. Ask your mother about it. Sold that big house yonder in 1952.

Back at Ray and Starr's I carry in my new jeans, socks, boxers, shorts, and a couple of short sleeve golf shirts from Hammer's. Starr's gone to the grocery store, leaving behind a note that I'm to call my mother at work.

Hey, I say, when Mom answers. What's up?

I'm afraid I've got some bad news.

What?

We found Pookie dead this morning. Out in the backyard.

No.

I'm afraid so. Tom thinks it was either a complication from getting her spayed or heartworms. We haven't had her checked in a while.

Well why not, I say, my voice harder than I mean.

I don't know Jason. Things have been so mixed up this summer, I guess we just forgot. I'm sick about it. I'm just so sorry it happened.

I know, I say, hearing her pull the phone away from her ear. I can see her doing it in my mind. She's about to cry.

I'll give you a call later on tonight or tomorrow, I say. I'll just see you tomorrow night. I'm playing golf with Dad and Pete up at Sewanee in the morning. I'll be back in Knoxville by supper.

I wait for her to say something, thinking she hasn't heard me. Okay, she says, I'll see you tomorrow night. Drive carefully, please.

I will.

And then I'm off the phone, heading upstairs to my room, where I lie on the bed until Starr calls me down for dinner.

In the morning I eat a couple of pieces of bacon and a bite of eggs, neither of which hits my stomach right.

My night owl's not used to eating this early, Starr says.

No ma'am.

Are you feeling okay honey?

I'm fine. I'm just tired. Don't feel like driving back to Knoxville.

Well stay here, Ray says, cornering the last bit of scrambled egg with a piece of toast covered with strawberry preserves, we'll find some kind of work for you.

You're not letting him eat salt on those eggs, are you Starr?

No. He still puts it on his tomatoes though.

Can't eat tomatoes without salt.

You need to watch that.

I'm watching.

When I'm ready to leave, Starr hands me a fifty dollar bill, what she calls just a little pocket money. We're so glad you came, she says. It was a great surprise.

I enjoyed it. I'm going to get it going Starr. I'm just sort of at a crossroads right now.

I know. Y'all got a mess up there in Knoxville. I just feel so badly for Tom. And your mother.

I do too.

You know we're always here. You can come stay with us if you need a change of scenery for awhile. Your grandfather's not been feeling well. I believe he'd enjoy the company.

I may do that. I may come down here for awhile.

Ray follows me out to my car. You need any money?

No sir. Starr just donated fifty.

She did? I wish she'd give me some money sometime.

I laugh. Ray already has his wallet out and is peeling off a hundred.

I don't need it Ray.

You might. You might want to take a girl out for a nice steak.

I appreciate it, I say, taking the bill and putting it in my wallet next to the other one. I may be back soon to visit for awhile.

He looks surprised for a second. Smiles. That would be good.

We shake hands and I'm on my way to Sewanee.

It's twelve miles from Winchester to Sewanee. In Cowan, halfway in between, I have to wait on a train. I think of Clay. Then of my father. My father saying, I finally told Daddy he should have played me in that Pelham game when Clay was getting so banged up. I was twenty-eight years old before I ever said anything. I was a freshman but if he'd put me in we would have won that game. They were putting eight men up on the line and just knocking the hell out of Clay whether he had the ball or not. We could have killed them by splitting Clay out and putting me at tailback. We could have passed them silly. Boy was I mad. It's the only game we lost in four years.

What did he say?

Said I might be right.

Might?

He knew.

At the golf course, Dad and Pete are on the tee loosening up when I pull in the parking lot. The cart's already loaded with their clubs so I'll be walking the first nine. Already the sun scorches what's left of the sparkling dew. It's going to be hot and I am going to play some bad golf. I walk to the tee box and drop my clubs with a thud.

What do you say there, Pete says, shaking my hand with much earnestness, patting me on the back, pumping my arm, knowing full well it's early for me. Ready to play some golf?

Oh yes. Hey Dad.

He comes over and shakes my hand, smiling because Pete's rubbing my neck like a fighter's trainer. Right on time, he says.

Looking forward to it.

I bet. How's the knee?

Good. About eighty percent I'd say.

Some walking should be good for it. Pete, you want to start us off.

Hey ho hup two, Pete says, high-kneeing it over to his clubs, razzing Dad a bit for chop chopping his ass. He tees up and knocks the ball a good ways straight down the fairway. My dad steps up and hits a pretty long ball. Then it's my turn. I walk up, put my tee and ball down, address the ball, take the club back slowly, and hit it a mile.

Good shot, Dad says.

It's the fifth hole and I've just yanked my third ball into the woods. You see that Pete, Dad asks, looking down the left side of the fairway where the ball has half boomeranged.

Went in right past that third oak. I think we can find it.

The sun has come nearly full up by now and I'm fading. I'll be walking down the fairway, thinking about Grandsay, about the time when Pete was five years old and holed an eighty-foot putt, Grandsay walking it off, measuring the distance, and me a little jealous. But I was more fired up than jealous, Grandsay with that look in his eyes like it was really something special, that putt, and like this was a special day, and Pete, shy and sort of mumbling around, embarrassed and proud. And I can't explain how my grandfather could smile, his eyes, it was like he was letting you in on a great secret, he was watching you catch on that there never was a secret. Eighty-foot putts? All you got to do is knock it in there. But it's not easy. It is all amazing, and it is all plausible, but when you knock it in from a long way out, you ought to step it off.

I've been walking up fairways on the verge of tears. The memories are too happy. And will my dad get his makeup time with some grandkids? He smokes too much. He doesn't understand what has happened, how I am the way I am, how he's here with me, watching my too quick swing, my head flying, back stiff as a board, and can't tell me what I'm doing wrong, there's too much water under that bridge, too many golf rounds that weren't fun, our sports albatross, a thinking man's game and Jason has a good mind, and he'll never be fast enough to be great at football or basketball, so I'll teach him golf. And I'm much too tired and scattered to be thinking such things. He's bitten his tongue so hard on my head jerking that he's started doing the same thing through some odd familial osmosis.

Pete takes off walking toward the woods where my ball went in, so I ride with Dad in the cart. I've not been watching where my balls go. The first time I went in the woods, Dad found my ball in someone's front yard next to a bird fountain. Last hole, I was about forty yards up the tree line, sort of halfass looking, thinking if I lost my ball I could just pick up and forget the hole, but there's Dad stomping around behind me, swinging his club through high weeds like he's fighting through the Congo until he finds the ball and I have to keep playing, and now, as we approach Pete, he's twenty yards into the woods and has found my ball down in a ravine, behind a monstrous-looking tree. Here it is, Pete says.

Throw it up here, I say. I'll just pick up.

You might have a shot, Dad says, smiling a little, not wanting to push it. Has he got a shot Pete?

Most golfers would.

So I packmule it down there to uproot a tree, Dad hollering behind me, we're gonna have to start charging him Pete.

They let me hit first on the next tee to change my luck, and I smack a tree that sits about forty yards up on the right of the fairway, the ball barely making it through the limbs at the top, then dropping feebly in the rough, leaving me a shot of about two hundred and fifty yards to the green.

I was up here one time, my father says, and Clay hit that tree and the ball bounced back behind the tee box. Me and Clay were playing Daddy and Coach Maxwell. It was a tight match and man were they were riding us, just yow yowing the hell out of us. His ball was behind the tee box I'm telling you. They thought they had the hole locked up tight.

What happened?

Clay hit it over the tree and put it on and birdied the hole anyway.

Pretty good shot.

Yeah, pretty good. And then we showed them how to yow yow.

At the break, Dad and I sit at a plastic table in the small clubhouse eating grilled cheese sandwiches and drinking Cokes. Pete sits at another table, talking to the golf pro. My dad tallies the scores, though on over half the holes I've announced no score. Can you believe I shot a forty-five on this course when I was fourteen?

Yes, he says. When you concentrate and loosen up and keep your head down, you can play pretty good.

I'm tired.

You look it. Things all right in Knoxville? I mean all right as they can be. Pete told me about your mother's boyfriend. I'm sorry to hear that.

Yeah, he's not too good. Smoking, I say, pointing at his cigarettes on the table.

Well, how's everything else?

All right. I've done better.

He nods.

I can't get it going.

He nods again, looking me in the eyes as if they might tell him something.

I'm not getting along with my friends.

Who?

Pel, Trick, I say, wanting and not wanting to say it. He always liked Pel.

Why not?

It's hard to say. I just don't trust them. It feels like they're messing with me lately. I don't know. I haven't been thinking very clearly.

He doesn't say anything, but reaches for his cigarettes. He frowns and looks out the window and I regret for a second telling him anything.

I'm getting out of Knoxville.

You can come stay with me in Nashville. We can find you a job doing something until you know better what you want to do. You're more than welcome in Nashville.

I may go down to Winchester and stay with Ray and Starr for a little while. They've got the room.

He hits his cigarette, but doesn't say anything.

I appreciate the offer.

He nods.

What do you think I ought to do about my friends?

I can't tell you that. I don't know enough about what's going on. So I can't say you're right or you're wrong or what's right or wrong for you to do. Right or wrong might not matter. It may just be a deal where you need to decide something one way or another then live with the consequences.

What consequences?

I don't know. It seems to me that either you keep hanging out with these guys, all the time worrying, rightly or wrongly, that they're putting the screws to you. Or you tell them all to just kiss your ass and be done with them for good.

I nod.

I wouldn't put up with any bullshit.

I nod again.

You know I'm here.

Yessir I know.

Pete, you ready to hit it? he says. Then he gets up and carries our plates and cups to the trash can and heads out the door to the golf course.

Driving back to Knoxville in the late afternoon, the sun fades behind me, marking the sky a light shade of pink in the rearview mirror. I have the windows down and the air is not too hot, cool even when I pass under bridges. I'm a bit sunburned on my face and neck. I've played some bad golf, though I didn't play quite so bad on the back nine. I've eaten a good lunch at my Grandmother Sayer's, with fresh tomatoes and corn and good corn bread. And it was the same at her house as in Winchester. Things were where I remembered them, where they ought to be. Pictures of Grandsay and Clay, dad and my grandmother. My grandmother's thimble collection, her spoons. Grandsay's pipes and game balls and photos of bird dogs.

I drive on toward Knoxville and I'm thinking about Grandsay, that if you have two pieces of pie and one is your favorite, then you should eat it first. That way you're always eating your best piece first.

I drive on, past Niota, Athens, then Sweetwater, past Loudon and Lenoir City. And Grandsay is telling me, you're faster this year Jason. You're really starting to burn that angle. Approaching Knoxville I come up on the Watts Road Exit thinking I won't look at the graffiti, but that seems chickenshit, so when I pass under I take it all in, and when I'm past, I reach for the rearview mirror to look at my eyes, then realize I don't have the need to look.

When I get to the community center, Beth's folding chairs. She's got her back to me, and the pool's empty except for Mr. Glassman who's knocking out his afternoon laps. It's a little cool out. It's still more summer than fall, but it's the time of day that seems especially sad this time of year, when, as a kid, you could see the night coming sooner, and school just days away, and at any moment your mother will call you home for dinner before you're finished playing.

Beth turns around and waves as I'm making my way down the walk. I come on around the pool to where she is and start folding chairs.

Still going at it, I say, looking over my shoulder at Mr. Glassman.

Still going at it, she agrees.

When do you close up for the summer?

Labor Day weekend. Then I come in the next weekend for cleanup. You know, drain and scrub the pool and all that. Then I'm finished.

You ready to go back to school?

I guess. Yeah I am. I always like the fall.

I nod, continue to fold chairs. Around the pool a few brown leaves have fallen. And the sky looks like fall, higher and clearer, the last faint purple streaking the clouds.

Do you have any plans?

Moving on, I say, moving on.

She nods, thinks about letting it drop. Where?

I may go down to my grandparents' for a little while. Little change of scenery you know. See what happens.

That might be good. You can always come back.

I smile, shake my head no.

You talked to those guys?

No. Well a couple of days ago I saw them. They're on their own.

She doesn't say anything, continues to fold chairs. In the pool, it's the slow steady splash, the patient breathing of air.

You've been a good friend to me this summer, I say. I don't know if you know that. But you have. I just wanted to say it.

I appreciate that.

And then Mr. Glassman is out of the pool, slow-footing it to his sandals. He sees me, flexes an arm, and points at me and then the pool.

I'm going to get back on it.

He nods, waves to Beth, and starts off for home.

I guess I'm going to follow him out, I say.

You're not heading out tomorrow or anything are you?

No, it'll probably be awhile. I'll drop by sometime tomorrow. Get back on the old rehab if that's okay.

Sure. I'll be here.

When I pull in Mom's driveway it's not yet fully dark. I get out of the car and head toward the back gate. The garage door is closed and probably locked and no lights are on in their room. The gate squeaks when I go through. It's quiet. Not the quiet of night where you can hear everything, but silent. Behind me the fan on the car whirrs and it's the only sound in the world.

Up on the hill, in the corner, the ground's been dug and filled in again, leaving a small reddish mound. I go and look at the pool. It's cloudy but not as bad as it's been. No rats or anything. Not a ton of leaves. I look up the hill again, where the mound is, and I start to walk up there. Instead I turn back to the house. Mom's at the sink washing dishes. I watch her through the window. She glances up and seems to look right at me. Then she cocks her head to the left up toward the hill and I know what she's looking at, though she probably can't see it for the easing darkness. Then I run on into the house.

Well hey kiddo, Mom says.

You look surprised.

You think you can surprise me by coming or going?

I guess not.

I grab a Coke out of the refrigerator and sit down at the kitchen table with the newspaper. What smells good?

I'm trying Tom's red beans and rice.

It smells good, I'm starving. Is Tom home?

Yes. But he's really weak. He's checking back into the hospital tomorrow afternoon.

She goes back to the bedroom and I start to read the paper. Then I go up and look at the beans cooking on the stove. Mom walks back in. We buried Pookie up on the hill, she says. I'm not sure if you saw.

I saw. Who buried her?

Jackie. By himself. Tom couldn't help. And that ground was so hard, and it was hot out. Jackie saved the day.

Yeah he did. I'm sorry I wasn't here.

I'm not. I'm glad you weren't here.

I put my hand on her shoulder. I'm fine, she says. You can wash the rest of those dishes for me if you want. Then she goes back to the bedroom again, and I hope she's not crying, and that if she is, Tom doesn't hear.

When she comes back in, we eat dinner. Outside, it's dark and the crickets have started. A breeze moves the wind chimes on the gazebo. The air conditioner clicks off and then the sound of water dripping. It's not as good as Tom's, Mom says.

It's good. Almost as good as Tom's.

She smiles. Thinks I'm lying.

Down on the track, a train blows its whistle one long clean time, then rattles faintly on, the low steady rumble of an ocean receding, waves crashing farther and farther away, until there is no sound but the absence of sound and forks scraping plates.

I'm going to move, Mom says. To California.

Good. I think you should.

Aunt Tippy said I could stay with her. There's a lot going on out there, a lot more opportunities for a woman my age.

I nod.

Tom's already told me he wants me to get on with my life. That I need to move on when he's gone.

He talks like that now?

Just the other day.

I nod, then take my plate up to the sink.

Mother says you may go down there for awhile.

I may. Got nowhere else to go.

Mom looks up at me, concerned.

I'm kidding, I'm kidding. I figure I can help out down there until I figure out what I'm going to do. Help Starr out with Ray. Get some kind of job. I don't know. Something.

Mother says Daddy's looking forward to it if you come. But I don't know how long you're going to last in Winchester.

Longer than I'll last in Knoxville.

Amen to that.

After Mom finishes dinner she goes to the grocery store. I sit at the table for awhile listening to the crickets, listening to hear if Tom is awake. Then I tiptoe down the hall as quietly as I can. I peek in the darkened bedroom. A baseball game is on the muted television. I'm standing in the doorway trying to decide if I should go in or not when Tom says, I could hit that fastball.

I come in the bedroom and stand next to the bed. That one that guy just threw or any fastball?

Any fastball.

I smile.

Don't ask about the curve.

I won't.

But I could jump all over a heater. Harder they threw it, harder I hit it.

I laugh.

Any more of them popsicles?

I think so.

We called em paddlepops back when I was a kid. I'd drive Taylor and Rachel crazy calling em paddlepops instead of popsicles. I guess they thought it sounded old-fashioned. I'd wait until they had friends over, a slumber party, you know, and come in and ask who wanted paddlepops. Used to aggravate the hell out of em.

He laughs and I do too. You want one?

Cherry, he says.

When Mom comes back from the store, I go out to the yard where Pookie's buried. Already the dirt feels too dry and I worry that the grass won't grow back. I go down to the house for the hose, but when I stretch it, it won't reach past the pool. I go to the garage and get an old mop bucket, then come back out again and fill the bucket up from the hose, and carry it up and pour it on the ground. I do this three times until the ground is muddy, then I take off my shoes and walk over the muddy ground until it's as flat as I can get it. I'm thinking that the grass growing around the grave will spread better if the ground is flat. When I'm finished I lie in the yard and run muddy feet through the grass.

I stay like that for a long time, every now and then raising up to see if Mom is still watching television in the den. I think about praying for Pookie, then think it's weird to pray for a dog, then I do it anyway.

Another train whistles down the track, and I think I should probably pray for Pel and Trick and Bobsmith and Jimbo. But I don't feel like it. Even if they're just regular guys screwing around, just messing with me because I'm crazy and a spoilsport on their party, it's still not cool to play ghosty with a friend.

Something flies past my face. It circles the pool, swoops, skimming the water for a drink, and off over the hedge. I lie back down and stare at the faint stars. A jet I can't see hums across the sky. The last honeysuckle of summer a memory in the hedge. It would be too cold to swim. I half listen for more trains to whistle, then wash my feet with the hose and go inside. And I did pray for the sons of bitches.

When I wake up, I hear Mom and some other people up in the kitchen who are going to ride with Tom to the hospital later on. I turn on the light and throw on my swimsuit and go to the bathroom to wash my face. A cricket sits frozen in the middle of the floor. I scoot it behind the toilet with my foot.

I head out the garage and walk down the driveway and look at the For Sale sign. Then on down the road, across Deanne Hill Drive, toward the community center. I get to the parking lot and see only a few cars there. One is Beth's. Another is a BMW with a Prince of Peace bumper sticker.

Beth is sitting on the edge of the pool with her legs in the water. Next to her Jody McDowell. A couple of kids are jumping off the diving board. Two mothers talk in lounge chairs. Beth and Jody are talking. They're talking quietly, watching their feet in the water, every now and then splashing water up on their arms. Jody says something funny and Beth looks at him and laughs, shaking her head as if she's just heard a corny joke. Jody is laughing too, fake slapping Beth on the back, hardy har har, slapping his knee, orange you glad I didn't say banana again?

I start to walk down, then change my mind. I turn and head back to the house. Behind me the spring of the diving board, splashes, running chatter along the concrete to get back in line. Far down the line, the whistle of a train. Good old Jody McDowell.

I get back to the house and head through the gate and up to the pool. The pool is just a little cloudy. Probably one chlorine shock will clear it up. The water is low, so I turn on the hose and put it in the pool. Then I jump in. I stay under for as long as I can, until I'm bursting for air, and then I pump out some hard laps until my legs and arms ache.

Inside Bobbie's talking about grabbing that so-and-so by the ass and saying, how do you like it buddy? And Mom and Rachel are laughing. When I open the door the voices stop. Hey, I say, sheepish about walking into a room of laughing women.

Well who raised the dead, Bobbie says, laughing loudly, looking around at Mom and Rachel to encourage them to laugh as well. Then she winks at me.

I go to the refrigerator and get a Coke, then lean against the kitchen sink. When's the baby due Rachel?

First of January.

How's Devon holding up?

A nervous wreck. He's just started his morning sickness.

I laugh. Is it a boy or a girl? Or do you know?

No. We want to be surprised.

And then they talk about the pros and cons of knowing beforehand and how Devon wants a boy and Rachel probably wants a girl and Mom and Bobbie talk about how once the baby's born, they'll be so happy it won't even matter. But Rachel and Devon know that and we all know that and what everybody is thinking but not saying is that it doesn't seem real that

Tom won't see his grandchild, or at least that's what I'm thinking. And I'm looking out the window thinking about that, checking to see if the grass is growing yet up over Pookie's grave and I'm noticing that the yard could probably use a trim, especially if the realtor's coming to show the house this week, and I'm checking out the angle on the hill, measuring the angle where earth meets sky, when Tom walks in.

Hey, he says, grinning, walking into a room of his favorite women, and what's Sweet going to do but grin?

I didn't ask you last night, he says. How was your trip to Ray's?

It was fine.

He must have come back early cause they were trying to put him to work, Bobbie says.

Tom smiles. Aw, he's just sowing oats. He's not the first to do that you know.

Lord knows that's the truth, Bobbie says.

He looks at me and smiles. You don't have to worry about this one Bobbie. He'll figure it out.

Then he goes over to the table and puts his hand on Rachel's stomach. Girl, he says. He takes one of Bobbie's cigarettes off the table and lights it. Well I'm packed up. Ready for them to chop off my head and put on a new one.

We laugh. Then the women get up and start moving around. Mom goes back to the bedroom, Bobbie calls her husband. Rachel stands up, but doesn't go anywhere.

So how's it going Jason, Tom asks, grinning. We have some joke between us that I'm not on to yet, though perhaps it is the joke of all this quick moving female action around him.

Good.

And Ray's treating you all right?

Yeah. I didn't piss him off this time.

You didn't try hard enough.

Rachel walks out of the room, shielding her face with her shoulder.

Tom looks in the refrigerator. How were the red beans?

Good. Real good.

I'm going to teach her to cook yet. So Ray's treating you all right, he says. He's not stopped grinning since he came in the kitchen and I have the sudden urge to cry. Not because I'm sad. He brushed his mother's hair when she was sick. He's the youngest and the wildest and the sweetest in his family.

Bobbie comes in. Sweet, you ready to go? she says, all big sister no nonsense now.

Ready to go, he says. Then I go back to the bedroom and get his bag and carry it out. And in a few minutes they come out and load up in Mom's company car.

I'll be down there later on, I say, and then they're backing out of the driveway, Tom smiling at me from the front seat, then leaning over the seat to say something to Rachel and Bobbie. Then my mother is laughing, and Bobbie and Rachel, and Tom looks back at me and waves.

Raised in Knoxville and a sixth-generation Tennessean, INMAN MAJORS now lives in Tullahoma with his wife, Christy. He teaches at Motlow State Community College in southern middle Tennessee, not far from the site of his great-grandfather's mule-trading auction yard.